Fabrice Humbert currently teaches literature at a French secondary school. In 2009 *The Origin of Violence* was published in France, where it was immediately hailed by the press as 'a revelation'. The novel won the first French Orange Prize for Fiction in 2009 and the 2010 Prix Renaudot Paperback.

The Origin of Violence

FABRICE HUMBERT

Translated from the French by Frank Wynne

The right of Fabrice Humbert to be identified as the author of
this work has been asserted by him in accordance with the Copyright,
Designs and Patents Act 1988

First published as *L'origine de la violence* in 2009 by Le Passage
Paris–New York Editions

First published in 2011 by Serpent's Tail,
an imprint of Profile Books Ltd
3A Exmouth House
Pine Street
London ECIR OJH
website: www.serpentstail.com

ISBN 978 1 84668 750 1
eISBN 978 1 84765 647 6

Designed and typeset by Crow Books
Printed and bound in Great Britain by Clays, Bungay, Suffolk

10 9 8 7 6 5 4 3 2 1

They say that Satan was God's most radiant angel. His luminous, meteoric fall bears the twin marks of greatness and betrayal. And I think that, somewhere in the meanders of my memory, I can just make out an image of the archangel falling from the empyrean to join the winding recesses of hell. This image from a children's bible, distorted perhaps by memory, has long haunted me: it is always the most beloved son who joins the ranks of Evil.

Years later, childhood now ebbing away as I prepared for one of the thorny competitive exams so favoured by this country, I remembered this image of Satan as I was taking notes on a book on early twentieth-century European history. Page after page of statistics devoted to the overwhelming dominance of Europe, in industrial, financial, military, cultural matters. It was the ascendancy of a fractured empire which conquered half the world, rival countries dividing it amongst themselves. Down the centuries, power may have shifted between these countries – the Spain of Charles V, the France of Louis XIV, the Britain of Queen Victoria – but they continued to rule the world. Through the off-putting pages of this history book I could hear the distant echo of a *fin de siècle* waltz, see gentlemen and ladies dressed in their finery in a great hall of some palace glittering and gilded. I could picture a man leaning against a mantelpiece, lighting his cigar before he spoke, a couple whirling on the dance floor, in the distance a young woman, head held high, as servants weave through the crowd and, in this clichéd image, the vast wealth of a peerless continent. It was then that I remembered the biblical image, and this glittering ball was superimposed with a carnival of the damned in which not once but twice – the second time without hope of reprieve – the values of this continent disintegrated, erupting in the blaze of two world wars and annihilating tens of millions of men in an unparalleled wave of barbarism. The fall of the brightest angel into the deepest darkness.

Time passed. The time of university exams had long passed and I no longer had to pore over history books. I was a teacher in a Franco-German lycée, I was taking my students to Weimar in Thuringia in Germany. We had spent several enjoyable days, going to the theatre, visiting Goethe's house, listening to the guides eulogise the great German writer, talking about his many loves – Charlotte in *The Sorrows of Young Werther*, Anna Amalia, his wife, and so many others – as though the only connection they could find with their national treasure was romance. The other topic was a meticulous account of his relationship with Schiller. And, sheeplike, we also visited Schiller's house, partly out of curiosity, partly glad to escape the early winter cold, often fierce in this region. These visits were by turns interesting, instructive, enjoyably grotesque and somewhat kitsch in the way Goethe and this provincial, rococo town were portrayed in the brilliant jewel-like colours of an Épinal print, because it was not difficult to understand that behind the portrait of the wise, benevolent writer was something more profound, and that there was more to the town with its cobblestones and literary walks than the arguments between Goethe and Schiller, a memory of something more turbulent, the metamorphosis of the Weimar Republic into the goose-stepping Third Reich.

After we had been there several days, a bus took us up the Ettersberg. The group was chatting and joking the way fifteen -year-olds do on a school trip. From time to time, looking at the bus's milometer, it occurred to me that the people of Weimar make this trip on foot – or used to, the custom is dying out now – every 11 April, the anniversary of the liberation of the camp. They form a procession, children and adolescents first, and march. It is already spring but they say it's always cold because the hill is constantly whipped by an icy wind. In fact, these pleasant woods where people like to recall the long walks taken by Goethe and Anna Amalia were also one of the most sinister places in the world since they hid the Buchenwald concentration camp in the beech tree forest. A camp established in 1937, eight kilometres outside Weimar, for political prisoners, homosexuals, 'asocials' and common criminals. Fifty-three thousand dead.

As the bus set us down so we could walk to the main gate of the camp, everyone fell silent.

I won't recount our visit to Buchenwald. I won't describe the barren plain, the torture cells, the crematoria or the measuring room where they pretended to measure Russian prisoners before putting a bullet through their heads. We walked around the camp for a long time. We read, listened, looked. All in silence. And then we were taken on a tour of the low-roofed building, took the narrow steps that led under the ground and there found a vast room, empty and cold, with hooks hanging about two metres above the ground; it was here that one thousand, three hundred men where strangled.

In this room, the image from my childhood suddenly

3

came back to me. Why did this image, this memory from an illustrated bible come back to me at this moment? The radiant fall of the angel of fire was linked to something I remembered from Dante, a reference which might sound precious or out of place, but it occurred to me at the time. And in that moment, Buchenwald appeared to me as a storehouse of Evil, a black hole drawing in all the terrible sketches and drafts in the universe. A dark maw, viscous, terrifying, devouring mankind. The point of convergence of absolute Evil. Going back up the steps to the fresh air, far from that stifling yet icy room, I clearly remembered the moment Satan first appears before the poet in the *Inferno*: the beast is motionless in the lowest circle of hell, the origin and source of all that is Evil. A colossal three-headed monster with the wings of a bat: "*s'el fu si bel com' elli e ora brutto, / e contra 'l suo fattore alzo le ciglia / ben dee da lui procedere ogne lutto*"; "If once he was as fair as now he's foul and dared to raise his brows against his Maker, it is fitting that all grief should spring from him".

Lines sadly relevant to our ravaged continent and to Germany most of all, this country which was the political laboratory of the twentieth century, testing every possible regime with terrifying speed. A house of cards falling and being rebuilt.

It is possible to imagine that Buchenwald transforms the streets of Weimar into a theatre set, simple cardboard flats painted yellow and green, transforms the statues of Goethe and Schiller into toys like the lead soldiers of long ago. The guidebooks are larded with mushy lies and children's fairytales. Yet this coexistence of great thought, great art and what is usually called absolute Evil is perhaps the image of Europe, thus it is not deceptive but actually reveals something about our history and our fate as a brilliant civilisation haunted by its mortal sin.

For me this was the third and last fall of Satan, the key image, at once childlike and mythical which governed the fate of our continent like the singular story I was about to uncover.

It is for each of us to find the source and the place of Evil. To seek it out, rip it out, and start again from scratch does not seem futile. It is the hope of the mad, the illusion of the naive and the demagogue, but it is also the supreme struggle.

Part One

I

What date can be set as the origin of this story? The simplest answer would be that visit to Buchenwald, since for me it was to unlock our box of secrets, in the form of a question admittedly, but a question so forceful, so urgent that it contained within it the beginnings of an answer.

But this is probably just an easy way of fudging the question. Because the origin is rooted in my childhood, because the earliest nights, if I could remember them, were probably already lost in the mysteries of this quest. Children sense such things. They quiver with questions.

Fear and violence have haunted me forever. I have lived in these shadows. I have always feared that I would be dragged away, bound, flayed like a dangerous animal. In endless nightmares I have glimpsed the jaws of wolves. Bright eyes glittered in the bedroom of my childhood.

Violence responded to fear. An animal instinct for self-preservation. Fear forever gripped me and forever I would defend myself. Not with some rational, equable resistance but with the violence of a panicked animal, slashing and biting to be free of a trap. The violence of those who bear the mark of fear. The fox in his lair, eyes flickering fretfully. As though childhood fear had brought the whole world crashing down. No more certainty, no trust, no peace.

Is Buchenwald the origin? Wagner, Sommer, Koch?

Years earlier, the first novel I published began with a murder and followed with a suicide. The first thing I ever wrote as a teenager was about a murder. Murder has touched the families of my two closest friends. A mother. A brother. It is not by chance that we are friends.

My memory recalls only violence and fear. Recently, on a trip to Croatia, the only story I remembered as I travelled through the magnificent, sun-drenched landscape was that of a couple murdered in the fields by a madman. This story had been told to me more than twenty years before.

I saw a film once in which, day after day, a boy lived out a terrible nightmare. At night, he did not sleep. During the day, reality was a piercing scream. He said he saw dead people. As he said the words, I felt a shudder run through me. That boy was me.

Fear. Always fear. And its corollary, violence. For years I boxed. I fought in the ring dozens of times. In the street, some weeks before my trip to Weimar, a drunk banged on my car. I wanted to get out. The woman with me stopped me. I was angry. Exhausted by the week I'd had, by our constant arguments. The man lashed out again, this time kicking the driver's door. I got out. His friend tried to drag him away. I heard this young guy shouting, I suppose he wanted to get his friend out of trouble, wanted to let me know that it was just the drink, that I shouldn't blame him, but it was too late. I lashed out in a fear fuelled by rage. I punched and punched again, my heart hammering, my whole body trembling, yet hard as steel. And when the drunk collapsed on the ground, I carried on, lashing out with my feet now, and it was only after some indefinite period that I heard another cry, the voice of the woman who was with me, who had got out of the car and was hitting me, sobbing, begging me to stop. When I did stop and stood in the middle of the street, helpless, trembling, almost sobbing myself as car horns blared, I saw her disappear, run far away from me and my violence. She never came back.

Once, in a book, I thought someone came close to answering my questions. A writer who claimed to write only about madness, murder and death and who believed that the origin of his obsessions was his Russian grandfather during the war. Reading those lines on the back cover, I felt a flash of recognition. I thought I had found a brother. I bought the book, read it. Disappointment. It was a good book, but it said little about his grandfather. Too little. He did not make enough effort to seek out his origins. Although there really was a murder, my fears failed me and the search remained unfinished. I had hoped this man would write my nightmares – he left the door closed. He had opened his own doors, not mine.

In any case, the visit to Buchenwald had already happened. Not the origin of this story, perhaps, but the origin of the question nonetheless. And of course no one but I could answer my own fears.

The visit to the camp, led by two German students, had just finished. I left the group to visit the museum at Buchenwald, an attempt to recreate the years of the Nazi regime. Lines of display cases with photographs and physical evidence from those years with, now and then, a telling phrase from Jorge Semprun, from his great work *Literature or Life*.

I was not really looking at the victims, the haggard forms in striped prison uniforms, but at the guilty. I wanted to see their faces, know their fates, find out whether they had been punished. I read the scant biographical details, pored over the photos, wondered whether it was possible to tell from their faces whether they were vicious thugs, trying in these photographs to discern the mark of Evil. But I found no mark. They had ordinary faces, hopelessly ordinary. There were a handful of brutish faces, like that of Hans Huttig, an SS officer sentenced to death in 1945, but most had unremarkable features. Just men, at least in appearance.

One of these men, Erich Wagner, the camp doctor, actually looked quite benevolent. And, in the old black and white photograph of him smiling, a full-length shot showing him slightly balding, wearing horn-rimmed glasses, he had the bright, radiant air of an intellectual. Imprisoned by the Americans at the end of the war, escaping in 1948, he had lived under a false name in Bavaria until 1962 when he committed suicide. Belated remorse, fear of being recaptured, illness? There were no clues.

Truth be told, I did not have time to think about it because at that moment my eye was drawn to another face. In the same photograph, a prisoner was staring at the doctor with singular intensity. I was struck by his features: they reminded me of my father. The resemblance was staggering, despite the prisoner's gaunt features, the hideously prominent cheekbones, the hollow cheeks. Since my father was born in 1942, and since no grandfather or great-uncle of mine had been sent to the camps, what I felt was no more than simple surprise, yet the photograph spoke to me, as though one of my family might have been here.

We headed back to Weimar by bus. I remember I looked in the rear-view mirror to make sure my hair was combed and immediately felt a twinge of shame: intent on my hair, I had forgotten a concentration camp... The rest of the afternoon was banal: a visit of the town, a couple of shops, a bookshop.

In the bookshop, glancing along the row of predictable

titles – classics, German, American and French bestsellers – I thought about the Buchenwald *Book of the Dead*. One line per name, one line per death. The names of all those of whom some trace was found and who had died in the camp. Futures snuffed out, unknown people executed... And then I looked at the stupid bestseller with a garish cover in my hand and the face of the camp prisoner came back to me, in black and white, the background somewhat blurred. He had no name. His true name had vanished into History. Perhaps he had been liberated by the Americans on 11 April, perhaps by then he was already dead. Just a face in a photograph next to a Nazi doctor who had killed himself. Just a stranger.

But a stranger whose features troubled me. He was the spitting image of my father; even the prisoner being slightly in the background and the image slightly blurred had something to do with the similarities I thought I had spotted. For example, I had the impression that the prisoner was somewhat shorter than my father. Moreover, I had to fill out the features since the prisoner's gaunt, emaciated face was a hazy spectre. So what similarities I detected were in the bone structure. But even allowing for such reservations, the resemblance was startling, to say the least.

The following morning, I got up early. I didn't bother to look at the itinerary for the day, carefully typed by the person who had organised the exchange visit. I vaguely remembered that I was supposed to join my colleagues at the theatre where French and German students were rehearsing Goethe's *Der Erlkönig*, a ballad as famous in Germany as *Snow White*, the tale of a night ride on horseback during which a young boy is ripped from his father's arms by the Erl King. Every German schoolchild learns the poem by heart:

"*Wer reitet so spät durch Nacht und Wind? Es ist der Vater mit seinem Kind*"; "Who rides so late through night and wind? It is the father with his child".

However, instead of turning left and heading for the theatre, I kept on towards the market and ten minutes later, without quite deciding to, I found myself on the bus to Buchenwald. Half an hour later I was standing before the photograph. And this time I was trembling. Difference in height, blurred backgrounds – tricks, illusions. The man in the photograph was the spitting image of my father. I stood, frozen, before the snapshot. I looked again at the doctor, Wagner, then back at the unknown man. At the surrounding photos in the case which might afford some clue. A group portrait taken with Himmler when he made an inspection of the camp, again with Erich Wagner, but without the prisoner.

I left the museum brooding. The camp, now deserted, was more striking than it had been the day before. There was not a soul. Blurring shapes, mist from the Ettersberg wound round the buildings in long grey trails, muffling sounds as it does in nightmares. I thought again of the Erl King, a shapeless spectre appearing from the mists like an illusion or a shadow. What was it the father says to his terrified son? "It is naught but the sound of the wind in the leaves…"; "*Sei ruhig, bleibe ruhig, mein Kind / In dürren Blättern säuselt der Wind*".

In the extraordinary calm of Ettersberg, the memory of the fifty-three thousand dead raised an army of silent shadows. I walked through the mist feeling slightly uneasy. Watchful, as though waiting for something. As I walked back from the museum to the gates of the camp, across the deserted Appellplatz, I felt as though I were falling in step with the prisoners of long ago. Time was swallowed up by the mist as it eroded eras and, behind the grey swathes, piled up images of massacre.

I see dead people, the little boy said.

As I left, I passed in front of the stump of the *tree of life*, the tree, now dead, was left standing by the Germans inside the camp perimeter; it was under this tree, apparently, that Goethe and Anna Amalia once sat. And once again, the memory of the great writer seemed to me unreal, theatrical. The prisoners marched under the tree, perhaps they too were told the hoary old story, and two minutes later they were shot dead. The backdrop to the lie; a piece of kitsch applied to tragedy.

As the bus brought me back to Weimar, I was careful, this time, not to look at myself in the rear-view mirror.

2

A week later, I was in Paris in a brasserie sitting opposite my father, Adrien. We'd met up like this regularly, two or three times a month, always at the same restaurant, for ten, maybe twelve years. It was one of the classic Left Bank brasseries with a beautiful retro interior, a menu that never changed and a somewhat overrated reputation. But the calf's liver there was excellent, and that was enough for me. Over time, the waiters got to know us and the *patron* would come over to say hello. My father always insisted on paying, though once a month, following an established tradition, I would go through the motions of reaching into my jacket for my wallet. At this point my father would reach over and stop me. That was enough. Once a year, on his birthday, he allowed me to pay. On those occasions I would choose some other restaurant in the area, because my father hated every *quartier* in Paris except the 5th. For him, the 5th *arrondissement* was the heart of the city and the only worthwhile district since it was the only one still teeming with bookshops large and small; other areas of Paris lacked spirit – I never quite understood what the word 'spirit' meant to him – either because they had no history or because they were the province of the nouveau riche. If there was a species my father could not tolerate, it was the rich. He despised money, pomp, ostentation. When people talked to him about expensive cars, designer clothes – something I occasionally did just to wind him up – he would roll his eyes to heaven. He did not own a car, went everywhere on foot or by metro, never bought clothes; in winter he wore the same old corduroy trousers and thick jackets, in summer a T-shirt and jeans. Since, in spite of his age, he was still tall and slim, he continued to look elegantly fashionable while others struggled to do so.

Given his beliefs, my father could reasonably have voted communist. But he despised communists even more than the nouveau riche. In any case, he never discussed politics, but on one of the few occasions the subject came up, he treated it with a contempt I found strange in a man usually so measured in his opinions and, more often, apathetic. Because this was my father's central trait: he didn't care about anything. Nothing, except art and an epicurean attention to the passing of time, interested him. Everything slipped by, incidents and accidents, political events and fashions. We never talked about it but he had a keener sense of ridicule than anyone. Everything to him was one big joke, slightly funny, slightly sordid. And he washed his hands of it.

That evening was not his birthday, so we met up in the customary place, with the customary waiters and our usual calf's liver. But in a brasserie in the dead of winter, is it possible to order anything other than calf's liver? While we ate, I told my father about the trip to Weimar. I explained my theory of the kitsch lie of the city, wrapping the concentration camp up in a literary and cultural past, shifting the focus of the crime by moving the city towards Goethe, the theatre, the friendship between two writers. He listened to me, smiling indulgently as he often did at my theories which were too impetuous, too one-sided for his taste.

"They're completely different periods, that's all," he said

finally. "Weimar was a city of great culture and it was also, during the twentieth century, a city next to a concentration camp. Other than demonstrating that culture is no defence against barbarism, I don't see what possible connection you can make between the two."

This was how my father was. Always moderate, always fair in his statements, at least on the surface. In truth, this moderation concealed demons. His humdrum life channelled his violence, and I saw much of myself in him. But his violence was more introverted: in my childhood, I'd seen him immured in terrible silences that could last for several days. There were storms within him whose force no one could measure and which emerged as migraines, vomiting, sometimes even problems with his sight. His body expressed his suppressed violence, passed on to me in his silences. We are father and son. Reflections.

I had hoped for a different reaction to my talk of Weimar. I had been struck by the photograph and, though a week had passed, had not stopped thinking about it. Now that I found myself sitting across from Adrien, the physical resemblance was incontrovertible. I had gazed at the prisoner, thinking of my father; now I stared at my father thinking about the prisoner. The same features. The same dark eyes, the same black hair, though greying a little now that he was over sixty, the same strong, square jaw. The difference in their ages – the prisoner had been about thirty – was incidental. Suddenly, it occurred to me that my father didn't look much like other people in his family. It was something I had never thought about, but it was true that my grandfather, a short man with a bald pate, a flat nose and chubby cheeks, had little in common with this tall, thin man with the stern, handsome face. It's true my grandfather was no oil painting, something that had always been a bit of a joke in the family. My grandmother, whom I had never known, must have been extraordinarily beautiful to compensate. That said, my father did not really resemble anyone, either physically or in temperament. Not even his brothers. In our bourgeois family he seemed out of place… But we were hardly about to go over this subject which came up at every family meal, celebration, ceremony, baptism… things he loathed and usually did not attend, allowing me, as he put it, to represent him.

"Have you ever been to Weimar?" I asked innocently.

"Never. But it's a fine idea," he said deadpan, "some future trip."

I smiled. My father often used this expression: "Some future trip". Everyone knew, he most of all, that he never stirred from home. He roamed his *quartier* on his daily constitutionals, ventured out from time to time to confirm the spiritual deficiency of other *arrondissements*, took the RER once a month to walk in the woods at Montmorency, always the 8.05 train. He was the most orderly man in the world, the most predictable in his daily routine, to the point that at any hour of the day, no matter where I was, I could tell what he was doing, from the invariable breakfast listening to France Inter to his time spent reading every evening, and everything in between – aerobics at 11, his daily walk at 2.30 p.m. It was so obvious to everyone that his predictable nature concealed a latent unease and unpredictability that no one would have been surprised had my father set off for Greenland one day; nonetheless, I could not remember a single time my father had been away. He was a singular metronome.

"You should go. It's an interesting city. You could decide

how pertinent my theories are," I said, smiling.

"That's true. I will go. I love to travel."

He gave me an amused look, as though mocking me, or maybe himself. We did not mention Weimar again. I made the mistake of mentioning Bauhaus and my father got carried away talking about Gropius, about design, declining values, the awfulness of contemporary art with that peculiarly reactionary mixture of knowledge and wit so characteristic of him that it became a pose. So I was treated to a lecture (nothing is more excruciating for a teacher than to have to sit through someone else's lesson) until dessert. As we went our separate ways, I delivered my Parthian shot: "Incidentally, I forgot to say. I saw a photograph of a prisoner in Buchenwald who looked extraordinarily like you."

Something in him froze. His eyes seemed to seek out some nebulous object in the distance; there was a silence. "Really?" he said eventually. "Interesting."

He kissed me and went on his way.

3

The life of a great family is lived to the rhythm of reunions, family dinners, for births, baptisms, birthdays, marriages, funerals… My family is no exception to this rule. In fact, it is not an exception to any rule. For the Fabre family, rules are rules.

That day, my cousin Lucie was having a birthday party for her son at the family home. It was an opportunity for some thirty members of the family to gather in Normandy. Our social typology is fairly simple: we're bourgeois. Not necessarily Flaubert's blind, stupid bourgeois, rather part of a liberal bourgeoisie, a family of traditional values but reasonably open and tolerant, in short a modern bourgeoisie based on money and family nonetheless. We have always been bourgeois, or at least since the beginning of the twentieth century, since Noël Fabre, an ambitious lawyer from Rouen, using the fortune amassed by his father, a former farmer who had become a landowner, managed to become member of parliament for a constituency in Normandy. He exerted no great influence as a *député*, being content to follow the orders and the edicts of his man, Clemenceau, but he was a *député* nonetheless, a role that represented the pinnacle of ambition for a farming family at the time. The financial foundations, indispensable to any great family, were laid down during World War I, when the same Noël Fabre managed to award his brother Jean the contract for supplying clothing for the army, in particular the famous garance trousers. This union of politics and industry, customary in our country as in many others, produced excellent results: by the end of the war, the Fabre family was one of the richest in Normandy. This wealth and influence was to continue throughout the century thanks to the ethic of work and success fed to us through our mother's milk. The Fabre family have practised the classic bourgeois professions: lawyers, doctors, professors, bankers, and have continued a widespread tradition of public work, since we fostered two more members of parliament (no ministers, unfortunately, to our great regret) and especially a long line of senior civil servants – department heads, prefects, ambassadors. This is something we excel at. Since the civil service no longer pays enough, our current strategy is to refocus on business and banking for which we are counting on the younger generation, my cousins' children, who are completely ignorant, utterly ruthless and devoid of scruples – in a word, modern. They are seventeen, eighteen, they go out all the time, go to wild parties and think only of following well-paid career paths that will make it possible for them to maintain our standing in society.

All in all, if we are not among the great families of the country, we are part of a middling elite, rich, moderately influential, thanks to our unity, quite intelligent, I think, though not to excess. Excess is anathema to the bourgeois. I would like to quote the first line of Gracq's novel *The Opposing Shore*. "I belong to one of the oldest families in Orsenna", but we do not possess that aristocratic, almost dreamlike, nobility. No, we are rooted in the tangible, emerging from a long line of farmers, and we defend what is ours tooth and nail. Even if my father, like me, is somewhat on the margins – he, because he was always on the margins, me because I am the intellectual of the family and have retreated to my ivory tower of Franco-German studies in a small lycée no one has ever heard of. I spend my time reading, preparing classes, correcting homework and writing novels. To quote a proverb: "To live happily, live in hiding." Yet at the same time, I can feel the power of the verb Gracq uses in his opening sentence: "I belong". We, the Fabres, belong to our family. Our past clings to us, constrains us, we are the past of this part of Normandy and a little of the history of the country. Our family is a building, a building buttressed with no crevices since we seal up every crack. Our strength is built on the long term and is constantly renewed. Though we are not perfectly adapted to the modern world, by our traditional mindset, our classical culture (we still have rather too much respect for literature, the arts, politics – values which are all now somewhat obsolete) we are still strong and we are wary of weaknesses: secrets, fears, defeats are never spoken of.

On this particular day, the Fabres had come together to celebrate the birthday of my cousin who wandered through the crowd bewildered, allowing himself to be kissed by all and sundry, never losing his composure. His mother, my cousin Lucie, looked rather beautiful in her black dress and, with her banker husband Antoine, provided a typical family sample. Though she was not a remarkable beauty, her pretty features (the result of careful selection by her ancestors), her excellent taste in clothes (an attentive education), and her understated make-up made her an appealing woman. I was fond of her: she was conventional, but pretty intelligent and could be funny when she shook off her role as wife and mother.

"Still no news from your father?" Lucie asked me.

"He never comes to these family gatherings."

"But this is his great-nephew's birthday."

"I don't think that means much to him."

My cousin nodded, more peeved than she was prepared to admit.

I went to join my grandfather who was sitting in an armchair with a glass of whisky.

"I see you're in good company," I said nodding towards the glass.

"You know the secret of long life, my boy: never add water. It's lethal."

He smiled with his yellow teeth. My grandfather had a first name that no longer existed (Marcel), grew uglier by the year, more cynical by the day, and yet, with my father, he was the only interesting person in our family. The others were nice, predictable people, who worked long and hard in business. He had another dimension, being at once supremely indifferent and supremely generous; showering his family with gifts without ever paying us any real attention. I think the love he felt for his family was a vast, vague emotion; he felt nothing particular for any individual, I don't even know whether he knew our names, he constantly favoured impersonal terms like boy, lad, dearest… From the head of the table, he encircled us with an amused gaze, his blue eyes his only arresting feature. He was the patriarch with no particular powers, who was invested with supreme authority. He never gave an opinion or an order: everyone was left to get on with things. But, if needed, he supported our efforts, with money or a phone call to some influential acquaintance. He had made his career as an important servant of the State, *sous-préfet*, then *préfet* of the department, later regional *préfet* for Normandy. He rarely talked about his work, which he seemed to have carried out with no passion but with a scrupulous sense of duty. It's true he rarely talked about anything. Sometimes, he reminded me of my father. Though physically very different, father and son resembled each other in their indifference, their penchant for secrets and their mutual love of literature, even if Marcel Fabre's education was redolent of Norman schooling at the turn of the last century, antiquated and yet so solid, so classic, yoked to Greek and Latin. The old man could still remember the rules of Latin grammar, sentences from Cicero and Homer. Most of all, he liked to recite poems to us, these were our only moments of intimacy with him. Ronsard, du Bellay, Apollinaire, Rimbaud, Baudelaire, Hugo. Long screeds, lengthy poems: *Le bateau ivre*, which, though I teach literature, I've never managed to learn by heart. One day, walking with him in the country, he recited the whole of *La chanson du mal-aimé* to me. The long dreary paths of winter in Normandy, this indefatigable old man with his gruff voice and Apollinaire's poetry. It remains one of my favourite memories of childhood.

"What about your pupils, how are they?"

He hadn't forgotten what I did for a living. Good sign.

"They're fine. I took them on a trip to Weimar last month."

My grandfather stiffened. It was palpable. It lasted only a second, but it was unmistakeable.

"Did you visit Goethe's house?"

Another evasion. I knew he was not thinking about the writer's house but about the concentration camp. Moreover, his reaction was understandable: a *sous-préfet* in 1940, he had not resigned but continued his career under the Vichy Régime, something which was hardly honourable, though he was never investigated after the Liberation despite the readiness of people to rush to judgement. We never spoke about it, the subject was forbidden.

The camp at Buchenwald was simply a red flag to my grandfather. If his actions had had consequences, it was to Buchenwald that most French political prisoners were deported, that the victims had been sent. Consequently, his sudden stiffening did not surprise me. But his subsequent *non sequitur* gave me pause for thought. Though I responded to his questions about Goethe's house with banalities, he suddenly asked: "Your father isn't coming today?"

I confess that the association of Buchenwald and my father did not seem accidental.

I said simply: "I don't know, Grandfather. He didn't tell me."

The old man seemed surprised to be called "grandfather". It's true it was something I had rarely done, even as a child.

Towards the end of the afternoon, after the meal and a Sunday walk with my cousins, I headed back to Paris. The day had been pleasant and unsurprising. I felt sated, a little tired and happy to be heading home.

As I drove, I thought about the man in the photograph. The simplest solution was to go back to the museum in Buchenwald. The following day, after classes, I called the museum. My question was very specific and I felt somewhat awkward asking it, forgetting that concentration camps receive thousands of similar questions. I was quickly transferred to the curator, who did not seem at all surprised by the question.

"We will try to find the source of the photograph in question. You say it's one with Erich Wagner?"

"Yes, but it's not him I'm interested in; there's a prisoner standing behind him, that's the man I'm interested in tracking down."

"I might as well tell you it's unlikely we'll come up with anything. We have a lot of information about Erich Wagner, but an unidentified man in a photograph… If you had a name, we might be able to do a search."

"Unfortunately, I don't have a name. That's why I'm contacting you."

"Call me back in a couple of days."

Two days later, the curator had little information to offer. "We have nothing on the man in question. We know only that the photograph was taken on 20 December 1941, in front of Barrack IX. There were about fifty men housed in the Block at the time, and we can only assume he was one of them. Obviously, that's simply supposition, but it seems likely the man just happened to step out of the barracks as the photo was being taken."

The man's eyes as he stared at the doctor did not seem to me to be pure coincidence. I didn't believe he had accidentally stepped out of the barracks at that moment. But the curator's comment, given the paucity of information, was not unreasonable.

"On the other hand, we have considerable information about Erich Wagner. I can send you a copy if you'd like."

I was about to say that I was not interested in the doctor, but then I thought again about the prisoner's stare.

"Why not? You never know. But the man in the photo…"

"It would be difficult to identify him. Not impossible. We're constantly trying to piece together information about the prisoners. If you can narrow down your search, we can do some cross-checking. We're at your service."

In all, I had a place – Buchenwald, Barrack IX – and a date – 20 December 1941. It was a little meagre but it would be possible to do some cross-checking. The following day I received an email with an attachment containing a biography of Erich Wagner which I glanced through quickly, noting that he had been posted to the camp in 1939. Also attached, and of more interest to me, was a list of the men in Barrack IX and a copy of the photo of Wagner and the unknown man. As I printed it out, the gradual appearance of the Nazi doctor and the slightly blurred figure behind him made me feel ill at ease, as if a foreign body from far, far away was suddenly bursting into my apartment.

As the curator of the Buchenwald museum had suggested, I decided to take Barrack IX as the starting point for my search. To go down the list of names and ask survivors to help me identify the man. For this, I would need a copy of the *Book of the Dead*, which I ordered from the camp bookshop. Like the photograph, and in a way that felt more sinister still, the book, which arrived a week later, represented the irruption of an *unreal reality* in my home. I compared the two lists: the fifty names and the names of the dead. It was a clerical exercise since the names meant nothing to me, but it was poignant. Utterly unknown men, with no flesh, no history, reduced to this single line, obsessively repeated:

Surname/First Name... Arrived (Buchenwald) on... Died on...

Many died at the end of the war, just before the camp was liberated, during the long marches in which the Germans, retreating in the face of the Allied advance, evacuated the prisoners, demonstrating one last time the frenzied, incomprehensible savagery that led them to kill, to kill for nothing, for no reason, when all was already lost. Of the fifty names, I found twenty-nine in the *Book of the Dead*. Twenty-one men had therefore survived, or more accurately there were twenty-one whose fates were unknown.

Of these twenty-one, I picked out the names that sounded French, of which there were six, and looked them up on the internet. I found all six, though I was worried that they might simply turn out to be people with the same name. I called them, retied the thread, reconnected the past and the present, the otherworldly and the peaceable everyday. And it was with difficulty that I stammered to the strangers on the other end of the line my questions about the distant past and a concentration camp called Buchenwald, knowing that the very words could only be received with pain. Five of the six people bore the same names but were not related. I never found out what became of those five sent to the camps, whether they were dead, which, so many years later was probably the case, whether they had left France or whether I had simply bungled my search. But Vincent Mallet responded. Working in Germany, he had been sent to the camps in 1942 for sabotage. He was not reluctant to talk to me and, though over eighty years old, he even had an email address to which I sent the photo. He called me half an hour later.

"I remember the man well. Under normal conditions, I would probably have forgotten his name, but I put it in my notebook because it's not the first time someone's contacted me about him."

"Are you sure?"

"Absolutely. His name is David Wagner, or rather was, because he died in the spring of 1942, a few months after I arrived. Strange, because he was a healthy man."

"You said that someone else contacted you about him?"

"Years ago, yes. A man phoned me, like you, I think he'd phoned a lot of people. He asked me for information about David Wagner, a man well known in the camp, a handsome man."

"So the person who called knew his name?"

"Yes, and as I remember, he had quite a lot of information about him. But he wanted to know more about him and Wagner, the camp doctor."

"They had the same name?"

"Everyone in Germany is called Wagner, it's like being called Martin in France."

"So David Wagner was German?"

"No, he was French, but he must have been of German origin. He spoke German pretty well."

"Why was he in the camp? Had he been in the Resistance?"

"I can't really remember now. He had a red triangle, so he was a political prisoner like the rest of the French. But I think he was Jewish."

"Was he a friend of yours?"

The man paused for a moment. "No. He wasn't a friend. I barely even spoke to him. He was in another barracks. But we knew him."

"Why?"

"Because there are certain characters in any situation who get known. And because Doctor Wagner despised him."

"Why?"

"No idea. But that's how it was. And Wagner might have survived if the doctor hadn't made him his whipping-boy."

This was a lot of information, but I wanted to go back to the phone call he'd received.

"What about the man who called you before, had he been in the camp too?"

"No. I don't know who he was but I'm sure he was never a prisoner. It was obvious. Besides, as I remember he was young. At least he had a young voice. Twenty, thirty at the outside."

"Voices can be deceptive."

"True. But I don't think I was mistaken. I quickly got the impression he was a young man."

"But why did he phone you?"

"Probably a member of the family. It's happened more than once, you know, years after the event. They want to find out something, some trace. Grieving is a long process."

I thanked him and hung up. The character was taking shape, the nebulous coalescing into situations, questions, names: Wagner the doctor, his hatred for David Wagner (which explained the latter's stare in the photograph), the young man who phoned years later. The identity harked back to others and that network gave rise to new questions. In short, the fabric that makes up a man's life was more substantial. But nothing essential, nothing selfishly essential had come out of it: the resemblance was no clearer.

With the crucial element established, a name, upon which is grafted all the destinies of the world, I now needed to find out this man's story.

4

"I was thinking about what you said to me last time, about the prisoner in Buchenwald. It's strange, isn't it?"

We were in the same brasserie, it was not my father's birthday. We'd had an aperitif, I'd ordered the calf's liver, winter was creeping through the streets of Paris. A winter that was not bitterly cold, but dirty and drizzling as so many we have known. We were eating our starters and here, suddenly, my father was asking this question.

"What's strange about it?" I asked.

What I found strange was my father's manner, a little playful, almost ironic, not worried, not interested, not wary, just ironic.

"The resemblance. You see a camp prisoner who looks like me and you don't think that's strange?"

"I do," I said cautiously, "that's why I mentioned it."

"Have you thought about it since?"

"A little," I lied.

"A little or a lot? It's strange, a doppelgänger."

"But, fifty years apart?"

"All the more strange. He must be a lot younger than me in the photo."

"Yeah. He's about thirty."

"But he looks like me?"

"The spitting image."

I placed the photo on the table. My father shuddered. I hadn't intended to show it to him. I carried it with me like a talisman. Face to face, one in my pocket, on paper, the other sitting opposite, in the flesh. Alert to any similarities.

"David Wagner, deported to Buchenwald concentration camp, died in the spring of 1942..."

My father studied the photograph in silence. For a long time. Then he sat back in his chair and said in a detached tone: "You're right, he does look like me. Or rather," he smiled, "I look like him, given the dates..."

"But isn't it strange... the resemblance?"

My father evaded the question.

"Why have you kept the photo? And how did you get it?"

"I asked the curator of the museum for a copy. Curiosity. Because I was so surprised by the resemblance."

"That's it? You haven't researched this man?"

"No. Why? Should I?"

My father shrugged.

"What do I know? You might get a book out of it."

I made a face.

"I'd feel like I was writing about you."

Now my father looked at me without a trace of irony.

We finished our meal rather quickly. When I left the restaurant and kissed him goodbye, I knew that I would quickly go back to my research about David Wagner. And I suppose my father knew it too. Though utterly indifferent, he was enormously perceptive, perhaps because, in being so detached, he could read people like books.

Cross-checking information from the *Journal Officiel*, which regularly published a list of the missing and the lists of those deported, I easily discovered that David Wagner had been born in Paris in the 2nd *arrondissement*.

A request to the town hall – in which it did not seem risky

to justify my request as being for family reasons – resulted in my receiving a copy of the official documentation for David Raphaël Wagner, born 15 September 1915, son of Ulrich Wagner, Romanian and Natacha Wagner, née Stawinski, a Polish citizen. He had a brother, Charles, and a sister, Sophie. Charles, Sophie, David: the names clearly indicated the parents' desire that their children should integrate. I was extremely interested in Charles and Sophie since they might well still be alive. And if they were not, it seemed likely I might find their descendants.

After that, things happened very quickly and unpredictably.

A week later, I pushed open the door of a small suburban house in Meudon and was greeted by the genial old man I had spoken to on the phone some days earlier, having failed to reach his sister who had been dead for some years.

Charles Wagner welcomed me and showed me into the sitting room. At eighty-five, he still seemed to be in good health, though he had trouble walking. He was tall, a little stooped, square-jawed. In spite of his age, I easily saw in his features something similar to his brother David Wagner, and, as I had been expecting, to someone else: his white hair, like my father's, was remarkably thick and bushy for his age.

He offered me a drink. I asked for a Coke. He looked surprised.

"I'm sorry. I'm from a different generation. I only drink alcohol."

I smiled. He sounded like my grandfather. I asked for a glass of wine.

"You look like your father," he said coming back with a bottle and two glasses. "The same bearing, though of course you're fair-haired."

"It's the French in me," I said, unsurprised to find that he knew my father. "My mother is blonde."

"So was your father's grandmother, Natacha Stawinski. My mother was one of those tall, beautiful Polish women, with rather austere features."

There had been no beating about the bush. Everything had already been said. I could leave now if I wanted, all my suspicions had been confirmed. I realised now why my father never came to family gatherings: the Fabres were not his family, he was a Wagner. But obviously, I stayed.

"I knew Adrien had a son, but I didn't know if I would see him before I died. I'm glad you've come."

"Did you know my father well?"

"I knew him once, but he vanished from our lives, mine and my sister's, a long time ago. I sent him a letter to let him know his aunt Sophie had died and inviting him to come to the funeral. He wrote a very polite response, but he didn't come to the funeral, which I can understand. Each to his own life. The Wagners are not the Fabres, not now, nor when their paths crossed before the war."

"But my father is a Wagner!" I replied.

Charles looked surprised. "No, of course not, his name is Fabre, he's a Fabre, obviously."

Now it was my turn to be surprised. "But you just said that his grandmother was Polish."

The old man studied me. "So you don't know? You don't know any of it?"

I shook my head. "All I have is a photograph. A photo of David Wagner in which he looks like my father. Since I found it I've been searching…"

Charles brought his hand up to his face, gently, his fingers splayed, the delicate gesture old people sometimes make. And he closed his eyes.

5

They were two, Ulrich Wagner and Natacha Stawinski, Jews who had come from the east, from Romania and Poland, in the hope of finding work, a better life, in France. They met in Lorraine, while working in a mine. They were married in synagogue in 1912.

They were three. When their daughter Sophie was born, they moved to Paris in search of better jobs, moved into a little apartment in the 2nd *arrondissement* and found work as labourers, work that was almost as gruelling. Then, when war broke out, Ulrich enlisted. Recent immigrants make the best volunteers.

They were four, at least when Ulrich was on leave. David Wagner was born in 1915.

They were almost five. But just as Natacha discovered she was pregnant, Ulrich was killed – hit by a stray bullet a few months before the end of the war. And so four they remained. Not the same four: the newborn was Charles Wagner. A mother and her three children, two sons and a daughter.

The harshness of her work, the meagreness of her pay led Natacha to open a laundry which faltered for a time before becoming established and later thriving. Of the slow rise of the Wagners from the misery of the mines to the relative comfort of a dressmakers' shop in the Sentier area in the midst of other Romanian and Polish families, Charles told me little. Perhaps he thought it would not interest me or that it was not relevant to my own story. Perhaps, too, he glossed over his childhood, over the three children and their mother out of a sense of modesty.

I said simply: "Your mother clearly meant a lot to you."

The old man looked at me. "All mothers mean a lot to their children. But it's true that Natacha was everything to us, she was father and mother, she was our whole family. We had no aunts, no uncles, no grandparents. We had our mother. She probably did not lavish the affection on us some children expect of a mother. She was not one for sweet nothings. She never said 'I love you' to us, I think she would have found the idea absurd. She didn't coddle us, we never played with her, never climbed into bed with her to sleep in on Sunday mornings. Because she was already up, already hard at work. But she was our rock, our hope, our spine. She held her head high in times of trouble, always, and though only later did we understand the difficulties she had had to overcome, we were expected to hold our heads up too. She expected much of us, especially at school. We were not allowed to fail, because we were Wagners, because we were Stawinskis. We were Ws and therefore foreigners. At school, they called us "the Germans", though only my father may have had some distant German origins that predated Romania. This was why our French had to be flawless and I think that few children could write as well as we could. And we all spoke very good German. The language of the east, too, the language of Lorraine, since annexed, where our parents had met. That was how it was: a Wagner had to speak perfect French and good German. Out of gratitude for our adopted country and out of allegiance to our name. Yes, she expected much of us."

He gave a curious smile, filled with gentleness and sadness.

"What can I say? She was our mother. My mother. She was the image of womanhood we took from our childhood."

Ten years passed and the little cubbyhole where once Natacha had spent every hour by the window to make the most of every last glimmer of daylight was now a bright, spacious shop employing three dressmakers. The shop that once patched, hemmed and mended has become a sought-after boutique which now makes clothing: shirts, blouses, skirts, dresses, suits, costumes. Natacha can do everything. Her reputation has spread throughout the neighbourhood and, thanks to word of mouth, some customers now come from farther away.

The apartment is above the shop. There are four rooms, a bedroom for Sophie, another for Charles and David and of course another, the largest, equipped with a private bathroom for Natacha. The living room, large and furnished in the bourgeois style, attests to Madame Wagner's social aspirations. She is keen that her daughter makes a good marriage and that her sons become doctors or lawyers following the current of the changing times in France: peasant grandparents followed by a transitional generation before being accepted into the bourgeoisie.

This may be the case for Sophie and Charles. The girl is a pretty, self-possessed adolescent with no particular brilliance but doll-like, with a pale complexion and blue eyes. She is a pale version of her mother as though inhibited by Natacha's presence and authority. It is easy to imagine her marrying in a few years. The youngest boy, for his part, is a thoughtful, studious child who enjoys school and books. He is obedient to his mother, to his teacher and will be obedient to his masters. His eyes are gentleness itself.

David is more worrying, but more promising too. Charles

will be a doctor, this Natacha has already decreed. David's fate, on the other hand, has not been drawn up. His mother foresees for him great victories and great defeats. At twelve, David is troublesome, rebellious, a mediocre student, always dashing about. It feels as though he might do anything, become anything. He is interested in everything, in nothing. He needs everything to move quickly: books, lessons, friendships, arguments, sorrows and moments of affection. He cannot stay still. When his mother lets him off the leash, he spends his time in the streets playing football, fighting, running. He has, however, a singular trait: everyone loves him. It is his great strength. In spite of his youth, he is a charmer, a seducer. He is handsome and funny, dark and muscular. Girls love him, women love him, grandmothers love him and he manages the extraordinary feat of not being despised by other boys. In her dreams, Natacha imagines him a statesman, a member of parliament, maybe even a minister. She sees him charming crowds the way he charms women. Of course he is Jewish, which does not help, but there have been exceptions, like Léon Blum. Natacha knows nothing about politics, but she knows about this man. It is not a name you forget if you are Jewish. So why not her son? Unfortunately, she can also imagine him being a pimp or an idler.

"You really think he could have been a pimp?" I asked Charles.

The old man burst out laughing. "I've no idea. My brother was thoughtless, you know. He had everything: he was intelligent, handsome, immensely charming. Everything came easily to him. For such men, life is not always without difficulties because they do not understand effort and suffering. Since they think of life as a bed of roses, they sometimes fall hard and never recover. But a pimp? I don't think so. A ladykiller, yes. You could say he was like Maupassant's hero Bel-Ami who succeeds, thanks to the favours of women."

His face clouded again. "But things did not turn out as my mother expected. And not just because of the war. In fact, the first fork in the path, and probably the most important, was his meeting the Fabres. It was something he never got over. The war did the rest."

David was seventeen when the Fabres came into his life. And they turned it upside down. Up until then, his existence had been carefree. From the moment he first stepped into the Fabres' home, anxiety, envy and misfortune insinuated their way into him.

It began unsurprisingly with the ringing of the bell in Natacha's boutique announcing the arrival of Marguerite Fabre and her son Marcel. These two names, which mean nothing to anyone, made me shudder since they referred to my great-grandmother and to my grandfather, whom I found hard to imagine as a young man. Marcel Fabre was twenty years old at the time and, having taken a law degree, he was about to enter the École des Sciences Politiques and had come to have two suits made for the occasion. On the advice of a friend of the family, he arrived at Natacha's shop with his mother, for though he hated the idea of her accompanying him to the tailor at his age, he had little confidence in his own taste.

David Wagner took an immediate dislike to Marcel Fabre. He later gave a variety of reasons for this, none of which were true since the real reason was envy. Marcel had everything that David did not, and vice versa. But the young bourgeois did not even take the trouble to acknowledge the teenage boy about to take his measurements, whilst David was forcibly struck by the wealth and self-assurance of his new client. Physically, one was tall and handsome, the other short and ugly. Marcel still had the glow of youth and did not yet have the toad-like appearance he would later acquire, but he could not be said to be handsome. Nonetheless, he was rich and had a promising future. David, who had not had the opportunity of going to the lycée, since in his world only the best students went – and he had been too lazy – worked in his mother's shop. There was nothing more to be said.

Ten days later, when David brought the two suits to the Fabres' apartment, his dislike became anguish. "Why not me?" David said to himself over and over as he moved through the opulent rooms of the building on the Boulevard Saint-Germain. "Why him and not me?" "Why them and not us?" Because they were Fabres, not Wagners. Because one was a long-established family which, having made a fortune at the turn of the century, had continued to grow richer through work, private income, marriage and connections, while the other had recently arrived from Poland and Romania. Everything might yet be reversed, but at that moment, this was how things were.

Having tried on the suits, Marcel declared himself satisfied. He was about to leave when Marguerite, who was not indifferent to David's charms, to use the expression of the day, offered the boy a drink. Marcel consequently found himself obliged to talk to him. But, as David would complain bitterly that evening over dinner, Marcel spoke to him as though he were a child. David was seventeen, he already had a job and was taller and broader than Marcel. He did not appreciate what he considered the latter's condescending tone – which in truth was probably simple nervousness, an intimation of the awkwardness my grandfather would suffer from his whole life in his dealings with other people, the result of his utter indifference to others.

"Have you always lived in Paris?" asked Marguerite, eager to get her handsome salesman to talk.

"Yes. My parents come from Lorraine, but I was born in Paris."

"From Lorraine? What is your name?"

"David Wagner."

"So you are Natacha Wagner's son? Her heir, one might say," she said with a smile.

The smile, which seemed sardonic, irritated him. The term heir was hardly appropriate, so why use it in this case, and why smile, thought David. She was mocking him. And in that moment he hated Marguerite Fabre as much as he hated her son.

By the time he went back down the stairs of the building some minutes later, he was not the same man. Perfunctory and clichéd as that expression is (it must be said that Charles, like all good pupils trained in the elegant, outmoded turns of phrase of the inter-war years, loved tired, pseudo-literary expressions), it accurately summarises the change in David who, within a couple of weeks, would become ruthlessly ambitious. But how can one have ambition without a future? How can one succeed? Earn money? How can one exude smug self-importance like the Fabres (or at least like the Fabres as he imagined them)? On the long journey home, he turned over these questions in his mind. The simplest solution was school, but that route was barred to him. Unlike Charles, who had been at the top of his class since childhood and whose future was already mapped out, David would never be a scholar. What then? How could he too become a Fabre – to David a generic category that included the whole of the bourgeoisie.

The answer was immediate: marry a Fabre. He seemed to remember seeing someone half-hidden in a doorway, a slender young creature, too well dressed, even from his fleeting glimpse, to be a maid. If she was a Fabre, he was sure that he could seduce her.

Having made this decision, the teenager's life moved along two axes: he tried to steer the boutique towards becoming a luxury emporium, likely to provide him with money and, more importantly, social standing, and he tried to get in with the Fabre family.

When David explained his plans for the shop to his mother, she immediately saw through her son's scheme and said simply: "You want to go up in society, son. That's fine, I have raised you all so that you might do so. But remember one thing: those who rise quickly and unscrupulously are like a monkey climbing a tree. All you see is his arse, and after a while you don't care any more. Ambition can be a great thing, but not in any form."

That said, Natacha agreed to reduce the amount of sewing and mending taken on by the shop in favour of more tailoring and dressmaking. In reality, she quickly realised that it would make little difference financially because what they gained in reputation and new custom would not offset the loss of their day-to-day clientele who brought things to be mended. But because she understood her son's needs and knew they were not losing money, she made no comment. And the profile of the shop's clientele did change, just as David hoped it would. Instead of local customers of modest means, the shop was full of well-heeled ladies – rather than men – though, in spite of his connections with Marguerite Fabre, it never attracted many of the aristocratic bourgeoisie of the 7th and 8th *arrondissements*.

Marguerite became a regular customer at the shop and introduced some of her friends to it – though unfortunately, only a few. David realised that Marguerite was the Fabre family's weakness. With the intuition of a ladies' man, an almost animal instinct of seeking out prey, he recognised that Marguerite was attracted to him. A woman of about forty, somewhat plump, rather pretty, Marguerite, after twenty years of a conventional marriage, without notable success or failure, had fallen victim to the common fate of women of her age in those times. Boredom, too much money and the anxieties of the age were three factors that would propel her into the arms of the first lover to come along. David had no intention of being that lover. He was too young. But he sensed a weakness in Marguerite and guessed that he could exploit it without actually becoming her lover. So he was charming, attentive, a little pompous too, so that he might seem older than he was: he regularly sent her cards, at New Year, on public holidays, when the shop released a new line, invited her to the few fashion shows he managed to stage and which, in spite of modest means, proved reasonably successful. He knew that he needed to see her as often as possible if he was to become intimate with the family.

It was during one of the fashion shows – which had little in common with the great fashion shows of the day like those of Coco Chanel and was simply a presentation of their new collection – that David made the acquaintance of the slim form he had glimpsed more than a year earlier in the apartment on the Boulevard Saint-Germain. Despite her name, Clémentine Fabre was the least appetising and attractive person he could imagine: she was pale, ugly, shy, something which did not suit David's plans. Firstly because, though ruthlessly ambitious, he would have preferred to mix business with pleasure and fall in love with a rich woman. Marrying a woman he did not love and would never love, given his physical needs – David was one of those insufferable boys who kiss the prettiest girls – was a very different scheme. Besides, when a tall, dark, handsome boy makes advances to an ugly girl, her family, who are unlikely to be stupid, are bound to question the intentions of their future son-in-law.

But David Wagner did not hesitate for long. Clémentine did have a beauty, a solitary but important one: her name was Fabre. The little Jewish boy from eastern Europe would get his hands on the heir to the Fabre family. The merchant with the shop in Sentier would be admitted to the salons of the Boulevard Saint-Germain. It was not purely mercenary but more a visceral desire for self-affirmation, for power, for revenge. And when this need unfurled, this lumpen young woman aroused in him an excitement that made him feel as though he might make love to, might posses a whole social milieu and dominate it, he knew he ought not to turn back.

"Would you like to see my collection?" he said to Clémentine.

She stood, speechless. It was the first time a man had ever spoken to her. And he was probably the most handsome man she had ever met.

At this point, we should pause, because Charles showed me his photographs. They are snapshots of the time, solemn, starched, posed as for a painting. David Wagner does not seem that handsome to me. He is clearly a good-looking man inasmuch as he is tall, thin, with masculine features and dark eyes (I immediately thought of the other photograph, the one from the camp, but I refuse to think about it: this David is not the other David). In that sense, he probably represented a masculine ideal of the time. But he did not have an exceptional build. That said, the men in Clémentine's family were particularly poor specimens, a fact that could only add to her admiration: I have already said enough about my grandfather and the only portrait that exists of my great-grandfather, in an old family album, shows him to be an absolutely worthy father of his son.

According to Charles, who I suspect knows little of such things and seems to be one of those men who have only ever been with one woman, his wife, his brother's attractiveness lay in his physique and in his determination. Lazy though David may have been, in love and in business he could be single-minded. He swept women off their feet.

This, however, is not how he set about seducing Clémentine, because this was not to be one of the brief affairs he was so practised in – he had started out seducing neighbourhood girls before quickly moving on to the dressmakers in the shop and then the models – this was to be the marriage that would decide his future and his fortune. His strategy was this: he needed to move quickly and slowly. Quickly find a place in her heart, slowly reinforce his position and gradually inch towards the wedding which he knew the family would oppose for as long as possible. Who would accept a little tailor from the Sentier? He had only to see how demanding his mother was with Sophie's suitors. Sophie, who was quite pretty, though hardly seductive, having little spirit and no experience, had been forced, by the age of twenty, to reject all the boys in the neighbourhood. People would tell Natacha the fable of the girl who refused every man who asked for her hand, determined to find someone younger and more handsome, only in old age to happily settle for anyone who would have her. But Natacha stood firm against La Fontaine: she had come from Poland, she had worked in the mines of Lorraine, she had lost her husband in the war, she had worked like a dog to set up her shop, all this she had done so that her children might find fortune in their new country. She was not about to let her daughter marry some neighbourhood good-for-nothing.

Having witnessed this, David knew how difficult the battle with Clémentine's parents would be. But he knew that she too would fight them. Because – and this came as a pleasant surprise – she was intelligent and stubborn. David had assumed her to be as stupid as she was ugly simply because she was shy. But he quickly discovered that behind her timid exterior, she was witty and clever. Though not clever enough – but who could be? – to grasp the motives of the man she loved so.

Because that was what it was: Clémentine's shrivelled heart blazed, as only the heart of an ugly girl shut away in a Catholic school for years and released to live a humdrum life devoid of male company could blaze. A man, a pregnant glance, a presence, that had been enough to spark the flame. There is no other way to describe it. Love is often the result of circumstances and Clémentine's condemned her to falling in love with the first man she met. If he had a handsome face besides and charms to which the most beautiful girls had already yielded, it is easy to imagine how Clémentine must have felt. And even if she did guess David's true intentions – as perhaps she did – she would not have loved him any less: it was better to be loved for her money than not to be loved at all. One has to be beautiful to be romantic.

The Fabres' mistake, as it turned out, was to have no clear strategy. They were faced with a young man determined to succeed and a young woman determined to love, a difficult alliance to overcome. The family was divided: the father was hostile to this terrible match, Marguerite had no illusions as to David's true feelings but she had a soft spot for him and, curiously, was not jealous that her daughter would spend her nights with a man – he was a man now – that she desired. As for her older brother, with his habitual cold, cynical lucidity he treated the affair as ridiculous, casually remarking: "If you want to sleep with a little Jewish social climber, go ahead! But why marry him?"

Between hostility, covert complicity and indifference, the Fabre family behaved absurdly: they refused to allow Clémentine to marry David but, faced with their daughter's tantrums and threats, allowed her to see him regularly and sometimes invited him for dinner. The only solution was to ban him from the house but they were too afraid that Clémentine, who was capable of risking everything, might elope with him and marry in secret.

That year, Sophie married a banker who was Jewish besides, which was pleasing, though over the years the Wagners had distanced themselves from their religion. Her new husband was from a good family, a nice man and a hard worker. Everything was going well; her eldest was now married off; Charles, who had won a prize in History at the *concours général* was a brilliant student with a great future ahead of him, while David, the little devil, seemed about to achieve his goal with the Fabres. Natacha was triumphant.

6

The magnificent thing about the microscope is that it plunges us into a world of vast hills and valleys with the fantastical contours of a visual story normally hidden from view. The thin translucent slide on which a minuscule fragment is placed suddenly reveals a whole universe so that the infinitely small encompasses all the riches of the planet. But at the same time, the eye, pressed to the black eyepiece, caught up in this new world, sees nothing of the old.

In dipping into the social and amatory byways of David Wagner's story, I forget that History is about to knock at the door. Natacha is triumphant, David bares his greedy fangs, but in the east, great forces are stirring.

And yet, David cannot see History, so caught up is he in his own schemes. Now, in the late 1930s, who cares if Poland dies! Like so many other people, he has more important fish to fry.

Slowly, weddings begin to take place. Sophie is already Madame Stern, it seems more and more likely that Clémentine will be Madame Wagner – a thought that makes her father shudder, and Marcel Fabre has given his name to a girl named Virginie. David was not invited to this last wedding, a fact that did not particularly surprise him, besides, in the trench war he was waging, he barely noticed such a detail.

The Fabres had gone back to their beginnings: Marcel had gone into the civil service and been appointed Secretary General of the *préfecture* of Rouen at the rank of *sous-préfet*. Living in

Normandy, like his ancestors, he had met a young woman and fallen in love with her – anything is possible – and managed to get what he wanted. In fact, it was common knowledge that Marcel Fabre usually got what he wanted. If David was ambitious and charming, Marcel was intelligent and cunning. One achieved his aims with charm, the other with skill.

One Saturday in December, David was summoned to the Fabres' house to meet Marcel and his new wife. He was in a foul mood. The previous night he had had dinner at his brother-in-law's *hôtel particulier* where he had seen his sister, radiant, pregnant with her first child, while his own plans for marriage were dragging on. Her parents no longer opposed the wedding, Clémentine said, but nor did they give it their blessing. Her father clearly hoped her feelings for David would fade and die. It was a vain hope since Clémentine loved David as much as ever and he, over time, had grown fond of his future wife for whom he had the greatest admiration.

The maid opened the door, David stepped inside and immediately saw Virginie. It was an image that would haunt him for a long time: a young blonde woman in a purple dress walking quickly to the window with a glass in her hand. He never knew why she felt the need to move so quickly at a cocktail party as deathly dull as the Fabres' but there lodged in his mind an impression of fleetness he would for ever associate with her.

In that first minute, countless feelings crystallised from which no one would ever be free. In the moment, nothing made sense, but everyone present realised that what happened later was simply an extension of the fleeting flicker – and then everyone understood its significance.

As David stepped into the room, eyes fixed on the young

woman, Marcel had an unpleasant feeling, which he put down to his dislike for his future brother-in-law, the same feeling that Clémentine would experience a second later seeing her lover's gaze. Then, closing the circle, Virginie turned and looked at David for a moment before smiling and lowering her eyes in a gesture that truly worried Marcel.

Not a word was spoken, not a thought formed, but the die had been cast. Over dinner, David found it difficult to tear his eyes from Virginie. Later, he would be incapable of explaining what it was about her that so attracted him: she was undoubtedly very pretty, but he had slept with more beautiful women who had not triggered the same feelings in him. Virginie was twenty, pale-skinned, her lips red, her eyes green. With these features a girl can be pretty or ugly, depending on chance. It happened that Virginie had been lucky.

According to Charles, his brother had been attracted to the young woman because she represented everything he had always dreamed of: she was tastefully dressed, witty, superficial – even if she would later prove to have other qualities – in short, to David she was the perfect woman, a fantasy of a happy, uninhibited life guaranteed to flatter his narcissism. And the fact that she was the wife of a man he so envied was an added incentive. Virginie was not simply herself, she was also, as are all women we genuinely desire, a collection of impressions.

That evening, two people of superior charm met and recognised one other. Afterwards, everything became complicated. But their meeting, in any other circumstances, would have been utterly simple: they saw each other, were attracted to each other, desired each other. Since the circumstances were far from simple, this complex rhythm exploded.

During the meal, David talked a lot. He was full of life, showing off. Clémentine and Virginie laughed at his jokes and even Marcel deigned to smile. But Virginie and David did not catch each other's eyes except for one brief moment and David saw in her amused expression that she did not find him unattractive.

Marcel, sitting next to Virginie, following the tradition that young couples should not be separated at table, regularly stroked her hand, her arm, her thigh as though these gestures would bring her back to him and mark out his ownership. He even kissed her tenderly. David felt a twinge. He wanted this woman. Until now, he had not clearly formulated the thought. Shabbily he took Clémentine's hand, without knowing why, perhaps out of guilt, perhaps as a response to Marcel.

When dinner was over, when they were alone in the library, where they often met, Clémentine said: "She's pretty, isn't she, Marcel's wife?"

He knew that she was asking him, very gently, to lie to her, to say no. He sensed her need, and because he respected this woman, because he was touched by her love for him, he wanted to please her. He could have said that Virginie was superficially pretty but not attractive, that she had no conversation, that you would have imagined Marcel would have married someone with brains. There were so many possible lies… Instead, despite himself, and because it was unfortunately obvious, he said: "Yes. Very pretty."

Clémentine bowed her head.

If Virginie had gone back to Rouen the following day, everything might have been different. Attraction is not deadly and in the absence of its object it fades. But she stayed in Paris for several weeks, claiming that she enjoyed being there and wanted to make the most of it while Marcel came and went between Rouen and the capital. Since she knew no one in the city other than Clémentine, her sister-in-law was entrusted with showing her around Paris. But instead of wanting to visit the Louvre or the Eiffel Tower, as Clémentine had when she was younger, Virginie wanted only to go to plays and shows. She wanted to have fun, something Clémentine had little time for.

David met up with them as rarely as he could: his attraction to Virginie could only be harmful and he could see no possible solution. But he was one of those men who cannot resist their passions. He would give in to it suddenly, walking out of the shop and suggesting taking the two young women on an outing. He took them boating on the lake in the Bois de Boulogne. The weather was sultry, hot and a little heavy, rounded like the clouds, the tops of the trees, the green roundness of the banks. David, in a shirt, his sleeves rolled up and his collar open, was rowing. He rowed hard, a primitive display of strength and stamina intended for Virginie. There was no point to this seduction since, although he desired the young woman, he did not want to do anything, but it was natural, because like an animal he needed it. Virginie watched him flirt and smiled ironically, the tangible distance separating them exciting David all the more, but sometimes her smile settled on him because she found him handsome and attractive. She herself could hardly have wanted more than this flattering display, but she would have been disappointed had he stopped.

"Aren't you tired?" asked Clémentine.

"I could row across the Atlantic," said David, puffing out his chest mockingly.

Virginie gave a throaty laugh for no apparent reason, a laugh of pleasure and abandon. She threw her head back, revealing her throat, and stared at the clouds as though lost in the heavens. Her hand dangled in the water, a liquid cut. David felt a shock. A desire such as he had never felt.

One evening, they went dancing. The dance floor was full, the room was stifling, the music deafening. It was the sort of club where all kinds of people mix and all three of them had dressed simply. But where Virginie's simplicity was artful, and David's showed off his muscular neck and chest, Clémentine's simplicity was simply banal. True, she was caught up in this desire that excluded her, felt an anxiety she refused to understand, seeing her sister-in-law being seduced but blind to the consequences.

First Clémentine and David danced together, a little stiffly, but gracefully since they were accustomed to each other. They chatted quietly, Clémentine smiled. Then, as it should be, David invited Virginie to dance while Clémentine went to get a drink at the bar before finding a seat. When she had sat down, she looked around for the couple.

They were dancing. The smile on Clémentine's face vanished. Nothing was happening, absolutely nothing, they made not a single ambiguous movement – they were simply dancing – yet there was such harmony between them, they looked so effortlessly beautiful that, to use the time-honoured expression, they seemed made for each other. Perhaps it was no more than a physical harmony but one so troubling that it united them, because quite simply there is a truth to bodies, a truth to the physical union.

"You're a good dancer," said David.

"So are you," said Virginie. "Better than Marcel. But I suspect you do a lot of things better than Marcel," she added a little sadly.

She said nothing else, but that was enough. David could guess what she had not confessed. He sensed the flaw, the discord in the marriage. Perhaps a simple crack but he knew how quickly a crack could deepen. He pictured the ugly, terribly serious little man, and saw this tall, beautiful, joyous young woman trapped at the age of twenty in the dreary role of housewife. The two images did not match. It was a photo one could rip in two.

Two days later, Virginie went back to Rouen. When she returned to Paris three months later for a two-week visit, the lovers were united. They had not seen each other, had not spoken, but time had done its work, crystallised their waiting and the desire. As David rushed to dinner, his palms were slick with sweat, and his heart ached like the teenage boy he was deep down. And this was what made him engaging: arriviste, hedonist, utterly devoid of scruples, David Wagner was also an innocent, capable of losing everything for a passion. For years he had been waging a battle which at one fell swoop was to give him everything: money, respectability, stability. For four months, he had been courting disaster, his passion for social status having given way to romantic passion. He realised he could lose everything: he didn't care. Suddenly, the possession of Virginie seemed to him more crucial than all the treasures in the world.

When he came into the apartment that evening, David did not know how she would greet him: she might have been cold, distant, she might have been friendly but indifferent, which amounted to the same thing. But when the young woman turned, cheeks flushed with emotion, in a tailored suit much too elegant for a family get-together, he had a strange feeling of cogs meshing, like a lock turning, heralding victory. Two desires meeting. They joked together. David went home humming and skipping.

Two days later, Virginie was at the shop to order a dress from a pattern she had taken from a magazine. She handed the page to David. Heart pounding, he watched the slender, slightly trembling hand proffering the pattern, though they both knew that this was not the reason Virginie had come. He opened the door to the back of the shop. They went up the stairs, talking inanely, pale from their passion. Their voices sounded strange, as though shifted somehow, the young man's voice out of tune at times. It didn't matter. They were barely listening to each other, aware that everything was being played out. And almost without realising how, they found themselves in each other's arms. But David knew exactly what he was doing when he took her completely and for ever.

Virginie was David's only love, a fact which I feel excuses many of his faults. He had had affairs, relationships, he felt a certain fondness for Clémentine. But, to the end, he loved only one woman. It is impossible to ever know a man. It is difficult enough to know oneself, as we have been told so often in philosophy classes, so what can be said about an ancestor disappeared half a century ago and brought to life by an old man's ramblings? A ghost, just a ghost, a fleeting cloud. And yet I believe David was one of those suicidal creatures who can only love when they know that it may cost them their life or their liberty. Deep down, they are people without a cause searching for an absolute. David had nothing in his life. He wanted only money, recognition, which are simply masks for some greater emptiness. When fate offered him the opportunity to lose everything, he leapt at it, because loss is an absolute: it gives one the sense of having something one has lost.

His loss had a charming face and a smile that would damn him: her name was Virginie.

They saw each other as best they could, which was both rather badly and also rather well. Badly because, like all forbidden relationships, it was unequal, volatile, difficult, with long periods apart and brutal periods of two weeks together. Good because their desire never faded and the other was sanctified by their absence. To tell the truth, I don't really know how it was and nor does Charles: it was just that, as David had sensed, the wheels were in motion.

7

Once war broke out, History regained the upper hand. No longer were there individuals, adulterous affairs, private lives; all these things were eclipsed by the enormity of the conflict. It was not that the individual disappeared, but that he and his personal concerns were subsumed by the common concern that was the war. On 3 September 1939 at 5 p.m., the world tipped into a violence, a barbarism that no one could have anticipated.

"Where were you when war was declared?" I asked Charles.

"Near Evreux, in Normandy," the old man answered, "staying with friends in a little village. The alarm bell was rung. We all immediately knew what was happening. Children jumped around shouting. But the adults gathered together in silence near the church."

"And David?"

"With Virginie, probably. I'm almost sure of it because my mother said she couldn't find him. They were probably in a hotel, they would only have found out later."

"Did you know Virginie?"

"Not at the time. They were too discreet, though my mother may have suspected, and besides the Fabres didn't receive the Wagners, so it was impossible for me to meet her officially. But at the end of the war, and once a year for many years after that, she would visit me to talk about David, maybe because she liked me. That was when I found out about everything.

Then she fell ill. I later found out she had died in 1952."

"Were you called up during the war?"

"As a doctor, yes. Actually, I hadn't even finished my studies, but they needed young doctors at the front. At first, I wasn't really much use and when the Germans attacked on 10 May, we were overwhelmed, we could barely look after the wounded. Afterwards, I was taken prisoner, I spent about a year in a camp before coming back to Paris. A few months later, I managed to get to London where I worked as a doctor with the French army before joining the troops in Africa."

"You didn't think twice about joining the Resistance?"

"No, for me it was the obvious thing to do."

"Why?"

"Because I'd become Jewish."

"You weren't Jewish before?"

"Vaguely. My family was culturally Jewish, from a religious point of view I was Jewish, but in reality I was no more Jewish than I was Parisian. But after war was declared, after Germany crushed France, I became Jewish. That's how Vichy designated me. They made laws to mark me out, imprison me, my brother was sent to the camps and killed. So no, I didn't think twice. From the first I knew that Jews had a duty to join the Resistance."

"Were other members of your family imprisoned?"

"My sister and her husband went to Switzerland early on. All the possessions were seized, they lost everything, but they were alive. After the war, they returned. My brother-in-law went back to his job and had a successful career. As for my mother, she suffered a sudden collapse during the winter of 1944. Like my father, she died just as there was light at the end of the tunnel. She had been strong her whole life, she had never weakened, not even when my brother was sent to Buchenwald. She loved him, you know, she was crazy about him. He was her favourite, he always had been. They worked together, lived together. She understood him, criticised him sometimes, but she always loved him. All through my childhood and my adolescence, I was jealous of that. But I loved him too, I worshipped him. He was my big brother. When he was sent away, she hung on. She hoped. She received two letters from Buchenwald, those typewritten forms in which prisoners were expected to tick boxes – 'I'm well/I'm not well' – and she wrote long letters back, not knowing whether David would ever get them. After that, there was nothing. But that didn't mean he was dead, just that he was nothing, less than nothing. Not a man, not even a number. Nothing. My mother waited, hoping for this nothing to reappear one day, just like that, to ring the doorbell. And they would fall into each other's arms. Yes, she still hoped, the news of the war was good, I'd sent her a letter to reassure her that Nazi Germany was going to be destroyed, that it was only a matter of months. But one day she suddenly broke. There were no workers in the shop, she had had to close up and besides she didn't care about the business any more. A neighbour found her the following day, collapsed at the foot of her chair, mouth open. This was a woman who, all her life, stood upright and straight and she fell just like that."

The old man made a curt downward gesture with his hand. Then he was silent. I knew I should leave. Which I did, somewhat awkwardly, as always. I've never known how to leave. In the street, I realised that I hadn't even asked him about my father. Perhaps because the answer was obvious.

Since the moment I discovered the photograph of that

man in Buchenwald, the pieces had gradually been coming together. Questions, scattered figures I had known since my adolescence, came together like salt grains in a rock cleft, to form a hard, white surface. In that sense, given that I was single and my life was pleasant but unpredictable, my search took over my life, gave it a purpose: I had *something* I needed to know. But at the same time, my world was not turned completely upside down, simply a slow crystallisation or rather a ripening. I was in no hurry. I was waiting. *Something* was happening. That he was the son of David and Virginie did not change how I felt about my father. On the contrary, I understood him better. Though I had got used to him, taking his quirks with me throughout my disjointed education, quirks I shared because in the end we are all our fathers' sons, my greatest difficulty had been fitting him into our family, the Fabres. Socially, psychologically, he was completely different and the Fabre in me rebelled against these quirks. Adrien Fabre was not how we were supposed to be, with our rather narrow, conventional morality, but still he clung to life, to his fundamental materialism. Adrien Fabre had no family of his own – he had barely lived with my mother, they separated before I was a year old – Adrien Fabre had no desire to succeed professionally, he did not care about money and more generally, though no one said as much, he didn't care about anything. The world barely existed for him. He was a tourist, casually visiting what other people call life. Seen like that, the question was: why was Adrien Fabre not like the rest of the family. When I discovered he was illegitimate, the differences made sense: a Fabre-Wagner or a Wagner-Fabre who had no blood ties to the patriarch, the foundation stone of our family, Marcel Fabre, had no reason to behave like a Fabre.

Had his quirks not run through me like a hairline crack, had I been completely true to the family moral code rather than a hybrid, an heir like the others in the family but one incapable of applying its moral code to my own life, I would have said: "Adrien F.-W. is not one of us."

His approach to life was actually quite typical of bastards. While some display an exaggerated need to be accepted, try to forge a place in the world, to leave their mark, others retreat into an inner world where they fashion a universe. Because they feel like strangers, and are people merely tolerated within their own family, they feel like guests in the world outside. Having learned in childhood to walk on eggshells, to do their best not to attract the attention of these strange yet familiar creatures around them, they carry this behaviour into their adult life, slip from place to place, from one decade to another like a shadow. My father was one of those who had forgotten the outside world perhaps because the world, with its animal brawls, reminded him of the fundamental morality, our family's morality of acquisitiveness. He had retreated into an inner world with its own arabesques, its own familiar outlines marked out even by his constant walks through Paris.

This behaviour, however, implied that my father knew he was not a Fabre. Bastards are only bastards if they know it, even if the family secrets – I'm proof of this – have strange effects on personalities that go beyond words, creating separations and differences in the subconscious. Adrien's absence at family gatherings was not the behaviour of a bastard who does not know but of a man who knows and draws the consequences. But I could not be sure. My father had always ridiculed these conventional gatherings, Christmas, birthdays, complained about the presents he had to find, the imagination required, especially for nephews, nieces, cousins he barely knew, a task all the more complicated when they were "irritating, ignorant" children.

I had a drink with him in the hope of raising these questions. He arrived a little late, which was very unusual. When he kissed me, I noticed a certain unease. I wondered what was wrong with him. We talked about this and that, while I was hoping to find the right moment. But how would such a moment arise? I had been told a story which drew together other fates than ours. I had been given a new genealogy. How could I talk about it?

I tried to approach it indirectly: "You've never really talked to me about my grandmother."

My father stared at me.

"Virginie Fabre," I said.

"Are you planning to write a book about her?" he asked a little sullenly. "Isn't my doppelgänger enough for you?"

The comment seemed uncalled for.

"I'd just like to know a little more about her."

"There is not much to know. Her life was short and without incident."

"Lives without incident are rare, especially in the mid-twentieth century."

"It all depends on how well you are protected. Virginie became part of our family, she married a future *préfet*, she took the name Fabre. That was ample protection."

"She died young…"

"Yes," my father said, "she died in 1952."

"You would have been ten."

He said nothing.

"What did she die of?"

"No idea."

"It must have been tough for all of you."

"I didn't realise you were so sentimental," my father interjected curtly.

I was not intimidated by his tone. I knew he was simply trying to push me away because I was getting close to something he kept to himself. In this, he was a Fabre: the personal was forbidden territory.

"Losing your mother when you're ten is hard. You don't have to be sentimental to understand that. It must have been hard for Grandfather too."

"He never got over it," said my father, happier to be talking about Marcel. "He seemed the same as ever, he had the same authority, the same passion for work. But I know he carried her ghost with him. Although he never cried in front of us, he was devastated. One day, a year after Virginie's death, I found him roaming around the house, he was standing, at the foot of the stairs, unkempt, his hair wild. He didn't recognise me."

"He didn't recognise his own son?" I said.

I still regret that heavy-handed allusion, that heedless treachery of an inquisitive son. But my father did not notice and I hope he did not hear the question. He was lost in his memories.

"Why have I never seen any photos of her?" I asked after a moment.

"I don't have any."

"Was she beautiful?"

My father was silent. The he said, "Very beautiful."

He said it regretfully. Then he went on, his tone hard and brusque: "Every since you found the photo of that man, you've been poking your nose into things that don't concern you. Being a writer doesn't mean poking about in other people's lives, it means having imagination, inventing things. You're a young man and you spend all your time among the dead. Ever since you were a child, you've been buried in your books, you don't live your life, you live by proxy. But this is worse. You're snuffling around the dead. This is our family history. I forbid you to write about it. You will not use it to promote yourself. I won't tolerate it."

And he left.

I sat there petrified. My father had not spoken to me in that tone since I was a child. The reason for his outburst was obvious: I was getting close to the truth and he knew it. Hence his nervousness, his flare-up. But understanding the reasons was one thing, the hurt remained. And I began to wonder whether I shouldn't give up my research. After all, what good would it do? I knew the basics. And it was not as though there was anything criminal in what I had found out. A man and a woman had fallen in love and had a child out of wedlock. My father was hardly the first bastard. Obviously for me it was momentous news, but looking at the situation dispassionately there was nothing earth-shattering there. Besides, he had been justified in raising the subject of publishing the story. What right did I have to write about such personal matters when it could only harm my family? At the same time, when I thought about my nightmares as a child, about how I felt marginalised in the world, about my father, himself silent, withdrawn like a man with no right to speak, I felt obliged to testify to the existence of the Wagners within the Fabre family.

I had a lot of work at the school at the time. Though I had the chance to teach gifted pupils, given the specific selection process of the school where I worked, the flipside was that my evenings and weekends were taken up with books, preparing classes and correcting homework. So it was easy for me to put the story of David Wagner to one side and focus on this year's syllabus: the political humanism of Montaigne and Rabelais. There was little chance I would stumble on any other grandparents or family secrets.

But still, in my dreams, I saw this faceless man. I didn't dream about him every night, but from time to time the anonymous form would reappear, nagging at me like a question. Yet I had a name to put to this ghostly form, he could only be David Wagner, but my nights disregarded such reassuring answers, and still the faceless man went on observing me. Though he had no features, no eyes, I felt him stare at me. Held spellbound by this absent gaze, bowing gradually to its authority, I returned to my search.

8

During my conversation with him, Vincent Mallet had advised me to contact a man name Serge Kolb, who, according to him, had been David's best friend in Buchenwald. He told me that Kolb was Jewish (on Mallet's lips, it sounded like a special category), but that was not the reason he had been sent to the camp. As a prisoner of war, he had twice attempted to escape and on the second occasion he had been sent to Buchenwald. And the Germans had never put him with the Jews.

Jew. This word which had become an obsession on Hitler's lips. This word which for centuries had been whispered in Europe and which the Nazis now barked insanely into the ears of the world like a man with a megaphone. During my adolescence, the word 'Jew' suddenly, without reason, became important as though I sensed that one day my life would be devoted to clarifying a page of our family history in a concentration camp. Proof of the prophetic power which some, including Victor Hugo, attribute to the act of writing, a power I believe in simply because this meticulous task, when every sense is focused on the page, causes inchoate secrets to rise, reveals hidden regions which are crucial and bound to come to light. This is why the strapping Jack London denied being his hero Martin Eden even as he highlighted the obvious similarities of their biographies. The crucial difference, he stated, is Martin Eden's individualism which makes it impossible for him to find hope in his peers. The proof, he concluded, is that he committed suicide while I have no intention of doing so. Years later, he surrendered to the same fate as his hero, rejoining the lines he had written and which his writing had secretly intuited.

The simple fact is that one day, without my knowing why, the Jewish question became a crucial one. I still remember my fascination with one of my Jewish school friends who, every Saturday morning, would fold his arms and listen attentively to the weighty philosophy lesson (three hours with the same teacher – a chore for any teenager), without taking a single note, having walked all the way from Vincennes – which as those who know how far it is from Vincennes to the Parthenon in the centre of Paris is a considerable walk. Even allowing that he was a precocious student who, in a class full of over-inflated egos, was proud to be different, the effort was remarkable and rather disconcerted me. So I naturally turned to this boy to give him the results of my "research", if I can use the word to describe the series of thoughts and disparate books I was reading at the time. The fate of the Jews seemed to me so terrible, so terrifying that I wanted to understand how such a hatred had developed. The history of the Jews was a mystery to me. I had read Sartre's *Anti-Semite and Jew** and a number of other respected books of the period (including Poliakov, I think) in a sincere attempt to find an answer. A deicidal people; a people intimately linked to money and usury ever since Christians had permitted them to become moneylenders; the arrogance of the chosen people – I had read many of the explanations put forward at the time and had come up with the idea that there was a deep-rooted hatred for the first monotheistic people, those who had replaced the peaceful polytheistic religions – so human, so anthropocentric – with a sombre image of an abstract, vengeful God. Sanctimoniously, I went and presented my theory to my classmate, who simply stared at me, half-alarmed, half-ironic. After that I replaced the relegated idea, like a toy I had outgrown, on the shelves of my memory.

"Do you know where Serge Kolb lives?" I had asked Vincent Mallet.

"Try Saint-Cloud. He used to have a large house out there. He is a big man, an industrialist."

"So he survived?" I asked stupidly.

"How could he not have survived? You'll understand when you meet him."

"Why? Is he particularly strong?"

Vincent Mallet shrugged.

"No. That would be of little use. He's something else. As I said, you'll see. The rich are like that sometimes."

"Everyone in Buchenwald was poor."

"Sometimes," the old communist sighed, "I wonder if being rich isn't a question of nature."

I didn't understand this description of Serge Kolb, with whom I would later have many conversations, yet the moment I met him, everything Mallet had said made sense. How could this man not have survived? From our first meeting Serge Kolb reminded me of the engineer Alfred L., in Primo Levi's *If This is a Man*, and our later conversations nuanced my sense of him, they never obliterated that first impression.

In the desolation of Auschwitz, beyond all society, man was revealed in his nakedness, in his essence. With staggering lucidity, Primo Levi forced himself, he writes, "to provide documents for a dispassionate study of certain aspects of the human soul". In his chapter "The Drowned and the

Saved" he presents two categories of man. If in ordinary life, he explains, the law, family, social structures tend to moderate human behaviour, making it possible for us all to survive, the concentration camp is a struggle to survive without respite. There is no possible moderation: you live or you die, you are saved or drowned. Unlike everyday life, there is no third way. And the easiest way to die is "to carry out all the orders one receives, eat only the rations and observe the discipline of the work and the camp". In other words, it is enough to take the path of least resistance, make no attempt to rebel, to plot, to look for solutions. Levi states that not *one* Jewish survivor of Auschwitz was an ordinary Häftling (prisoner) in a normal Kommando. They had all had special specific roles, thanks to their skills (cooks, doctors, tailors…) or responsibilities within the camp. Levi then describes, in a phrase of terrible lucidity, some "particularly pitiless, vigorous and inhuman individuals, installed (following an investiture by the SS command, which showed itself in such choices to possess satanic knowledge of human beings) in the posts of Kapos, *Blockältester*, etc." The ordinary individuals become *Musulmann* a term of uncertain origin which marked out those destined for death and for the ashes of the crematoria.

Amongst the saved who were able to adapt, by force or by cunning, Primo Levi describes the case of the engineer Alfred L. which shows "how vain is the myth of original equality among men". Alfred L. had previously run a factory of chemical products and as soon as he arrived in the camp, using a very determined strategy, he did everything he could to prove his superiority: never complained, kept himself perfectly clean even in the worst conditions, worked with zeal, behaved like one of the guards because "to seem strong was half way to being strong". When a Chemical Kommando was formed, he was immediately named technical head, responsible for new recruits, which made it possible for him to eliminate possible rivals. And Primo Levi concludes: "It is quite probable that he managed to escape death, and today is still living his cold life of the determined and joyless dominator."

Serge Kolb was anything but pitiless. And Auschwitz, an extermination camp, cannot be compared to any other. But at first glance, in his vast, impersonal mansion in Saint-Cloud, this tall man with his hard, emaciated features reminded me of that superiority. I don't know how he seemed to David Wagner when he was still young but I imagine that he was exactly the same, confident and full of authority even without the weight of years. At the time that we had our conversations, Serge Kolb had, in theory, handed over the running of his famous pottery works to his son, though in fact no major decision was taken without him and he continued to pay close attention to the business. Every morning, he got up early and went running, came back, showered and had breakfast. His whole life was marked by this rigorous discipline. During the terrible carnage of Buchenwald he might very well not have survived but if any man gave the impression of being indestructible, it was him. He exuded a cold, impressive vitality.

But this coldness, which commanded distance and respect, did not exclude friendship, something I later realised. No one would have patted this man on the back, it was not his style, but he was nonetheless the kind of man who could be relied on. He was, in any case, the most loyal friend of David Wagner.

I hesitated as I wrote the word "friend". Was it possible to have friends in a camp? Is friendship not something that demands time, trust? I don't know, to be honest. If Levi speaks of friends, Semprun talks about companions though he also uses the term brotherhood. And I have always been struck by the fact that Malraux's phrase, with its succinctness and its mystery, provides the epitaph for the books of both Styron and Semprun: "I seek the crucial region of the soul where absolute Evil confronts brotherhood." In the desolation of the camp, brotherhood may have been the only way not to slip into despair, which led directly to death.

Serge Kolb provided that brotherhood for David Wagner. In spite of his modesty, that is how I understood their relationship. They supported one another. By a quirk of the railway networks, and although Kolb was coming from Germany, they were both on the same train to Buchenwald and it was there they first saw each other. What struck Kolb that day, in spite of the fear, the thirst and the general panic (though large convoys of prisoners were not yet being sent to the camp, a group of about thirty prisoners of different nationalities from German prisons had been rounded up), was the young man's apparent impassivity. He did not move, did not speak, he did not even seem concerned.

"I've sometimes been told I'm a cold man," said Kolb. "But in all my long and full life I've never met anyone as inscrutable as David was that day. Not that he was like that by nature, but I later noticed that in extreme circumstances he would become like that. Danger made him retreat into himself. He showed nothing, neither emotions nor affects. I don't even know if it was a good thing, I just know it was how he expressed anxiety, like animals that retreat into their shell when they're in danger."

They met at the camp. They were about the same age, they were both French (and in 1941–2 there were few French prisoners in Buchenwald), Jewish and Parisian, they hit it off. Meaning that even in the tragic conditions of the camp, friendship could be sparked in the same banal way as in ordinary life.

"When I got out, it was a long time before I could talk about the camps. I was one of those who said nothing. It's a classic distinction," said Kolb with an ambiguous wave, as though apologising for all that was known about the camps, "among those of us who were in the camps. There were the ones who couldn't talk and the ones who couldn't stop talking, those who needed to talk in order to survive and those who, for the very same reason, could not bring themselves to. I didn't say anything. Not a word. When I got married, it was a year before my wife knew that I had been in a camp. And then one day my children were grown up. And I thought it was my duty as a father to pass on the memory of what happened. Because there are not many witnesses to that horror left."

"I'm obsessed with this idea," I said. "I've tried to get to grips with it, but I've never experienced anything like that. I represent the third generation. We don't even try to understand our fathers' history but our grandfathers'. Once you're gone, all that will be left are the documents. There won't be a living soul who saw Ettersberg under the Nazis."

"You're right, unfortunately. But that's not what I was getting at. It is my duty to transmit what I experienced, however tenuous it is, for the generations who did not live through the reality of the camps. However, one of the problems of transmission is getting people to understand that Buchenwald was both utterly other but also rather banal in its impulses. Death was omnipresent and I could describe scenes of absolute horror: violence, decomposition, sadism. Truly, if you haven't experienced it, you don't know what evil means. But at Buchenwald we got to eat, albeit not much, we chatted, we even laughed. I've never seen a film set in a camp where prisoners laugh. Everything is grey and solemn. But I laughed in Buchenwald, which might sound shocking, but it's true. I can even tell you that in Buchenwald I laughed while chatting in the latrines, that's right, I laughed while taking a shit, excuse my language. On Sundays, I even listened to lectures by teachers and people interested in books. I read philosophy books in the camp. And that's what I can't pass on to my children: the abject horror allied to a banality that made it possible to shit and talk about literature while dying. And it was easy for people to get along because they liked football. That wasn't true of us. David and I weren't remotely interested in football. But our friendship started like all friendships start: we had things in common. It was cemented by our hatred of the enemy and when the doctor, Wagner, appeared on the scene, though I was powerless, I did my best to help him."

9

A strange incident comes back to me as I try to piece together the gist of my conversations with Serge Kolb. A bad reporter, I never recorded our conversations, convinced they would be engraved on my memory as on a clay tablet. It also seemed to me that the details were unimportant since I was looking not for a story, which is a coherent collection of details, but for a truth. The glaring light of truth. And if I was to know the truth about David Wagner, the truth about this too much-loved upstart turned martyr, the details, I thought, would simply get in the way.

But the conversations were longer and more numerous than I could ever have expected. Before my conversations with Kolb, I felt like a fraud. First, because my father had forbidden me to go on investigating. And then because concentration camps are an emotive subject and one, it sometimes feels, that only those who were in them can talk about. Besides, some people say that the enormity of the crime means no comment or story is possible unless it is direct testimony. I admit that when such comments don't come from people who were in the camps, they don't move me. And I truly believe that art has a gift of clairvoyance and that my childhood fears, my violence, are a means of access to Buchenwald. But I feel uncomfortable with this alien, unknowable past.

Thankfully, Kolb took the mantle of deception from me. I had the right to know, and more than that, I had the right to write about it if I wanted to because I was the grandson of his friend David Wagner. True, there remained the fundamental impossibility of transmitting something I had not experienced. No, I had never seen Ettersberg under the Nazis. To me, Ettersberg was the historical awkwardness of Goethe's Oak and Anna Amalia, the Nazis, the communist camp and that throwback that was the memorial to the camp. It was a deserted camp with watchtowers, a vast gate inscribed with the words *Jedem das Seine* – To Each His Own – and a museum. But I could transmit a different form of experience. And in fact, if memory died as generations died, humanity would no longer exist.

Nevertheless, and this did nothing to reassure me, the strangest memory of our conversations leaves me feeling uncertain. Was it really something that happened in the life of David Wagner or a fact I gleaned from one of the countless books I was reading at the time about Europe under the Nazis? Sometimes I seemed to remember that the protagonist of the story is not my grandfather but a teenage girl, as though fates were superimposed. I hesitate, memories blur and everything disappears into the void and Serge Kolb, as I write this, is no longer here to support me because he died two years ago.

Yet memory is crucial because at that moment a life was being played out. My grandfather – or at least the character I think of as my grandfather – was about to be deported to Buchenwald. The roll-call had already begun. Perhaps David was not fully aware of it but he should stay put. It was important that he not leave. To what extent he realised that his former life no longer existed, that he had no support, that he could not wriggle out of things as he had always done before, by some charming ruse, I don't know. But maybe he thought he was going to a prison camp… How could he even have guessed the reality of a concentration camp?

He found himself – or at least a young man named David found himself, unless it was a teenage girl – that morning, standing in front of the latrine and he told himself that he had to dive into the cesspit, to escape from the convoy, disappear where no one would ever find him. Through the thin wooden partition, he heard the names being called one by one in a loud, gravelly voice. It was important he did not answer, that they did not find him. If his name was erased from the lists, everything became possible. His heart in his mouth, he stepped forward, stared into the dark, repulsive, reeking hole as though staring at the water before taking his life. He stretched out his hand, his face… but he couldn't do it. David or the adolescent girl, these two deportees, these two disappeared, could not bring themselves to do it. They left and they died.

It is incredible that I don't remember the origin of that story. But it's true. Perhaps it's just a reconstruction, maybe I've grafted a true story onto David Wagner's life simply because I so desperately wanted him to escape the camp. It's possible, it's something I've done before. All through my adolescence I was convinced that as a child I had saved one of my classmates. I must have been seven or eight years old when my friend Richard was bullied by a little thug and his gang. It was pure sadism, probably because Richard was gentle and overweight. One day, they made him follow them into the far corner of the playground and took down his pants. It was at that moment that I arrived, like a knight in shining armour, and threw myself on the gang's ringleader. That's how I saved Richard.

In my dreams. Because in fact I stood there terrified and did nothing as they dragged him away. I wanted so much to help him... but I couldn't. But I realised this only years later, certainly some time after I turned twenty. One day, I realised that superimposed over the image – what Freud calls a screen memory, I think – of the blond knight leaping on the bad guy was the other image of Richard coming back from the corner of the playground crying and pulling up his trousers. This is how I managed to lie to myself for years, out of cowardice, how I genuinely believed I had saved my friend. They didn't rape him, obviously, they didn't really touch him, but he had been humiliated, bare-arsed, surrounded by the gang. That's what they enjoyed.

Of David Wagner's life sadly there is nothing to be saved except perhaps his memory, which is part of my life, and I leave it to psychoanalysts to explore the significance of my forgetting or my reconstruction. In any case, shit pit or not, David got on the train, his eyes met Serge Kolb's and they both vanished into the night, with the dogs howling and the lashing of the SS batons.

From this moment on, nothing that I tell you has any meaning. I'm an intellectual, a teacher who wears glasses and most of my life, with all the doubts that that entails, consists of giving meaning to the actions of men, to memory, to emotions. But what meaning can be given to the concentration camps? As a teenager, the first book I read about the camps made me cry. Since then I have met former camp prisoners, read many books: doubtless I became hardened and have not cried. But I have never become inured because the litany of horror is absolutely infinite and each time we believe we have gone beyond the bounds of crime, some new fact, ripped from the imagination of a sadist, comes to add another circle of Evil. And I never found any other meaning for this madness than the pleasure of death. All those who went there talk about the hell of the camps. This apparently hackneyed image is probably the most appropriate because it seems to me that the religious representations of heaven and hell are simply projections, as on a screen, of human fantasies. The vast medieval imaginary of hell, the hell of Dante and of Bosch, gives form to human folly in its most hideous. The concentration camps are hell made flesh because the terrible mixture of iron discipline and the vilest human urges created here on earth everything imagined in those secular representations. The camps are Man. To enter one of the camps is to penetrate an icy madness devoid of any meaning save destruction, suffering and death. And sometimes, in spite of the testimony, I doubt that any brotherhood could have confronted absolute Evil.

Sometimes I am wary of words. So I will speak in figures. We all believe we know the camps when, in fact, we cannot even imagine them. More than eight million people passed through the concentration and extermination camps. And yet there were never more than a million people at the same time in all the camps put together, be they the twenty large concentration camps or the thousands of smaller Kommandos, to which we need to add the extermination camps whose names everyone knows: Auschwitz-Birkenau, Majdanek, Treblinka, Belzec, Sobibor. There is only one explanation for the discrepancy between these two figures: at least six million people died in the camps, particularly in Auschwitz, the greatest nightmare in all humanity. The Kommandant of the camp, SS Kramer, did not miss a single execution. People say he laughed and slapped his thighs. The head of the crematorium, Moll, amused himself hanging Jews up by their hands and pulling until their arms broke and the body fell to the floor. Then he would hang the victim up by the legs and begin again, then he would toss the dying torso into the burning pit. The SS were able to beat all records: in a single day, they managed to execute thirty-four thousand prisoners. They told them to undress, to fold their clothes and put them in piles, a sign said that after the shower they would be served black coffee. They were told to tie their shoes together so as not to lose them. So as not to lose them. The name of the SS in charge of the camps is not remotely ambiguous: Totenkopf-Standarten – Death's Head Units.

Did David see the skull on the jacket of the SS officer hitting him? I don't know. Even if, now, I know a lot. Even if, in my interviews with Kolb, I felt both more conscious and more a part of that fate. Even if I know that, arms in the air, David ran from the station to the camp, reeling and staggering beneath the blows. A man collapsed. He was beaten. A little farther on, another. He was kicked and beaten with truncheons. When the third, an old man, stumbled and fell some minutes later, a soldier shot him dead. He was a boy. Serge later discovered that he had only been at the camp for ten months and at first he had been almost shy, he had even given a prisoner a cigarette. And now he was a part of it, he had become an animal like the others, his face as he fired was almost demonic in spite of his blond hair, his pale skin, his slender adolescent neck. An Overscharführer said simply: "He was too old. He would have been no use for anything."

After that, no one fell. Even the shouts of the SS were less harsh, as though they had satisfied some secret wish. The group arrived at night. The gates of the camp did not open.

David was thrown into a tiny cell with ten other prisoners, including Serge. Some still did not understand. Despite the cramped train, despite the running. Some screamed: "There's no room. We can't get in." He was pushed inside with truncheon blows, blood trickled from his head onto the clothes and the faces of those around him. The cell was narrow, dark and overheated. There was a cry: "They're trying to suffocate us." There was no air. They were cramped, crowded. "Take your clothes off," said a voice. A mass of bodies writhing in slow, weak gestures. The heat was intolerable. Several people fainted. Then everyone slipped into a sort of queasy stupor, an asphyxia that was the last stage before death, from which they were dragged, screaming, in the morning.

Some woke from their stupor weeping. Among the men, of various nationalities, there were Resistants, communists who knew what they were fighting for and who had been living hard lives for years now. But there were men who did not know why they were there, who only a few days earlier had been living contentedly, well fed, well dressed. Those were the ones who were crying. Because they had been ripped from a life that was normal, despite the war, and hurled into hell. Because from the first interrogation, everything was done to try and break them. And because it generally succeeded. All their moral strength collapsed at once. David did not cry: as Serge put it, his inner destruction saved face. It was as though he were frozen. Not a word came from his lips.

Afterwards, the group waited for several hours, kneeling by the barbed wire, arms crossed behind their heads, prostrate. Soldiers marched up and down the line screaming at them, sometimes beating them. A fat non-commissioned officer ran past them knocking them down like pins. A man sobbed, face pressed to the ground. When he righted himself, flecks of mud fell from his head. David watched, fascinated.

A man came. He was barking orders, a list of warnings punishable by death: attempting to go near the barbed wire, smoking, escaping, eating during the work Kommandos, stealing, resting, lying, going outside the perimeter.

"So, basically, living is punishable by death," someone muttered.

The man who had earlier been sobbing and now stood, drained, motionless, hunched over like a statue of pain, suddenly began to whimper. And then his moans grew louder, his mouth opening in a harrowing, horrible scream, a death-rattle flecked with spittle. The scream went on and on, there was no end to it, because he realised that he was lost, that all was lost and so he howled in infinite pain. Everyone stared at him and shuddered, frozen with fear, waiting for they knew not what and still the scream went on.

A colossal SS officer in shirt and braces came out of the building. With a single truncheon blow he left the man unconscious, then warned them: *Bald werdet ihr aus gutem Grund schreien!* "You'll have good reason to scream soon enough." Even those who knew no German understood the threat.

After several hours they were forced to get up and run. They went into a dirty room where they undressed. All these pale, naked creatures seemed desperately frail. One after another, they faced the barber who shaved them completely, which made them even more frail, their long necks bare, their eyes suddenly bigger, more frightened. Opposite, the soldier watching them, rigged out in boots and helmet, seemed like an indomitable machine. Then they were pushed into a tank of disinfectant, a viscous liquid full of dirt and decomposing matter that burned their skin. Afterwards, they had to bend over in front of the officer, legs spread. A soldier was laughing. He suddenly lashed out, kicking one of them in the buttocks. The man fell forward, laughing pathetically. Next, they were given a scalding shower, their one respite for days. David closed his eyes. When he opened them again, he was already being pushed towards the store room where he was given a tattered prisoner's uniform but was lucky enough not to get a pair of the wooden-soled shoes whose ridges quickly hurt the feet and made it difficult to walk. A man who could not walk was no use in a work camp. And a useless man had no reason to live.

At this point they were stripped of everything of value: watches, wedding rings, medals. Their luggage was tagged: "they will be returned to you after your period of internment". David had to give up his wallet containing his money, his identity papers and a photo of Virginie. Everything had now been taken from him: by force of screams and blows he had been stripped of a part of his identity. By a process which the Nazis had perfected, he had been stripped of his former life which, after the prison and the train journey, was now only a vague memory, a sort of fleeting, reassuring tremor. Nonetheless, he could not help but mourn this symbolic disappearance. He had nothing left, no identity, no love – if that word had any meaning whatever in the dense block of madness that encased him.

I don't know whether in this description of David Wagner's arrival, I have managed to give any sense of what a concentration camp was like, at least as it was described to me by Serge Kolb. I think there is little point giving a detailed description of the living quarters as David saw them, the crude bunk beds, the prisoners herded together like infectious animals. I think it is easy to imagine David slipping between the other bodies to begin his first night in that jumble of shapes and smells.

But what it is difficult to imagine is the ceremony the following morning, the tragic farce for which credit must go to the camp Kommandant, Plaul of cursed memory. He it was who had decided, a month ago, that the prisoners were to live according to the sporting regime of Hitler's Germany. Consequently, reveille was rolled forward half an hour for morning sport, a frenzied gymnastics led by Plaul himself, a scrawny, stooping, heron-like figure, and enforced by his sub-officers. And so these weakened, walking skeletons waved their limbs grotesquely, clumsily following the barked orders, lifting their knees, tottering, falling in the chill morning air. The spectacle, in the misty dawn, of these thousands of frenzied, disjointed bodies seemed all the more like the visions of Dante at his most macabre and mortal when two were left dead by the exercises.

This was merely the beginning of the day. Wheels had been set in motion, like lunatic cogs slowly grinding into gear and a trap as grotesque as it was implacable was slowly closing. A death urge disguised by the coldness of discipline, the camp was a madness run by madmen.

Serge, who, as a prisoner of war had managed to make some contacts within the camp, had warned David that he had to present himself as a "specialist" when positions in the Kommandos were being allocated. So, when those newly arrived were summoned before the head of the work details, when the command came for "specialists", both men stepped forward. Serge explained that he was an engineer and was posted to work in the weapons factory. David said he was a tailor. The officer, for some unfathomable reason, stared at him with hostility. With the arbitrariness of absolute power, he barked: "Quarry Kommando."

David blenched. He knew this was the worst Kommando, nicknamed "straight to heaven". Most newcomers were posted there.

Curiously, they were not dispatched that same day, but spent the day in the block sleeping on the straw mattresses, dreaming, sinking into sleep as into the gluey liquid disinfectant. At evening roll call, they went out. What they saw as they emerged, what made them stop in their tracks, stunned, was even more hellish than the morning: men staggering home from their day's work exhausted, some being carried by others, all marching like the living dead while grating festive music, played by an orchestra of grinning prisoners, screeched and wailed. Perhaps, it was then that they realized they were in hell and had no more chance of getting out than if they were dead.

After roll call, after the wait of more than two hours during which the names of those present were called one by one, with the implacable Nazi obsession for administration and bureaucracy, five of those who had arrived the night before, including David, were picked out without being told why. Among them was the man who had screamed. Seeing him, the others remembered the words of the SS officer and began to tremble. They were led off. There a trestle had been set up, a table on which the prisoner was made to lie face down, legs dangling on the ground. As soon as they saw *der Bock*, the group knew that some form of punishment was to be administered.

The man who stepped forward that evening to administer the beating – the same SS officer who had come out of the

Bunker the night before – is one of the men I have thought about most often during this period of my life. His name is Martin Sommer. Unknown to almost everyone, he is nonetheless a nightmare because within his circumscribed domain he reached the limits of horror. It was only later that David heard the stories of his hideous exploits and he congratulated himself on emerging alive from his one encounter with the man. Shortly afterwards, after an incident that bears telling, Sommer left Buchenwald. But the fact remains that, much more than Kommandant Koch – to whom he was linked and about whom I will also speak – Martin Sommer consumed my thoughts perhaps more even than the doctor, Wagner. Is it possible to imagine a professional murderer? A man more savage than any animal? A man who did not commit mass murder using gas or cannon fire, but who murdered individually, by strangling, hanging, poisoning hundreds of prisoners. Sommer's kingdom of blood and murder was the Bunker, the prison house. The rumours about the place are of utter horror, though it is difficult now to image that narrow corridor, to the left of the main gate, that grey corridor lined with tiny cells from which would emerge Hauptscharführer Sommer's towering form, his broad shoulders, his powerful body, before going into a cell and beating a victim to death with an iron bar, blood spattering his shirt, with such fury, such hatred that sometimes arms or legs were severed from the body.

I remember a photograph of Sommer. Strapped up tight in his SS Totenkopf uniform, he points furiously towards two prisoners hanging from a tree by their arms which are bound behind their backs, a punishment that dislocated the shoulders and led to illness or death. Facing the strapping, powerful man, these emaciated prisoners in striped uniforms like pyjamas, the pain on their faces unclear because of the poor quality of the photograph, but obviously terrified, seem small and weak as adolescents. And once again, though my memory is not perfect, I can make out no mark of Evil on Sommer's face. Just as during my visit to Buchenwald, nothing proclaims the presence of Evil, nothing in the face screams "I am a monster". If there were not two men hanging next to him, Martin Sommer would look like a former wrestler turned soldier.

And yet, according to what we hear from the testimony of those who survived, Fritz Männchen, Kurt Leeser, or the servants who worked in the Bunker, Richard Gritz and Roman Haldemeyer? So many atrocities that it would be impossible to set them all down here. But there are some details that haunt me still. Not, perhaps, the most brutal, but the most gratuitous.

Why did Martin Sommer immediately butcher those prisoners who looked out the window or read a few lines of the newspaper that served as toilet paper? He would spy on them through the peephole, throw open the door and kill them.

Why, one day as he was walking along the corridor carrying a jug, did he suddenly go into a cell containing seven Jews and, in a rage, knock two of them out before ripping a piece of piping from the radiator and killing the others?

What prompted the vile sadism that led him to put laxatives in the prisoners' food and provide them with only a tiny chamber pot so the whole cell would be covered in excrement? Then, feigning disgust at such filth, he would murder them all.

Why did he drag out the martyrdom of Pastor Schneider for eighteen months, whipping him with a bull's pizzle and leaving the wounds to become infected, never dressing them, never allowing the pastor to wash, and flooding the cell with a few inches of water and a constant flow of blood, water and lice? Why did he tenderly wrap the pastor in blankets, leaning over him as he covered him up when the blankets were freezing and served only to further weaken his heart? Why, since the end was inevitable, did he not simply kill him?

I understand none of this. It goes without saying that there are no answers to such questions save for the futile, unsatisfactory explanation of sadism. These questions echo still because Martin Sommer was not always a butcher, neither before nor after these events. Of this, I will talk later.

It was this man who now moved towards the little group. He was going to beat them because one of them had screamed. The others had been chosen at random. But he might just as easily have beaten them because they had blue eyes or brown eyes. Or because he did not like the way they stood still. Or for any other reason. The silence deepened as he passed. Butchers apparently carry with them this aura as though accompanied by some deadly peril. He bent one of the men over the trestle and slowly, methodically, began the beating. The man did not cry out. A little blood trickled from his lips as he bit them. A second man, the man who had screamed, was placed over the *Bock*. This time Sommer did not beat the buttocks but hit the kidneys savagely. The man struggled. Sommer continued his brutal beating to the end. The man had to be carried back to the block where he died three days later. David, terrified, followed him on the trestle. But that day the executioner did not want to kill him. The ten blows were administered to his buttocks. Every blow ripped through his whole body. But he was not seriously wounded. This was simply a warning: "Today is when the punishment begins."

When the ceremony was over, Serge came up to David and spoke to him.

"Look at me," he said.

"What?"

"Look at me. You're not looking at me."

It was true, David could not look him in the eye. Because he no longer had an identity, because he no longer felt he was a man. And it would be days and days before he regained something of his composure with his friend's help. In fact, it is astonishing that he managed to retain a certain calm in this nightmare because, though Serge, as a skilled worker, worked indoors in relative warmth at precise tasks before becoming leader of the team two months later, David was to experience the direct route to heaven that were the quarries.

Imagine a diabolical painting. Look down at them from the heavens. Put yourself in the position of the sun some hundreds of metres above them and watch these tiny, scattered creatures in a chalk-white funnel, this myriad of identical slaves with no faces, no features, labouring ineptly with their picks as others lift too-heavy stones and yet more, in groups of ten, push the carts under the watchful eye of armed soldiers. They have had a crust of bread to eat, a sip of some tasteless liquid, and they work all day, with half an hour's rest at midday to eat what remains of the bread – if anything remains. A ladder leads down into the depths of the quarry but Kapo Müller, the prisoner leading the Quarry Kommando, every bit as sadistic as the SS, did not allow those newly arrived to use it that first day. He pushed them towards the slope and they stumbled, rolled, one of them broke an ankle. He held out for two hours because everyone told him to hold out and then Müller came over and suggested that he go and rest behind the sentry line. A man whispered something, trying to ensure the Kapo didn't overhear: "Don't go. Whatever you do, don't go and rest."

The other man looked at him in surprise, not understanding, and hobbled away with Müller to the top of the quarry and off towards the line of guards. Two prisoners next to the cart turned. The line opened, the man managed another ten paces, then he was shot in the back, "died during an attempted escape". A soldier gave Müller a packet of cigarettes as a reward which he smoked blissfully as he watched them work.

David did this work every day. He got up to go to the grotesque gymnastics which would be stopped some weeks later, after a curt report from no one knew where, about the number of deaths caused by the practice; drank his brownish liquid (coffee?), joined the long line to the Appellplatz, found his tools, went down into the quarry, lifted rocks, pushed carts, came back to the Appellplatz at night, stood there for two hours, joined the scrum of people for food, sometimes managed to get a rotting potato as well as the soup. Every evening after the final whistle, he talked to Serge Kolb and tried to look him in the eye. Their conversation was one more ritual in his timetable, a duty he accepted for better or worse but one which, at Serge's insistence, he always accomplished.

The reasons Serge befriended David are not obvious to me. But the fact is he took him under his wing and tried to keep him alive. He had a remarkable strength of character, as we have seen and his life in the factory was much less harsh that than that in the Kommandos (in fact, the others envied him, considering the factory a sort of forbidden paradise), so he still had some strength to give.

"Why were we friends?" Kolb said one day when I asked him. "Why do people become friends? There's no particular reason."

"There are always reasons," I said. "What did you like about him? After all, he wasn't exactly a likeable person…"

"You're wrong. David was very likeable. He was a charmer and even the pale, weak version of him at the camp still had something of that charm. You're judging him without ever having known him, basing your judgement on some trivial love affair. You've said several times that he was ambitious and a liar. Maybe that's true. But it came from the fact that David was weak, he lacked singularity."

"What do you mean?"

"He had no singularity, he bowed to other people's views. A charmer is malleable because he adapts to what others see in him, women mostly, but men too. He is self-regarding but does not really value himself, which is why he tries to provide the image of himself that people expect. That was his weakness, I'll grant you that. But if you really want to go back to his relationships with women, I can tell you only one thing: David only ever loved one woman."

"Why do you say that?"

"Because of that girl. I don't remember her name. A beautiful blonde girl. There were men there who wanted to buy the photograph from him… they just wanted to rest their eyes on her."

"The photograph of Virginie? I thought that was destroyed during the initial search?"

"Of course it wasn't! The Nazis didn't destroy anything, everything could be sold on. Besides, we're not talking about the same photograph. This was one he got later in a letter. He always carried it with him."

"A letter?"

"Of course. We were allowed to receive letters. Sometimes they were tossed on the fire, sometimes not. David received a number of letters from his mother. And this letter. And I don't think anything could have made him happier than that photograph. I can still see it… She was a very beautiful woman."

"This sounds unbelievable. A photograph from the outside world in a concentration camp!"

"Yes, it was something of an anomaly, like the food parcels we were allowed later. A flaw in the system of destruction, but it only goes to show how crazy the camp was, much more absurd and illogical than people imagine. A sort of vast killing machine riddled with fierce inconsistencies. Some people took advantage of them. And David is a symbol of that madness: the madness saved him at first and in the end it killed him. But at least that photograph gave him some strength. He was French – and our government's policies since 1938 hardly made us popular in the camp – and Jewish, this always came out eventually; luck wasn't exactly on his side."

"But you were French and Jewish too."

"Yes, but I was an escaped prisoner of war which earned me some respect. Besides, I was working in the factory, which meant I made interesting friends, men who wanted to be part of the team. Most importantly, I wasn't detailed to the quarries. So I was stronger than David. That's all I thought about: giving him some of my strength. That's why I liked that photograph. That's why I insisted we talk every night. To keep him close. To give him advice too. I was beginning to understand how the camp worked. I realised that if you weren't clever, if you didn't fend for yourself when it came to work, to food, you were headed for death."

In reality, Serge had little time to spend with his friend. Things moved quickly in the camp. The initial shock – not only physical but psychological – was so brutal that a man could be broken in the first weeks, or at most in the first few months. If he survived that, it meant he had adapted. After that, if his body did not betray him, if he wasn't caught by an SS officer or a Kapo, he might become a *concentrationnaire*, one of those hard, solid creatures inserted in the system, ranged against the enemy.

The danger was that David might become a *Musulmann*, a dead man walking, with no vision, no future, an emaciated scarecrow staggering towards death without seeing it. In the Block, three men went mad. One day, they simply lost their minds, their spirits broken by suffering and despair. Reality slipped away from them, they would scream for no reason, or they would sit silently: the camp had devoured them. When one of them began to rant one night at evening roll call an SS officer threw a bucket of water over him and pushed him into the electrified barbed wire. It is this psychological dimension of torture in the camps that cannot be communicated. The concept of absolute Evil, that slightly abstract, sometimes even rhetorical idea comes, to my mind, from the moral torture of the camp. It is from this that it takes its meaning, which is why it is at the heart of the experience of prisoners like Semprun, who regularly mentions it, and why it pains them that they cannot communicate it. Absolute Evil was not an idea but a torment: one felt Evil inside oneself. Because the camp did not simply destroy the body, it destroyed the spirit, it deliberately set out to break men and turn them into submissive, mindless slaves. Madness was only the most extreme result of the Evil. Everyone, to some degree, was touched by it.

The disintegration of David's heart could be seen in his bowels. Like many prisoners, he felt a constant need to defecate. He ate almost nothing, but when he did it passed straight through him. Within a few weeks, he had lost twenty kilos, and he had never been fat. I've seen a dozen photographs of David: the first one, the original one from Buchenwald which is at the root of this tale and which established so many links. The photograph of the handsome heart-throb in the pre-war style of Harcourt's photographs, a posed Hollywood portrait of the handsome rake. I have already talked about these two photographs. There is another of the two brothers at the beach taken on holiday or on a weekend away which Charles Wagner had shown me. Charles, a young man, is lying on the sand, limbs rigid from the exertion of holding up his brother, legs splayed as in gymnastics, prominent abdominal muscles, slim and well-built. I find that photograph moving. Perhaps because it shows the two brothers together, perhaps because it shows David hale and strong. Or perhaps, like any photograph because it surprises and suspends for all eternity the fleeting thing that is life. Whatever the reason, it is also proof that David was not a single kilo overweight. It is easy to imagine what losing twenty kilos in a few weeks did to him.

It was after a morning roll call, having twice soiled his trousers, the warm flow down his legs filling him with a mixture of fear and shame, that David, terrified that he had dysentery, signed up with the infirmary. He expected nothing but a little warmth and rest which might calm the diarrhoea.

The very idea was absurd, but David could not know that. Though those newly arrived did not know it, unless one had connections in the camp (because Buchenwald was a mystery difficult to fathom, and the first selection depended on knowledge, something veteran inmates could not risk communicating to those who had arrived for fear of stumbling on a traitor or an SS informer or something simply because they didn't care), the infirmary was a dice roll with death: the only medicine was aspirin, prisoners were despatched to make room for others, or SS doctors experimented on them before Doctor Hoven, Erich Wagner's superior, eliminated them.

Serge was not fully aware of these things. Nonetheless there had been frightening rumours about the infirmary and he tried to dissuade David from going there. But he had no real justification. And so, through a chain of coincidences, David Wagner received permission to leave his work Kommando, was seen when he first went to the infirmary by a less than supportive prisoner and found himself face to face with his namesake, Erich Wagner.

I can picture the doctor stepping into the room where David is waiting, I can only imagine him, but the features are his, those in the photograph, his glasses, the slightly receding hairline, the intellectual air. But perhaps because I know too much about it, know what he condemned his victim to, I cannot help but see him as having a more sallow air, more malevolent, more vicious. The more so, since I am better acquainted with his biography. I know that at the moment Erich Wagner stepped into that room he was thirty-seven, he had a wife and two children living with him outside the camp. They lived in a comfortable little house with a garden and even if the smoke from the crematoria, blown by the wind, sometimes smelt of burning flesh, even if Erich was sometimes a little harsh with the children or with his wife, they were living a perfectly agreeable life. It was an enviable position, being the doctor at one of the most important concentration camps in Germany, not far from the charming and prestigious town of Weimar, with its theatre, its museum, its memories of Goethe and Schiller. All the more enviable since Erich Wagner had never been a doctor, having failed his medical exams three times, to the shame of his family, where from father to son there was an aristocratic line of doctors. But he had joined the NSDAP as early as 1930 and there showed a dedication equal to his earlier failure, displaying an utter lack of scruples and a brutal devotion – especially with a cudgel – to National Socialism. This, needless to say, was more than enough to make him an eminent physician, appointed to Buchenwald in 1939 and quickly conferred with the title of doctor when one of the prisoners, Paul Grünewald, an actual doctor, was forced to write on his behalf a medical thesis entitled *A contribution to the subject of tattoos*.

No one was present at this first encounter between the two Wagners, or rather between Prisoner 8007 and Hauptdoktor Erich Wagner. Perhaps the doctor stepped into the room with the words: "Welcome to the chamber of death, you filthy Jew", or maybe "Dear Jew, I feel like cutting out your liver and feeding it to the dogs. The Jews yesterday looked a little jaundiced, their flesh was overripe, the poor animals had to go to sleep hungry." Or maybe "Sir, we are so glad you could join us because this morning we have decided to infect you with a new strain of typhus we've just received which, combined with a number of other deadly infections, should allow us to develop first-class vaccines for our soldiers. If, of course, you are agreeable, Mister Jew."

I am, of course, getting ahead of myself – and doing so in rather bad taste. Even so, this is what is being played out in the infirmary. It is here that the red triangle – hence a political prisoner like all the French in Buchenwald – becomes a Jew by stupidly going to see a doctor where his nakedness immediately exposes him.

Yet that in itself is not enough. Many French Jews, sent to camps for political reasons rather than that of race – otherwise they would have been sent to Auschwitz – wound up in Buchenwald without incurring any particular hatred from the SS officers. Only the generalised hatred of a system of destruction. Erich Wagner certainly realised during this visit that David was Jewish, but that does not explain his hatred, particular as he had never been a virulent anti-Semite. We can take it for granted that he considered the Jews to be evil, but it is less probable that he personally despised them.

Doctor Wagner's attitude therefore supposes that Prisoner 8007, far from simply being one of the shifting, unknown, undifferentiated mass of prisoners, acquired a human identity, become a person. For some reason or other, Erich Wagner recognised the existence of his namesake and decided to make him his victim. And even if I do not know his motive, even if I can only imagine that, wandering along the rows of bunk beds in the infirmary during one of his rare visits, the doctor happened upon his enemy, some incident – however small, since I cannot imagine anything important could have happened between a sick prisoner and an SS officer – must have taken place.

The strangest thing about this story is that the real tragedy did not take place between the two Wagners. David is lying in a bed in the infirmary, I am eager for some incident, some encounter, but at that moment even the camp prisoners are interested only in another prisoner. If the infirmary had any significance in the camp that day, among the most important prisoners who did not know or care about David, it is because another murder was to take place, one which had nothing to do with David Wagner.

In the room next door Grogorij Kushnir-Kushnarev, a White Russian immigrant, director of the prisoners' secretariat (and hence himself a prisoner) was in isolation. He had come to the infirmary on the same day as David, unsuspecting. However, this was the moment the political prisoners had been waiting for for years. Kushnir had been an informant for the Gestapo and had betrayed to the SS hundreds of men of the camp resistance. Almost from the first, the camp had been a battleground between the political prisoners and the ordinary criminals on whom the SS relied, since there were too few of them to oversee everything. Gradually, the political prisoners had taken control of a number of key places in the camp, notably the infirmary. They did not control the place, obviously, and the SS carried on with their murders, but things had improved somewhat. Whether out of stupidity or overconfidence, when Kushnir felt ill he had gone to the infirmary. The political prisoners immediately announced that he was infectious and put him into isolation. There, he was murdered.

If I mention this episode, it is not to boast about the great feats of the resistance movement within the camp, but to demonstrate the tragic solitude of David Wagner. In the midst of the teeming network of parallel lives that is a concentration camp, where fates could be decided with terrifying speed, in the inevitable isolation which a life-and-death struggle entails, David Wagner's destiny was sealed in that moment and nobody cared. In the camp, everybody was thinking about Kushnir, someone about whom no one was thinking on the outside. At that moment, the news which was occupying the world was the German advance in the east, since the outcome of World War II, though no one knew this at the time, was to be decided in Russia, where millions of men clashed over the fate of millions of others.

But I want to remember a single man. On that day, a man of no importance, a man whose name no one knew, of whom only a single anonymous photograph remains in the camp in Germany, would meet the man who would kill him.

10

It is all a matter of name. The unknown man in the photograph was given a name and around that identity dozens of other names clustered. The living and the dead. The living who helped me to recreate the memory of a man and the dead who haunted his fate. If I include among the latter Erich Wagner, Karl and Ilse Koch and more tangentially Martin Sommer, whose role is probably more important to me than to David by the significance – or the lack of significance of that lethal lunacy – that he acquires, I will have mentioned the most important.

I have already mentioned Sommer, and his paths and David's have briefly crossed. But I have only mentioned Koch in passing and need to dwell on him, though he is less important in this tale than his wife Ilse Koch.

The history of Buchenwald can be split in two: the period under Colonel Koch and the period after he left in 1942. Obviously he is not responsible for all the developments: the terrible conditions under which the camp was constructed in 1937 and the way in which it was organised in the years that followed also contributed to its harshness. But on the other hand, the rapid collapse of Germany during the last year of the war goes some way to explaining both the shortage of food and the gradual disintegration of the camp, which led at the same time to terrible casualties and to prisoners taking over some control. What went on in the camp therefore escaped the control of Karl Koch. Nonetheless, he presided over the harshest years in the camp, it was under his command that Sommer held his post, while corruption in Buchenwald was endemic, all to the detriment of the prisoners. His expulsion came as a relief.

Koch was a typical example of the outcasts in the SS who made their careers through violence, misappropriation and crime and whose adherence to Nazism was as much a result of temperament as of social climbing. Born in Darmstadt in 1897, he was the son of a minor civil servant. After less than brilliant studies he was mobilised, though he did not actually fight more than a few weeks on the front regardless of his later claims – he fought for only a few weeks at the front. But from 1920, he was prepared for what was to come next: a demobbed soldier, hungry for revenge and for glory, anti-communist, involved in the early fascist raids against workers' associations, an insurance salesman, he was an ideal recruit for the Nazis. This portrait was completed by a number of minor counts of fraud against his employers and a prison sentence. When he got out in 1930, he was almost a vagrant, divorced from his first wife, father of a child institutionalised for mental illness, he was one of the social outcasts prepared to do anything to become the spearhead of the Nazi movement. In 1931, he joined the NSDAP and so began a meteoric rise in the SS. An officer in the Allgemeine SS, he was transferred to the Totenkopf units and became in Berlin head of the Columbia-Haus, the prison where political prisoners were held. Noted for his efforts (for the number and the cruelty of his tortures), he came to the attention of Eicke, Concentration Camps Inspector for the SS and the man who assassinated Röhm, head of the rival SA. Koch was appointed watch-commander of the first major Nazi concentration camp, Esterwegen, in the marshy region of Emsland, and later Kommandant of the camp, before taking over the running of Buchenwald in 1937 to build one of the most famous camps in Nazi history. A few months later, he was joined by his second wife, Ilse Koch, whom he had married in 1937.

This was the woman whom David encountered in the lanes around Buchenwald and it was this incident, coinciding with his meeting Erich Wagner, which was to seal his fate. After a week in the infirmary having to prove he was suffering from diarrhoea – a ritual in which every day, those suffering from dysentery had one minute with a basin in front of the nurse to provide visceral liquid proof of their condition, failing which they were ejected from the hospital block, the Halle Revier – David emerged more or less cured. In fact, although his encounter with Erich Wagner would prove decisive to his fate, it had made little impression on David. At most, he had seen an SS doctor – we do not know whether he was aware they shared a name (in fact, I should add, having checked the records, that in the history of the camp there were four unrelated prisoners named Wagner at Buchenwald, to whom we need to add SS Untersturmführer Wagner).

David went back to the quarries. Every day, three or four exhausted men were "shot while trying to escape" there. David himself, according to Serge Kolb, was becoming a *Musulmann*. One day, when he got back from the quarry, Müller ordered him and one of his work colleagues to go to the weapons factory to get some tools. As the two prisoners were walking, a soldier following behind, they heard the noise of hooves.

"Don't turn round."

"Why not?" asked David.

"It's Kommandant Koch's wife. Don't turn round, don't

look at her. She hates us. When she passes, stand to attention but whatever you do *don't look at her*."

As the Kommandant's wife drew alongside them, the soldier lashed out with his rifle butt, forcing them to bow. Unfortunately, Ilse Koch did not just simply go on her way – invariably a bad sign. She stopped her horse.

"What are you doing here?" she asked.

"We were told to go and pick up tools for the quarry," David answered in German.

"Work-shy, that's what you are. I'm taking your numbers."

She noted down their numbers and put an asterisk next to David Wagner's.

David's companion, a man named Weiss, was devastated.

"We'll be on the *Bock* tonight."

"Why? We were carrying out an order. She knows that, there was a soldier with us."

"You don't know her. She's completely insane, she's worse than the SS. She doles out punishments all the time. Sometimes you only have to look at her – or not look at her – to end up on the *Bock*. She had a number of prisoners killed while her villa was being built. All you had to do was break a vase or a branch to be sent to the Bunker. And when you got there, Sommer would take over."

"She's pretty," said David.

It was one of the rare words from "before" he had uttered since his arrival in the camp, a casual, careless aesthetic comment.

Weiss looked bewildered.

"You saw that jacket she was wearing?"

"Yes. Amazing."

"She had a gypsy killed the day he arrived so she could have his jacket. And the boots."

"What about them?"

"They belonged to a Polish priest."

That evening, David was called to the main gate. Often, such orders were terminal, those called to the front gate never returned. Weiss shook his hand.

"This is something to do with the Kommandant's wife. I don't know why she only sent for you."

David crossed the camp. In the darkness, snowflakes were falling with a soft whisper. A muted light came from the blocks but David was alone. Later he would say that he truly thought he was going to die that night and that as he walked he felt a mixture of fear and relief, breathing in the night, the stars, the moonlight like a last icy gift of life. The joy of those last minutes mingled with a feeling of perfect chance: in that, the camp had done its work. Without breaking him, it had nonetheless convinced him of his uselessness. A man was going to die. That did not matter. People around him died every day and every one of those deaths was accepted, sometimes welcomed. If not a friend, death was a resolution of sorts. What was to be feared were the last moments, the torture, the bullet ripping through your skull, but certainly not death itself. David was afraid of Sommer, he was afraid of the minutes that were coming, but for weeks now he had been prepared for death. At some point he realised he was trembling and he knew it was not simply the cold.

But it was not Sommer he found waiting for him. At the main gate, a drowsy Kapo explained to him that at 5 a.m. the next day an SS officer would escort him to the Koch house. Though the news was unbelievable, David had enough experience of the camp not to be too happy. An encounter with the

Kochs could very well end up with him in Sommer's custody. But there was an advantage: one day when he did not have to go to the quarries.

The following day, Weiss was astonished to see him, but David barely had the time to tell him he had been summoned to the Kochs' villa. Weiss nodded sadly. Some minutes later, at the main gate, an SS officer escorted David to the villa on the outskirts of the camp near the road leading to Weimar. They arrived at the door of a large house built of dark wood surrounded by a garden and tall trees. The soldier knocked. No one answered. He knocked again. Nothing. So, they waited for an hour outside the door, almost motionless, hoping for some sign of life in the house. But David supposed that the Kochs did not get up early.

At dawn, a car drew up outside the villa. It had to be the colonel's driver. (Koch never rose above the rank of colonel. Ilse Koch was known as the Kommandant's wife not because her husband held the rank of Kommandant, but because, being in charge of Buchenwald, he was a *Lagerkommandant.*) Fifteen minutes later, the door opened and a man in uniform appeared. David immediately stood to attention. The man stared at him astonished.

"*Zu Befehl!*" said David, saluting again.

The man shrugged and walked past him. Since the door was still open, the soldier pushed David in and stood guard outside. Inside the house, nothing moved. No servant, no soldier, no prisoners. Or else everyone was asleep. The first room was a large reception room in a terrible mess, the vast table was covered with leftover food, wine stains, a number of chairs and armchairs were upended and there were glasses everywhere. David stood in the middle of the room, knowing he did not have the right to sit down. But when he finally realised there really was no one, he righted one of the armchairs and sat. It was hot, he was alone and, as always since his arrival in the camp, exhausted. His eyelids were heavy but he knew that if the Kommandant's wife got up and found him asleep in a chair, he would be sent straight back to the quarries. At best. The struggle between fear and sleep was an unequal one. David dozed off. Luckily, some time later he was woken by a sound. Still deeply asleep, he jerked to his feet, tottering, dizzy at this sudden return to consciousness. Ilse Koch had opened her bedroom door and was coming down the stairs. Hazy, like a sleepwalker, still wearing her nightdress. Her red hair was tousled. David, terrified, did not know what to do. What if she was angry at being surprised in such a state? A single look could be punished with the *Bock*. Seeing her like this, barefoot, in her nightdress!

Ilse Koch moved through the living room. She walked without seeing anything, her face dark and sullen. She stopped, stared at a still-full glass of wine then drank it. David did nothing, he did not move. He did not dare make his presence known, didn't dare leave. Then she saw him. She didn't seem surprised. She simply did not know why he was there. She asked him his name in her usual bad-tempered tone.

"David Wagner."

She came over to him. Studied him. Then she nodded, seeming to remember.

David still did not understand. Why had she had him come? The Kommandant's wife turned and wandered through the room again. She told him he was to be her new *Kalfaktor*, a word he didn't know and struggled to work out. Why the title? Then, sitting down in one of the armchairs, she stopped speaking. Her heavy, haughty gaze contemplated the sitting room as though it were some ruined splendour. In truth, she was not pretty. She looked like a butcher's wife, a little vulgar, plump, buxom, but oozing contempt. Her nose was like an eagle's beak, her eyes hard, her lips thick, even her hair, which was dishevelled, everything about her made him dislike her. She could inspire a desire mingled with hatred, but she was not pretty.

. The thin, shaven, humiliated man opposite did not have the strength to judge her. He settled simply for being afraid while still wondering why she had asked him here. And then suddenly, moved by some inspiration, he began to tidy the room. He began by righting the armchairs, then he cleared the table, put the glasses and the plates in the kitchen. At first, the Kommandant's wife remained in her chair, then she disappeared. At about 10 a.m., a woman arrived.

"*Du bist der neue Kalfaktor?*" she asked curtly.

"*Ja.*"

Hearing the word for a second time, he realised this must be why he had been told to come. It clearly meant some sort of servant, since he spent the morning with this fat woman of about forty who was as contemptuous of him as her mistress, making beds, washing dishes, doing the cleaning. This work, in the warmth of a house, especially the time spent lighting the fire, almost swallowed by the flames as they licked him, together with the leftovers he found to gorge on, and there was always plenty, made a marvellous reprieve in his life as a prisoner. He would hide in order to savour these moments since he knew he was forbidden from eating and that more generally any pleasure would be severely punished: in the quarries, any man who rested was beaten, a man who smoked could be killed. In the Kochs' villa, at the centre of the system, there was no reason for the rules to be any different.

That evening, after he had gone back to the camp, still escorted by an SS officer, David told Serge about his day. Kolb thought carefully for a long time, then gave his opinion.

"I've heard a lot about Ilse Koch. She's bad. I'll try to find out more. But the truth is the job is interesting. If you really are working as a servant for the Kochs, that means the end of work detail, of cold, maybe even hunger if you can manage to steal food. Obviously if you make the slightest mistake you'll be sent back, but for the time being, it can't be bad. I think there's just one question: why you? I can see you being a servant, you're personable, but why not choose a German? Other nationalities are rarely allowed into SS houses, they usually work in the gardens."

"I don't know why she picked me. But anything is better than the quarries. And I might not be German, but I speak the language well."

This was a possible explanation; being able to speak German was the first factor when it came to survival in the camps. That said, the following day, having asked around, Serge came up with something that might explain things. The Kochs were indeed looking for a servant. Kurt Titz, the previous *Kalfaktor* (a word barely used in everyday German which usually refers to a prison drudge) had been found drunk by the Kommandant's wife. She even accused him of dressing up as a woman, something Titz denied. Not that his denials counted for anything, he had been locked up in the Bunker for several weeks. Other *Kalfaktors* had been tried, but when they did not please the Kommandant's wife they had been punished by being assigned to the harshest work Kommandos.

Wary of frightening his friend, there was much information Serge did not add, and it is possible David never knew of Ilse Kochs' terrifying past. Before Buchenwald, this had been nothing remarkable. Contrary to her fabulations (she claimed to be a prostitute's daughter raped at the age of twelve...), Ilse Köhler was the daughter of a factory foreman from Dresden, a militant social-democrat. As a secretary, the young social-climbing woman enrolled in the NSDAP where she met her future husband, the rising SS star Karl Koch. And though he once confessed that he would never have married her if she had not hounded him so much, the fact is her stubbornness paid off: Ilse Köhler became the wife of Kommandant Koch. From that moment on, her life became monstrous. But she was more open to reason than a man like Martin Sommer, and the litany of her crimes never plunged me into the abyss as Sommer's did. There is something utterly impenetrable in that man's cruelty and sadism. The cruelty of the Kommandant's wife was mostly indirect: she killed by jotting down a prisoner's number. Her sadism, for the most part, was purely Nazi perversion, by which I mean that she did not simply marry Koch, she married a system of destruction of the other. This vulgar, ruthlessly ambitious woman suddenly gained absolute control, the power of life and death over tens of thousands of prisoners. If Sommer is one of those subterranean incarnations of grim folly, a brutal Nazi madness hiding out in dungeons, in prisons, Ilse Koch is the public face: the negation of the other, it is the contempt, the treachery that leads to death. Sommer carried out the vilest deeds for Ilse Koch and in that they are indissolubly linked. They are linked too by their similarities: heavy, strong, the one conspicuously virile, the other excessively opulent and feminine. Perhaps the two were even lovers, the Kommandant's wife was so free with her body. But once again, Ilse Koch's depravity does not allow us to penetrate the convoluted twists of insanity and one can guess, however careful one should be about such things, how her mediocrity was transformed into perversion.

I will talk again about the fate of Ilse Koch because, though my family history is on the side of the victims, the will to understand draws me to the guilty and I have wanted to know how they were punished. Not out of a desire for revenge: as I think you will have understood, I'm not on my grandfather's side. I feel no love for this man I never knew and who probably deserved none. Lost and gone, dust to dust, all that will remain of him, in spite of the testimonies, is a shadow. But I am committed to the memory of David Wagner, a notion more abstract and thorny than love. I wanted to know what became of the guilty because the memory of the dead has two faces: that of the man who died and that of the man who killed him. Around them is the system that made the crime possible. It is these three aspects of memory that interest me.

For the moment, it is enough to know that Ilse Koch was tried three times. Shortly after her second trial, the one at Dachau, the American prosecutor William D. Denson wrote an article for the *Frankfurter Rundschau* of 8 October 1948: "Ilse Koch is the epitome of sadistic perversion. Gradually I realised that Ilse Koch is not a woman in the ordinary sense, but a creature from a different world, something utterly inhuman." I don't share his view, which seems to me to rely too much on rhetoric. If the Kommandant's wife truly was from a different world, it was not Mars or Neptune, but Buchenwald, which is all too human. Ilse Koch was not inhuman and the post-war trial, based on the underlying metaphysics of Evil, frantically searching for absolute Evil, misunderstood this. On the contrary, this woman should be considered the epitome of mediocrity, vulgarity, pettiness, sexual desire brutally trans-muted into absolute power. Tragedy sprang from this conflict.

The evidence against her was set out in the Augsburg trial in 1949 by Judge Jagomast. I will simply recapitulate it. It is easy to understand why Serge did not want to say too much. In the testimony, it is explicitly stated that the Kommandant's wife, when she went out riding, beat the prisoners she encountered with a club or a riding crop. She would also note down certain numbers and have the prisoners punished – on the *Bock*, by being strung up from a tree by their arms or in the where many of them died. The judge goes on to cite several murders which she personally ordered. There, in a long paragraph, he goes on to detail a monstrous practice by the Kommandant's wife: after the summer of 1940, having seen photographs of tattooed prisoners taken by Doctor Wagner in the course of his 'research' (his thesis, you will remember, concerned tattooing), Ilse Koch demanded that she be given the most beautiful tat-toos, which meant killing the prisoners and removing the skin to be tanned. The judge notes that the Kommandant's wife would sometimes note the number of a prisoner when she saw a tattoo she liked. These skins were used as lampshades, book bindings, shoes. The last charge against her related to the fate of twenty-four prisoners taken to the quarries in the spring of 1941. Along the way, SS officers began firing on them. The Kommandant's wife, on horseback, killed them with a pistol.

This was what David Wagner could have found out. And happily he did not learn it, at least not before beginning to work for her, because it was this same arbitrary life and death power of the executioner which was to save him for a time.

Rather than working in the quarries, in the cold, suffering the harsh discipline and hunger, every morning he went to the villa Koch. He tidied the dining room and when the Kommandant's wife woke at about eight she would tell him to look after the children. Artwin, a boy of four and Gisela, a little girl of three were surprisingly gentle. When they woke, their eyes a little bleary, he found their delicate movements touching. Sometimes the little girl, who was pale and blonde, would stare at David wide-eyed as though trying to understand. What? He did not know. He also fed the dog, Artus, a wire-haired fox terrier, who was given meat from the SS kitchen, a portion large enough to have made soup for ten prisoners. Sometimes David stole some but it wasn't easy because the dog would bark in protest.

Another *Kalfaktor* worked in the garden. He never came into the house. Besides, David jealously guarded his position, it kept him alive and warm. He would not have allowed a rival on his patch.

At about ten, the maid would arrive. Her name was Gudrun and she spoke to him as little as possible. If she had a chore she found repulsive, she would call David. One day when Artus had done his business in the kitchen and she had slipped in the excrement, she ordered David to clean her shoes and wash the floor. He did not say a word. The maid was German, she was free, she lived in Weimar. Consequently she belonged to a different world, the world that began outside the camp gates. For this reason, regardless of how stupid she was, she was de facto a superior being. Sometimes she would talk to Ilse Koch about what she had done the night before. She would laugh. These brief glimpses of the other world, of family, children, freedom, were deeply painful for David. But he knew too that his sadness was a good thing, for he never felt such things when he was working in the quarries. The desolation of his soul left no room for gentleness. More and more often now he found himself thinking of his past life, of his family, of Virginie. His solitude swelled with memories.

At noon, Ilse Koch would emerge from her room. The noise always made David shudder, because the Kommandant's wife was prone to violent fits. Curiously, these rages were more often directed at the maid than at him. But for the moment, Gudrun kept her position. It was common knowledge that maids did not last long at the Koch house. After a quick inspection, whose outcome had less to do with the quality of the housework than with her mood, Ilse Koch would order a meal from the SS mess hall, which always made her their finest dishes. She ate alone or with friends. David would serve them. It was pointless to try and sneak food in the kitchen since Gudrun was watching and would have informed on him. He could never even have tasted what he served. He made up for it in the mornings, eating leftovers while the family were still asleep. Obviously Ilse Koch never offered him anything to eat or drink. That went without saying. Besides, he had to be careful about what he ate since he was not allowed to use the toilets.

In the afternoon, Ilse Koch would saddle her horse. She would ride for hours through the woods, surveying her kingdom, whipping the prisoners. Her domain stretched out before her, always the same, endlessly renewed, with this human tide in her power.

She sometimes received friends or even lovers. She made no attempt to hide anything from David, since he was nothing. Perhaps that was why she had chosen him. Prisoners, especially foreign prisoners, were insignificant. Even Titz, who wore the black triangle of the asocial, had been German. Doctor Hoven, Wagner's superior, and Florstedt, Koch's deputy were her regular lovers, though this did not preclude casual affairs.

Yet there was something troubling about the impassive gaze of the Kommandant's wife. Sometimes David felt as though he did not exist, as though he had been expunged from the world of the living. Since his arrival at the camp, it was clear he had been stripped of his status as a man. When he had given up his clothes, had his hair shaved, he had handed over his identity as one might a coat. He was nothing now but an element in the destruction. Yet the Kommandant's wife's blank stare was a new experience. Every day, every night he had felt his loss of humanity. And yet he had not felt this absence. Artus had a much greater presence than he, obviously, but so would any stray dog. The Kommandant's wife could have made love in front of him without feeling embarrassed. In the mornings, when he went into her bedroom to get his orders, she was half-naked. She would have had any prisoner who stared at her killed, yet she flaunted herself before him. On several occasions he had seen her abundant red pubic hair and felt a poisonous excitement at the forbidden sight. He was so certain that he would be put to death if he made the slightest move or stared too insistently that even this glimpse seemed like blasphemy. But the Kommandant's wife did not see a man, she barely saw a thing.

David sometimes wondered if she was not toying with him. It was possible that he was not simply this absence and this thing, but also a man that she could despise, that she could excite and put to death if he betrayed his arousal. Perhaps it was a deadly game she liked to play. But the days passed and he had to face the facts: the Kommandant's wife did not so much as blink when he passed her. He no longer had a body, a shadow, he was no longer made of flesh. He was a ghost.

He did not feel humiliated by this. Just once it occurred to him that, in Paris, he would not have spent so much as a night with this woman. An afternoon perhaps. He would almost certainly have rejected her advances (and it was obvious that she would have tried to seduce him). This made him smile. It was another normal thought, a thought from "before". The ghost thought like a ladies' man.

It was strange. In certain respects, he recovered the thoughts he had once had and through them an identity. The *Musulmann* retreated. His spirit was stronger, his gestures more alive, he began again to believe in the future. He told himself he had to hang on. Often, he behaved like an automaton, his mind elsewhere – in the workshop in Paris, in the Bois de Boulogne, at parties in the capital. Next to him, a woman was laughing, a tall blonde woman whose photograph he still had, still gazed at constantly. He encountered her in hotel beds, pursued her, met her in his room above the workshop. She was gentle and passionate, angry sometimes. All this he could feel in the silence of the large villa, especially at dawn when the soldier took his leave and he started on the housework. And he emerged stronger from these trips into the past.

But on the other hand, his thoughts were steeped in death. He had brutal, morbid visions as though the fabric of seeming normality was ripped apart, releasing monstrous dreams. Every morning, when he went into the children's room and they woke up, he would stretch his hand out to their throats and imagine these tender fragile creatures, their necks broken, like white flowers strewn across the sheets. And when Ilse

Koch lounged in her bed, his eye would fall on the lamp stand made of a human bone and in a sudden explosion the room would be filled with bones and it took all his strength not to scream, not to hurl himself at this woman in front of him, to punish her, not for her cruelty, but simply because violence and death exploded within him. He would go into the kitchen, smash Gudrun's head, blood flowing, flowing, drenching the floor and Artus would lick up the rivers of blood. The world had exploded and when he went back to the camp he would hear the dull rumour of death, a vast groaning which perhaps was not imaginary but simply the knowledge of the murders taking place. Because the exhausted lines of men at roll call, the living dead, their faces gaunt, skeletal, because the bodies stretched out on their bunks as on their deathbeds, what were they but death itself, stolen from dreams? So perhaps it was fitting to mete out some violence and some death to this privileged family. Perhaps, too, blood had to be made to flow by his own hand. Let the ghostly Jew, the enemy, the pervert, the scourge of humanity, actually play his role.

But he did not play it. Did not act on these visions. David never seriously thought of killing the Koch family, perhaps because he still hoped he might live, while a murder would have sealed his fate. Or perhaps simply because he was not a murderer – even in the terrible flickering between life and death.

This drunken wave of visions became more marked one morning. He was working in the house when he felt a presence behind him. He turned. A teenage boy was standing there, mouth open. He was pale, immobile, staring. David said hello. The boy did not answer, did not move. David went on with his work, glancing around from time to time. He offered the boy a drink. No reply. Still the teenager watched him. David took a broom with a floorcloth and began sweeping the floor. The boy seemed intrigued. At some point, they found themselves next to one another and the boy reached for the broom. David stopped, handed it to him and the housework was passed into other hands. With awkward but energetic movements, the teenager began sweeping up, pushing the floorcloth under the furniture, into every corner. With meticulous attention, he examined his work, sighing from time to time.

After about fifteen minutes, fearful of reprimands to come, David tried to take the broom back. It was futile. The boy grunted plaintively, muttering *"Will nicht, will nicht"*. Confused, David went into the kitchen but as soon as there was no one to watch him, the boy stopped sweeping. He stood as though daydreaming, leaning on the broom, made a few dance steps, letting the broom fall, came towards the kitchen. Cautiously, like a cat, he peered inside.

A scream sent him scurrying away.

"Manfred!"

It was the Kommandant's wife.

"Get out of here! Don't hang around the kitchen."

Arms dangling by his side, the boy went to the far end of the living room. Then he sat in an armchair and closed his eyes.

Manfred, the child of Koch's first marriage, packed off by his mother-in-law to a boarding school in Gera, was staying at the villa for a week. So David spent a week under his fixed, slightly bewildered stare in the suspended reality occasioned by the boy's mental dislocation. What with the Kommandant's wife barking orders, the rare, furtive visits by Koch in his black uniform, Manfred's fixed stare and the murderous visions,

David had his finger on the madness of the camp. Yet, in spite of the visions, he did not feel that he was mad. But he realised that madness had come to the camp, that it was not simply the lunatics who were quickly murdered by the guards, madness had become a part of the lives of everyone in the camp. An all-encompassing madness that touched the skeleton in rags tied up and foaming at the mouth looking like a medieval drawing, to the nagging executioner, by way of the meticulous, attentive, obsessive camp prisoner, the spectre of survival at any price.

If events had taken a somewhat frenzied turn, this was also because the Kochs were on the wane. David watched their decline. Obviously, Koch was still the undisputed master of the camp but the wheels that were to crush him were already in motion. David never had a clear idea of what happened and, though every network in the camp had been trying to find out for weeks, since it had a bearing on the future direction of Buchenwald, even Serge did not find out until after the war. Historians have spent much time studying the Koch trial, which in effect was the trial into corruption in the SS camps, and I don't propose to go into the details. Nonetheless, to briefly outline the facts, it seems that all the allegations were the result of hostility and rivalry between Koch and the Prince of Waldeck-Pyrmont, the SS officer in charge of the Weimar district. For as long as Koch was protected by Eicke, the general inspector of the camps, it would have been impossible to oust him. But when Eicke went to fight on the Eastern Front, where he was to die, the prince attacked. In the autumn of 1941, Koch was interrogated by the tax authorities about undeclared taxes relating to the canteen in Buchenwald. This was the beginning of his fall. At first, it was slowed by the support of Reichsführer

Himmler: not until 1942 was the colonel transferred to Lublin, to the extermination camp known as Majdanek. But the Prince of Waldeck-Pyrmont and Judge Morgen, who was determined to root out fraud in the camps, had gradually been digging up damning facts. The whole camp, putrid with corruption, was bringing in considerable money, most of which went to Koch: food supplies diverted from the prisoners, monies extorted by various means (which was why families were allowed to send money to prisoners) including blackmail or punishment, misuse of work details, exploitation of the craftsmen in the camp for personal gain. To get rid of the evidence, Koch's administration had all the papers burned. But Judge Morgen discovered that the colonel had also had two infirmary Kapos, Krämer and Peix, killed by Corporal Planck because they knew too much about the financial exploitation of the Jews.

"The courts never worried about the execution of prisoners in the camps. Why were they interested in these two men?" I asked Kolb.

"I think Krämer's personality had a lot to do with it. He was a forceful man who had done a lot to improve conditions in the Halle Revier, which even performed surgery, astonishing given that he was a lathe operator by profession. The fact that the infirmary was infiltrated by political prisoners was partly thanks to him. He was well known in Buchenwald and though David and I arrived in the camp after his murder, the story was still doing the rounds. Actually, what Judge Morgen was interested in was the motive for the murder. Executing two prisoners was barely worthy of notice, but these two had been murdered because they had evidence of fraud, which was a very different situation."

The charges against Koch mounted. Himmler's waning

support resulted in a new transfer, which saw Koch moved to Bohemia-Moravia in August 1942. His fall was accelerating. A year later, Koch was imprisoned. Investigators had discovered devastating proof: with SS Köhler threatening to reveal everything, Martin Sommer and Doctor Hoven, on Koch's orders, had murdered him. Karl Koch, Ilse Koch, Planck, Sommer and Hoven were thrown in jail.

We were not yet there. When David was working as *Kalfaktor* with the Kochs, their fall had not yet begun. It had clearly been looming since the autumn and Koch did what he could to save his skin. It was at this point that he cleaned up the camp. But if I have outlined these facts it is because, aside from their historical interest, the photograph at the origin of this story is explained here. The photo was taken on 20 December 1941, the occasion of the visit by the Reichsführer, come to support his protégé and warn the Prince of Waldeck-Pyrmont.

In the archives at Thüringen, there are a number of photographs taken in the glaring winter sunshine that day. The visit of the Reichsführer was always an event but on this occasion it took on a special importance since Koch's future was at stake. Himmler, a short, fat man with round glasses, arrived with his usual escort, accompanied by two or three senior civil servants of the Reich, Saack, the Prefect of Thüringen and Lachmann, the local Landrat (equivalent to a district administrator). In the photos, Koch and Himmler are shaking hands and seem very cordial; Koch is wearing a permanent, almost stupid smile. Saack is expansive, making grand gestures, arms flung wide, body bowed while the Landrat, Lachmann, stands slightly apart, probably because he is younger, despite his formal pose, his balding pate and his junior rank. There are a number of photos of the camp officers, four of the doctors, one as a group, then individually. And suddenly, there it is. The original photograph, the one in the museum at Buchenwald. Doctor Wagner and, behind him, looking smaller because of the distance, a chance decision by the photographer who was more interested in the Reichsführer than a mere doctor, David Wagner. In spite of my research, I have never discovered the name of the photographer. I know all the people in these photographs, I could talk about them for hours, but I do not know the name of the man who captured them in photo.

By this date, 20 December 1941, nothing had apparently happened between the two Wagners. A sick prisoner had encountered an SS doctor in the Halle Revier, and later, as a domestic servant, he had met him again at Koch's villa. So what? In fact, the die had already been cast. Some days before 20 December, as Serge told me, a crucial conversation had taken place between the two men. The conversation is known as the Parable of the Jew. I call it this in my notes because this is how Erich Wagner referred to it.

The conversation began pleasantly enough in the living room of the villa where the doctor had come to take coffee with Ilse Koch. The Kommandant's wife had gone into the kitchen, as usual, with a long list of complaints about things that needed to be done. Erich Wagner had remained alone in the living room, a cup of coffee in his hand, distractedly stirring with his spoon. Then, whereas usually no one ever spoke to David except to bark orders, Erich Wagner, who had visited several times and never seemed to notice him, started to talk to him. He asked if he was happy with his new duties, if everything was going well. Then he told David how much he liked France, admired its culture, especially its literature which he considered the richest and most diverse in all the world. Obviously he loved the great nineteenth-century writers, but he also admired Diderot, Rabelais and contemporary writers such as Gide and Malraux. This last name alerted David Wagner: he knew very little about literature, but he knew the name Malraux, as many people did, for political reasons and knew that since the Spanish Civil War, the writer had been one of the most outspoken opponents of fascism. I personally find this profession of French faith somewhat suspect. I never believed it, never believed Erich Wagner had read the authors in question. He probably knew their names, hardly difficult for a man of even mediocre education, but the fact that he named an antifascist like Malraux was surprising, unless it was a supreme vice, a bait intended to trap. I believe Erich Wagner was a con man. He was not a monster, he should probably be classified with the lapdogs and the liars, the two-bit conmen who are overtaken by the results of their acts and become killers by accident, by the wretched gratuitousness of chance. This was how he had come to have a thesis written by a prisoner, how his pathetic research on tattoos had led him to cut away human flesh and tan it. All in all, I would classify Erich Wagner's homily as what in rhetoric is called *captatio benevolentiae*, a form of speech intended to flatter and persuade the person one is speaking to.

After this introduction, they talked about their shared name: David Wagner; Erich Wagner. Curious coincidence. Where did it come from? Wagner was not a French name. David, who preferred not to talk about his Polish and Romanian origins, claimed he did not know but had good reason to think that his ancestors had come from Germany.

"It's certainly possible," said Wagner thoughtfully, "there

used to be a lot of Jews in Germany. I mean, you are Jewish, if I remember rightly from your visit to the infirmary."

David nodded.

Erich Wagner then began to elaborate his "Parable of the Jew". He compares the Jew to the country rat which wanders and flees as winter approaches. Winter came, and with its white cloak (we can appreciate Erich Wagner's metaphors) covered the whole country. The rat would have liked to stay in the warmth of his burrow, but, urged on by hunger, he was forced to go out. Blinking and shivering, the little animal looked about for help. But winter stretched as far as the eye could see. So the rat hopped, walked, hobbled for days and days without finding a crumb to eat. He was about to die when he saw a dark mass in the distance. Seeing it, he got some of his strength back. As he got closer and the snowy mist lifted, the rat saw that it was a farm. Unable to believe his eyes, he had gone in, and to his amazement, heard a horse whinny. He headed for the stable where he found three big horses, there was straw on the ground which they trampled, whilst feeding on cereal and oats. Heart pounding, he rushed to the trough and ate his fill. For weeks and weeks, the rat lived on the horses' food. He thought that winter would pass before anyone noticed him. He was wrong. The farmer had quickly noticed him and one day as he was greedily swallowing a particularly fat grain, the horses being a little way off, he began to feel tired and numb, his limbs became paralysed and his eyes were clouded by a dark veil. And so he died, a victim of his appetite for poisoned grain.

"Did you understand the 'Parable of the Jew'?" Wagner asked, getting to his feet and smoothing his uniform.

David nodded silently.

"The important thing," he went on, "is to understand that even if the rat thinks he's safe, he always dies in the end. Thanks for the coffee."

There is nothing harder for a man than hope disappointed. David thought he had found a glimmer of humanity in the doctor only to discover he was just like all the others, determined to destroy him. For several days after the conversation, he was devastated. He couldn't stop thinking about it.

The Parable of the Jew was the last piece of the puzzle of the photograph. Names, dates, events, explanations, everything was now in place. That day, 20 December 1941, which seemed to be the apogee of Koch's power, ended with Himmler being invited to the villa. Ilse Koch, disastrous as a housewife, but adept at exploiting the talents of others, had prepared everything perfectly. A veritable banquet was laid on for the twenty-two guests. The table, covered with a pristine white tablecloth and festooned with gilt decorations, took up most of the room. The expanse of white was broken up by beautiful floral arrangements. Each place setting had large plates, silver cutlery, eight glasses of different sizes and shapes, heralding the feast that awaited the guests. Four waiters, prisoners dressed in white jackets for the occasion, stood to attention at the four cardinal points. Ilse Koch had made them take hot showers in order to minimise the foul stench that clung to prisoners. The food came from the two finest shops in Weimar, from the butchers, Daniel, and from Fisckkettel's. The wines and spirits had been requisitioned in France. The menu included petits fours, foie gras served with white wine, a succession of dishes with marinades, several capons, four large legs of lamb with potatoes on a bed of salt, cheeses and a dozen different tartlets.

One chair remained empty, that of Landrat Lachmann who

excused himself, claiming pressing work, which Ilse Koch accepted with bad grace. She said something ill-tempered. The prefect whispered something to the Reichsführer who nodded as he watched the Landrat leave, then said: "*Es war doch ein verheißungsvoller Mitarbeiter.*"

However, the promising collaborator, in Himmler's words, had departed. This, however did not change the bacchanalian nature of the evening, which left the men flushed and panting, slumped in the chairs, shouting and laughing coarsely as the prisoners continued to serve wines and meats. David served Himmler on several occasions, and simply knowing that the slightest mistake would have him sent to the Bunker filled him with such a mixture of fear and hatred, that every time he returned to the kitchen he almost fainted. He was haunted by visions, imagined himself spilling sauce on the Reichsführer's shirt, the man roaring as the Kommandant's wife got to her feet, a fatal mistake, and he cut Himmler's throat with his carving knife, the little pig's blood spilling onto the white tablecloth, mingling with the sauces, the guests screaming and running, but it was too late for the pig, who had fallen to the floor. The prisoner in the white coat stood, knife in hand, wild-eyed and covered in blood.

When the visions faded he was left breathless, as though he really had just committed murder and needed a few moments in the kitchen to compose himself, the flood of images having ebbed. Hands trembling, he went back in to the dining room and tried to avoid the Reichsführer.

Happily, Himmler left quite early, with the two men in his escort and Prefect Saack. As he left the table, he embraced Koch, who smiled blissfully. With the Supreme Head of the SS gone, those left, officers and non-commissioned officers, allowed themselves free rein. They drank and stuffed themselves, throwing pieces of meat at each other which they fetched from the kitchen. Some of the women looked disgusted, others laughed heartily. One climbed on the table and began to dance, showing her legs. Lips curled back over red gums. It was very hot. The Kommandant's wife had turned the music up full blast. The room began to smell. Wine was drunk straight from the bottle. At some point, three whores from the brothel in Weimar suddenly appeared in the arms of the two non-commissioned officers, blouses undone, kissing voraciously. In the kitchen, David had drunk some wine. The room was spinning. He had not eaten, he was too weak. Colours throbbed, music shrieked, mouths gaped like the jaws of wild animals, Ilse Koch was dancing in the arms of her husband, her red hair seemed to blaze. Florstedt stared at the scene enthralled. A woman's fat, heavy breasts were completely exposed. David felt exhausted, his eyes were closing. He did not feel well. He was gripped by a warm smell. The heat of the fire, the bodies. He moved aimlessly about the room, only to be tripped and fall to the floor. He got up and went into the kitchen where he found the other three prisoners. Screams and moans came from the dining room.

"We're better off here than in the camp," said one.

"It's hot."

"And we missed roll call."

In the middle of the night, they were escorted from the villa to the camp by an SS officer. The stench, after the cold pure night air, was overwhelming but they were asleep before their heads hit the straw mattresses.

II

The evening was the Kochs' last triumph. Two weeks later the colonel would be transferred to Lublin – given the importance of the camp, this was not a punishment but a warning, which Koch clearly did not understand since he continued his embezzling to the end. His wife did not go with him – the couple did not get on – and in Buchenwald until 28 August 1943 when she was arrested, but she was increasingly absent – it was important that she be seen on her husband's arm from time to time. She led a very free life, with lovers, parties and horseriding. Sometimes, when arriving at 5 a.m., David would find her shambling the house, drunk and dishevelled. One bottle of cognac followed another. She would get up very late and when she called him into her room, which now reeked, she was almost naked, her body heavy yet alluring in its abundance. Ilse Koch was still young. It was easy to forget, given the cruelty, her imperious manner as the Kommandant's wife, but she was only thirty-six. And the invisible *Kalfaktor*, crushed by the omnipotence of this woman, by the distorted arbitrary system which made of her a sort of sombre, bloody god, could not but notice her. With a gaze devoid of desire, yet trembling, the wild trembling of weakness, of powerlessness, he drank in an image of her body that stayed with him for hours.

The situation was becoming worrying. David's life depended on the presence of Ilse Koch and if she were to leave the camp, or was absent too often, he would be sent back to the quarries. Even as things were, his position was threatened. The Kommandant's wife no longer needed him. Gudrun was more than capable of taking care of the house. Some weeks, when Ilse Koch was in Lublin, he would wander through the house, stretch out on her bed and sleep all day.

Winter passed; David had gained time. The hardest months were almost over. It is said that the spring breeze from the Ettersberg could be as cold as the winter winds, but the newly arrived did not believe it, the sun could not but be a staunch ally. Roll calls became less painful, less cold, the days grew longer. This, however, meant that work details were longer.

One afternoon, David encounted Wagner who walked past whistling.

"Winter will soon be over, little rat…" Wagner said.

One morning, David found Ilse Koch sprawled in the corridor outside her bedroom. She had collapsed drunk. She lay, mouth open, snoring. Her nostrils were pinched, pale, a little yellow, there was rouge on her cheeks. That evening she left for Lublin.

The following day, David tidied the house, which took him barely an hour. Outside the window, the ashen day passed. He stepped into the bedroom of the Kommandant's wife, stared at the tangle of sheets, slightly soiled. He lay down and slept. It would be his last sleep in the villa Koch. That evening, he was summoned to the main gate where he was informed that, owing to the frequent absences of the Kommandant's wife, he was being transferred, at the request of Doctor Wagner, to the infirmary. The farmer had caught his rat.

For a month, David tended to the wounded and the sick. Kolb told me that he was a good nurse, attentive and sympathetic. Strangely, this was perhaps the most bearable time my grandfather spent in the camp. He seemed detached, Kolb told me. Rather than weighing on him, the Parable of the Jew had set him free. Now that he had resigned himself to the inexorable, he was no longer afraid. For months, David had been afraid. At first he had lived in abject terror as they broke his body and his spirit; he felt a crippling fear of death, of suffering. That had faded now. He did not expect to suffer; he knew more or less how he would die, eating poisoned grain. Kolb tried to keep David's spirits up. Since Doctors Ding-Schuler and Hoven were carrying out typhus experiments, Kolb slyly suggested David might 'accidentally' become contaminated, which would mean being sent to isolation in Block 46, a place where Erich Wagner, being terrified of disease, never set foot. David shook his head, smiling. The suggestion seemed absurd. In any case, Kolb was helpless. No one had ever succeeded in preventing the death of a condemned man. It's true I've since heard stories about certain prisoners disappearing, expunged from the lists and hidden in isolation Blocks, but that happened in the last months of the war, when the end was already clear. That was still some way off. The winter of 1942 was drawing to a close. It was the middle of the war.

On 20 March, Wagner declared: "Today is the last day of winter."

It was clear what he meant.

On 21 March, David woke early. He spent a little time with Serge, who talked nineteen to the dozen, trying to drown his fears in the torrent of words. Then he went back to the Block and wrote a card to his mother. All that was permitted were a few cold, official lines about family matters. Personal letters were destroyed. He wrote that winter was almost over, asked for news and said he loved them all. At the end of the letter, he wrote simply: "Give my love to Virginie."

During the afternoon, David walked in the camp. He refused to have anyone go with him. A cold drizzle was falling. His silhouette became blurred. He walked slowly, hands clasped behind his back, not even feeling the rain. This would be his last walk. He walked all around the camp in a diluted reality in which the lack of fear and the certainty of death melted his thoughts and his visions, in a sort of vague mist which joined him with the Ettersberg. He had lived twenty-six years – he had spent his last birthday in a quarry – and images of those twenty-six years came back to him in the crepuscular colours of the winter rain. Images of school and his schoolfriends in stark black and white as though they were photographs, the playground and the classroom, his brother and sister. And his mother, in the shop. A Christmas dinner. The small family gathered at the table, the four of them joined by an old friend. The candles and turkey. Why this dinner? Why this particular Christmas dinner? Just a family meal that made his heart ache.

David stopped in front of the barbed wire. Ahead of him, the woods rustled. "*Sei ruhig, bleibe ruhig, mein Kind / In dürren Blättern säuselt der Wind.*" It's just the rustle of the wind in the leaves. He thought he could hear groans as though the trees remembered the dead. As though they retained the memory of the faltering, emaciated men murdered beneath the cover of their foliage, *Sei ruhig, bleibe ruhig, mein Kind!*

Twenty-six. He had been born, had grown up, he had been a popular rogue, he had loved a woman and then he had been caught. Like a rat. This was his life. The life of David Wagner.

He walked along the line of trees, stood in their shade, proceeding slowly, counting every step like an invalid. A grunt-ing sound caught his attention. The pigsty. A number of the pigs had come out of the pen and were snuffling in the dirt. Big, well-fed, well-tended pigs, their bellies black with mud, obscene in their feverish gluttony. He stood motionless, the image fascinated him.

Then he walked on, sad and thoughtful, sometimes look-ing up at the watchtowers or at a guard on duty, a machine gun slung over his shoulder. Grey shadows passed him in this rain-like mist, walked by without even looking. Other rats, thinner than he was, weaker. He would die in good health. He would die at the end of winter, in the wilful randomness of these massacres, suddenly condemned by the whim of a doctor. Men everywhere were falling and from everywhere rose the muted groan of death: gaunt bodies lay dying in the Blocks, tomorrow men would be unable to heft the rocks, the heavy burden slipping from their hands, refusing to be lifted onto their shoulders, they would try again, fail again, the rock would slip and a soldier would explode their head with a bul-let. David Wagner would not die weak. He would die healthy. He repeated the word to himself: healthy.

Virginie's skin was white. So white. The skin of a blonde girl.

The rain was heavier now. David sat on the ground, in the mud. The memory of her skin engulfed him. The grain of her skin, soft and slick with sweat after lovemaking. The shim-mering smoothness of it in the sunlight.

Farther off, lashed by the rain, the main gate opened like a pair of jaws, like a gaping maw which had swallowed those sent here. The camp had opened its mouth so the rats would tumble in, one by one, in a slow massacre. And they had all fallen. The dead were everywhere. The soldiers disposed of the bodies but everyone could see them still. There were the dead at every step, dreamlike traces, and soon he would be one of these bodies that had been taken yet remained.

And, as though this prospect frightened him, as though reluctant to bring forward the hour of his death, David got to his feet again. He walked more quickly now, still following the barbed-wire fence, circling the camp, towards the closed mouth of the main gate. He could not leave, no one could leave, it was a road of no return, a walk from which there was no way back. All one could do was keep on and slip into the darkness, into ever more terrible nightmares, ever darker forests. *Sei ruhig, bleibe ruhig, mein Kind.* So David walked on and came to the brick buildings accessed by a little flight of steps that was sinking into the earth, and which he knew he must avoid at all costs, even if his punishment was a bullet in the head, because behind the hidden door swung hanged men, naked, emaciated like animals on hooks in an abattoir.

David closed his eyes. This was the end of his walk, truly the end. He had come to the boundary – there was nothing else, nothing but the butcher's hook.

Then, he went back to the Block, came out again and spent what time remained with Kolb. He did not seem particularly sad. He even joked once or twice. Serge did not leave him for a minute.

That evening, he was called to the main gate. Serge watched him walk towards the entrance. It had begun to rain again, it was dark, the figure of David quickly disappeared, but Serge continued to stare at the darkness.

Serge Kolb passed quickly over these last points. His tone more brusque, his sentences shorter. He did not want to revisit this end. Relating these events, I've felt a terrible tiredness. Once the circumstances of the photograph were known, everything else seemed to me to be heavy and gruelling. I knew Doctor Wagner killed my grandfather. The details mattered little to me. Or rather, having amassed so many details, I did not want any more, as though I were so stuffed with details I might vomit them, as though I wanted to leave the camp. As it turns out, I was not finished and other details would be added to these; they were, however, different in nature; unlike this inertia which made it difficult for me to write, they would speed up my telling of this story. Proof that this grandfather I've said so often mattered to me, that my duty was one of memory rather than love, meant more to me than I had thought.

Before closing this chapter which has become so painful, I need to talk about the fate of some of those I have mentioned. I've already said that when I looked at the photographs in the museum at Buchenwald I wanted to *know*. One of the people had mattered more to me than the others, but those in uniform had also attracted my attention. As I have said, the guilty interest me as much as the victims. Some of the internal violence of the Third Reich seeps into their fates.

Kapo Müller was killed outside Buchenwald by his own work mates.

The Koch trial resulted in three death sentences: Hoven, Koch, Sommer. Wary of delving too deeply into the corruption, the SS were content to get rid of the worst elements. But Hoven was later released only to be arrested by the Allies and hanged after the trial of the SS doctors. Karl Koch was executed by firing squad a week before the liberation of Buchenwald on the order of the Prince of Waldeck-Pyrmont, who would later be sentenced to life imprisonment by the Allies. His fate demonstrates the shifting nature of opinions and therefore of justice: his sentence was initially reduced to twenty years, then to five years, then to… nothing. In 1950, he retired to his estate, Schloss Schaumburg. Martin Sommer was also sentenced to death. Eugen Kogon, a former inmate of Buchenwald and a historian specialising in the concentration camps, writes that he was hanged, and he was happy to have thought so, having almost been his victim, but the truth is very different. After sentencing, Himmler offered Sommer the opportunity to redeem himself on the Eastern Front – something Himmler often did (he had done as much for his own nephew). There, Sommer lost an arm and a leg. After the war, he went into hiding, using a false name, and was not arrested until 1950; he was freed shortly afterwards. But when he married a young nurse, had a child and demanded that his military pension be reinstated, the German courts decided he had gone too far and prosecuted him. When a journalist asked this man in the wheelchair if he felt his sentence was adequate, Martin Sommer burst into tears. This man who had never shown the least compassion, whose sole role in the camp had been as a killing machine found sufficient pity to weep for himself… One witness, a former inmate of Buchenwald, the journalist Pierre Durand, bitterly reports that despite being sentenced to life imprisonment for the 101 murders to which he confessed (the real number is incalculable), Sommer lived a free man using various medical pretexts and was even interviewed in 1980 while voting for Strauss, the controversial leader of Bavaria.

Ilse Koch, as I have said, was tried on three occasions. In the SS trial she was accused of being an accessory to embezzlement and also of sexually exciting the inmates, but was acquitted for lack of evidence. The second trial in 1947, before the American military tribunal at Dachau, sentenced her for the crimes mentioned above (charges which were again made at the third trial in Augsburg), but in 1948 General Clay commuted the sentence to four years imprisonment. Ilse Koch had already claimed she was still beautiful enough to find a protector among the American or French officers. Though there was an attempt to hush up the facts, an American journalist published them and the resulting scandal forced the West German courts – harsher than the American tribunals – to reopen the case on the basis of crimes against German citizens (particularly in the period 1937–9). The Augsburg trial, whose charge sheet ran to 130 pages, once again sentenced Ilse Koch to life imprisonment, in spite of the denials, the fits of rage and the feigned madness of the accused. When sentence was passed she screamed: "All the others are free! I want to be free too!" She was incarcerated in Aichach women's prison in Bavaria where she hanged herself in 1967 after being refused a pardon.

My grandfather, for his part, was given no trial. Erich Wagner simply injected him with poison. The indictment was the Parable of the Jew.

Part Two

Violence has never left me.

I am the nicest man in the world. With first- and second-year students at the Franco-German Lycée, I am the gentlest of men. In all my years as a teacher, I don't think I have ever got angry with them. They make me laugh and I find them incredibly touching and funny, so magnificently childlike, about to embark on the great journey of adolescence which will shake them up for years. In ordinary life, I am calm, almost phlegmatic; in the street I walk slowly, my nose in the air like a half-wit.

But on the flipside is the other man. The one who feels threatened by a harsh word, worried by a raised voice, like an animal at bay. The man alert to a sudden movement. The one who wakes in the morning filled with fear and has to organise his thoughts, reflect on his life to say: "There's no reason to be worried, calm down."

And consequently the man who cannot bear the harsh word, the loud voice, the sudden movement. Someone who feels violence well in him like a fury. Who would be prepared to lash out as he has done in the street when someone banged on his car. Someone so ashamed of this violence that he tries to bury it deep within him until it eats away at him, until it invests every sentence of this work of the unconscious that is writing. I constantly talk about violence, constantly write about violence. My dream has always been to write comic novels, why then do I create half-crazed characters overcome by the intoxication of destruction?

I once tried to write a novel about the murder of a young woman on a housing estate in the *banlieue*. As you can tell, I specialise in happy stories. For various reasons, the book was a failure and I gave up on it. But I well remember how obsessed I, like the central character, had become with the young victim, as though our fates were being played out in the fictional exhumation of that teenage body when it was nothing more than that, a fiction, one not even based on a true story. But my mind – and even more so that of the character I had created – lived only for this ghost, this broken body woven out of the imagination. I had invented this girl whose body is found on a patch of waste ground, invented the character haunted by his past trying to solve the murder, and yet the blurred face of this fictional character never left me and my one regret is that I never had the strength to bring her to life.

In retrospect, after my obsessive account of my grandfather, how can I not understand that that young girl should be added to a long list of victims whose fate, like those of the killers, I am trying to uncover?

How can I not understand that even a failed, abandoned story, one of the embryonic novels writers keep in their desk drawers, a story with no connection to my grandfather, still strives to connect with the buried stories of family violence?

I am incapable of writing about anything other than this: violence. The violence we inflict on ourselves or that we inflict on others. The only truth that really resonates in me – and consequently my only convincing subject when I write – is the childlike whisper of violence, oozing from my early years like poisoned water.

A violence with no boundaries, no limits, a violence that quietly advances down the ages, occasionally raising its hissing, snake-like head. And although the origin may be found in my family destiny, the violence was passed on to me, probably hidden in my father's silences. Through the strange and fascinating meanders of childhood, that period in which consciousness is established for life, violence was my inheritance. I am my grandfather given over to executioners, I am my father trembling with suicidal violence, I am the heir to an immense violence which haunts my dreams and my writings.

In my childhood dreams I invented chivalrous knights to battle monsters. I have already told how all through my childhood I believed I had saved one of my primary school friends from humiliation, a clear sign of nagging guilt. I could not bear the fact that I had done nothing. I did not save Richard. In my memory, everything revolves around the little patch of greenery at the far end of the playground, almost invisible in the mists of memory, to which the gang drags its victim.

Its victim. Its victims. My grandfather and his many avatars: the young girl, Richard and still others, fictional and real. I intervened only after the battles had taken place, in belated and pathetic attacks of writing. But I should have reacted. In my years as a teacher, I could have saved Richard again. And once again, I did not, out of blindness this time. Because I didn't see that patch of greenery at the far end of the playground.

It was in a *banlieue,* one of those places where teachers are sent to learn the hard knocks of school and life. A mission made all the more difficult by the fact that a thousand indicators of language, attitude and clothing suggested I was bourgeois. It is pointless going over those rocky years which were no different from what has been written in a host of magazine articles or by certain teachers. It's enough to say that for the first few years of my teaching career I was a sort of extra-terrestrial in a suit and tie, popular for the most part, astonishingly treated as something of a local star, with pupils asking for my autograph or screaming my name in the playground like demented fans. But the hazards of my work took me into the labyrinth of dark corners in the housing estates, to the heart of a desperate violence and I was hated as I have never been hated, simply because I was different, precisely because I was *bourgeois*, and consequently an animal to be killed.

The incident took place during one of my first postings in a reasonably quiet lycée in a deprived area, the worst pupils being in the other school in the town, out by the industrial estate. It was a long commute to get there: metro, train, bus, and the frequent bus strikes meant I often had a long walk. In spite of the vile atmosphere among the teachers, I had spent quite a pleasant term with pupils who were not particularly gifted but nice.

At the end of the term, the head teacher, asked by the school board whether there were any particular problems in the class, received a note from a pupil whose identity was never known: "Someone in the class is being bullied." After an investigation, it was discovered that two pupils had attacked a third as a joke. Claiming they did it only to teach him, to toughen him up so he could deal with life, they had been beating him up for several months. The worst thing was that they probably really did mean no real harm. They were having fun. Having fun throwing him down the stairs, or putting him behind a door and running at it. No one knows why, but a ping pong table was their favourite place, they would tie their victim to the table and play funny games, like jumping on him, playing ping pong with his head, hitting it with a bat.

"We were trying to toughen him up. Life's tough. It was for his own good."

I had noticed nothing. This time, I had the authority to do something and I had been blind. I hadn't suspected a thing. The guilty parties were likeable enough, contributing in class, always smiling, sometimes joking with me after lessons – before going to beat up their classmate. And I liked them better than I liked him who, though he was a mediocre pupil, was arrogant and very withdrawn. This was hardly surprising, he retreated behind his status as a victim, suffering less from the physical pain than he did from loneliness, the feeling of helplessness and loss. His friends were his torturers, the only people in his class he ever talked to. No one else spoke to him. From the beginning he had set himself apart, his solitude had led to his rejection, with the exception of the one sympathetic pupil (though I had no reason to think so, I always assumed it was a girl) who wrote the note. I now saw even his arrogance in a new light: it was the arrogance of the victim, the head held high of those humiliated every day who wished the ground would swallow them. What could he do but despise everyone when he himself was so despised, so scorned. He didn't even dare talk about it to his parents, especially his father, a strapping authoritarian fireman who, at his age, would have sent the two boys packing with a quick slap. Or rather, who would not have had to do it since he was clearly loved and respected.

When I talked to the two teenagers, they said: "Honestly, it's not like it was anything serious. It was just a game."

Just a game. And even if this incident doesn't haunt me the same way as my childhood dream of the knight, I am still astonished that I could have been so blind. Pupils like a deck of cards lined up on chairs in front of me. I think I know them, I don't know anything. I think I know what they're like, I don't know anything. A game of cards whose rules I don't understand.

A game of double-sided cards. Because the relationship with violence – and this is its perversity – is almost always two-sided: violence suffered, violence inflicted. It is this dual nature of violence that struck me during my years teaching in the *banlieues* of Paris. Sometimes, thinking back on the peripatetic period, I'm reminded – with a healthy dose of irony thankfully – of the desert and the cliff of Azazel. It was here, according to Leviticus, that on Yom Kippur, having laid hands upon two goats and imbued them with the sins of the year, the high priest sends away the second goat, the *scapegoat*, having sacrificed the first. And it was from the top of the cliff of Azazel that the animal was cast down.

My cliff of Azazel was the Lycée P. My personal fall into the ambivalence of violence. Having been working at a secondary school, I arrived a month into the term, replacing a teacher who had resigned. He, I later learned, had been teaching at the Lycée Chateaubriand in Rome and at the end of his contract he had been recalled to France and, entirely at random, posted to the Lycée P. Regularly classified bottom of the league tables, the school taught only courses in industrial technology and vocational training, which might have made it more stable since there is some hope that these might lead to something. But this was not the case. One entered the dark building with its ruined hallways, its broken strip lights, and one realised that for the goat burdened with all the sins of society, the worst was inevitable. It was not for lack of money, the lycée received more than enough, but no one could replace the lights as quickly as pupils broke them. As soon as I arrived, I sensed things would go badly. But I had been posted here and, a conscientious public servant, I was going to do my duty, which, if you strip away the rhetorical flourishes, simply meant that I was going to suffer in order to guarantee public peace. The first lesson went badly, which is always a bad sign, because usually the worst classes don't show their colours until the second day. After twenty minutes of class, a small, stocky black kid who was leaning back casually in his chair said: "Why isn't there more action?"

He was rebuked, put in his place, but the first salvo had been launched. Within the first twenty minutes. I won't list the many attacks that followed. If I managed to deal with things more or less in the other classes, this one waged war that was unrelenting, though thankfully for the first months inconsistent. I fought alone; there is no other choice for a teacher constantly alone in front of thirty people. It should be said that most of these pupils were over eighteen, all of them were men, with the exception of a single girl (who did still seem like a teenager), and many of them were as strong as me and certainly more dangerous.

At night, exhausted from the stress, I was a zombie. But on days when I did not have that particular class and regained a little strength, I would go boxing at my club. I've been practising French boxing since I was a teenager. Having tried a number of other combat sports, I discovered that this one suited me. I like the intelligent nature of the fight. During that year at Lycée P, I boxed as often as I could. I wanted to build my body, channel my violence. People wanted to destroy me, to break me like so many of the teachers I saw slinking through the estates, bent over to avoid being spat on, like the shadow who took the class next door to mine on Wednesday mornings, whose class was constantly out of control and whose pupils despised him because he did not have the strength to fight back. He had been broken. Me, I beat out my frustrations on a punch bag or my sparring mates at the club because I wanted to be equal to the threat. The body held up the spirit. At one point, I did break, but the pupils knew nothing about it and I went back into the fray and kept taking the tablets given to me by a psychiatrist: the doctor told me I had turned the violence in on myself, because I could not react, because I had to teach my classes, talk about Stendhal, make them write, whereas what was really at stake that year was taking power, overturning authority. My own violence had created a short-circuit. "Like a pinball machine when it tilts," the doctor remarked.

One Wednesday morning, I remember, a day the class considered to be torture, two hours of maths followed by two hours of French, the worst almost came to pass. The maths teacher, a gentle soul and a philosopher who had been working for ten years on a thesis on epistemology, did his best to give classes above the noise and the chatter. I took the class after him, considerably less philosophically. That morning, the class was particularly noisy and wouldn't pay attention. There was a kid at the back, lazy rather than bad, who was talking a lot. Then suddenly he shouted something to a friend across the class. And at that moment, though this was nothing terribly serious, I felt my fist clench and I strode towards him. He immediately realised I was about to hit him and curled up and in a strange voice, fatalistic and resigned, he said, "Don't hit me." The anger drained away from me. I went back to my desk.

This was what caused me to break. Because obviously I couldn't lash out, because obviously I could not be so stupid, so brutal. But violence does not simply dissipate, it needs a target. And that target was me.

When the pupils banded together to attack, at the end of the year, not in small random attacks, but intent on completely stripping me of power, symbolically throwing my coursework on the floor and putting my chair out in the hall after I had cut their marks in half, having found out they had copied, they finally won the battle. But they never realised they had won because the ringleader was suspended for three days and because in their presence I remained stony-faced. In truth, they had won. They now held the power. For the remainder of the year, I had to very carefully tack between what the possible and the impossible, and make no demands of them. But they had left it too late, there were only a few weeks to go which in the end took little out of me.

The ringleader was the stocky little black kid I mentioned earlier. Despite our initial encounter, he was the only one in the class I rated. Firstly because he was a boxing champion. And I know the talent and the sacrifices it takes to win a championship in France. He was a fostered child and moved from one home to the next because everyone hated him. He was uncontrollable, violent. Always ambivalent. Starved of love, he didn't love. Rejected, he lashed out. It was the only reaction he knew, though he wasn't really bad – just unbalanced. He was a terrible student whose grade never made it past a twenty-five even in a class that was marked up and in which few students could write more than a short paragraph. Yet he was quite intelligent. He contributed in class and when he bothered to wake up, his contributions were interesting.

As the year wore on, he often slept through class. He worked in the markets at dawn, he spent his evenings training for matches. Class was the only time he had to rest. Besides, his mind was all over the place. His homework was a nightmare, completely disorganised, almost illiterate. And all his essays had one thing in common: they were all about him. In every piece of homework he found a way to show himself off. He needed to talk about himself all the time, even when he was asked to comment on a text. Such a terrible need to exist. To attract attention. Not to be the reject, the dunce, the marginal. He thought of himself as brilliant, funny, popular. He was careful in his dress. His face was covered in scars: at the end of secondary school, having been given a stern lecture by the careers guidance officer, he had thrown himself out of a window to escape and the broken glass had scarred his face. For all these reasons – yes, absolutely all of them, his repressed violence and the desperate need to exist – I rated him. We would sometimes chat together in a friendly way.

And, obviously, he was the one who betrayed me. He hadn't handed in any homework, I gave him a zero. I had rejected him. He hated me for that. I had become one of a line of fathers who had rejected him. So he stirred the class up against me – they were primed and ready – and all hell broke loose. The following year, after I left, the violence of this class got so bad that the police had to intervene.

These anomalous years provided the backdrop for the body of the young girl I've mentioned earlier. Over and above my obsession with the murder itself, I tried to depict the mixture of terror and compassion I experienced in these totally impoverished – more spiritually than materially – places. I never managed to finished the novel, for aesthetic and personal reasons both of which led to my failure. One of the reasons for my failure was the overwhelming bitterness I felt after I left the Lycée P which made it impossible for me to think about the happy aspect of the *cités* which over the years had attracted me, the joy and the energy I had been accustomed to and which, though I was blind to it, can so quickly turn to violence. I wanted nothing more to do with the *banlieue*. I could no longer deal with this social disaster. I was eaten up by rage. And that was not good for my book.

I remembered the shots fired at my train as if this was the Wild West, my colleague who had told me she had almost been raped by a gang on that same train, remembered her comically describing (someone should do a study about the laughter in Evil, about that magnificent distance laughter provides in times of adversity) how she'd been grabbed by the neck like a goose, one of the thugs saying they had to rape her now and the other telling him the train was coming into the station and the police were about to arrive. I remembered a visit to La Verrière, a psychiatric institution for teachers, walking through the grounds with a colleague who had lost his mind: he couldn't go on any more, he had been broken, the same game of domination, or crushing those who were weak and this man had clearly been fragile. Gradually he had fallen apart, he could no longer do anything, couldn't give classes and there was nothing anyone could do for him. At some time or another, the door shut and he was alone in the classroom. The moment he stepped into the lycée he broke out in a sweat, beads of sweat trickling down his face.

And so the body of the young girl was swathed in an unwholesome violence. Everything around her shimmered with my rage. A rage both personal and social which might have given better results but which, poorly channelled, simply resulted in writing that was too tense, as though I had a score to settle. Not only had the fictional naked body of this girl, raped on a piece of waste ground, become something personal, something I had inherited from my childhood, but the city around her was now also my cause. I had too much to say, too much to prove. And I knew that to write a good book, it would be better if I did not have too much to say, almost nothing in fact, so that the images, the words could speak for me, as if by magic.

So the abandoned body was set aside, forgotten, and the city with it. The whole novel slipped into the troubled waters of half-dead memories. But the young girl, of course, reappeared in the shape of my grandfather whose fictional representation she had been – the body to be found and buried.

2

I had emerged from all that. The reign of power no longer concerned me. One evening, at the Franco-German lycée, an exceptional school in many respects, for the standard and the kindness of its pupils, I told my colleagues, much to their amusement, that I had become a third-rate boxer because I no longer had the aggression in me: my life was calm and peaceable. As we have seen, this was far from being the whole truth. But it did reflect a real improvement.

It was at this point that a news story erupted, a sinister echo of my unfinished book, that became the talk of the country.

I read in a newspaper that a gang from one of the *cités* had tortured to death a young Jewish boy, Ilan Halimi, in an attempt to extort money. He had been found naked, handcuffed, his body covered in burns from bleach of some kind, with four stab wounds to the throat. This story crystallised the intuitions in my story. In my life, I had circled news stories as a dog circles its food because I thought that our society revealed itself in such brief flashes. I had written an academic piece on a young Japanese man who died after playing a video game non-stop for several days without sleeping, and a teenager who had killed his parents, imitating the details of a horror film he had just watched. This interweaving of the real and the virtual fascinated me. But the Halimi case was of a different nature. The more newspaper articles I read, the more I learned about the gang, their methods and their past, since it turned out they had been operating for several years and been involved in a number of cases of extortion. One of them had gone to a doctor's surgery to ask for a sick-leave certificate for an imaginary knee problem and they subsequently made a grotesque attempt to extort money because of this certificate. After that the gang moved on to more serious things; they planted a bomb in another surgery, sent several threatening messages and attempted blackmail by pretending to be a Palestinian or Corsican terrorist group. It didn't work. Then they came up with the idea of taking hostages using a bait. A young woman was used to lure the victims – all Jewish – into the *cité* de la Pierre-Plate, in Bagneux near Paris. It was at this point that this unlikely gang came up with a strategy that was to puzzle the police. Their first choice is the father of a music producer. The girl used several pretexts to arrange meetings, mentioning demo tapes and after the meeting, she asks to be driven home. When the father finally does go back with her to Bagneux to pick up the demos, two members of the gang are waiting in the stairwell. But the man fights back, screams for help, the neighbours call the police and the attempt fails. On two subsequent occasions a different decoy – a young blonde girl in love with one of the gang members and whom they have promised 5,000 euros – tries unsuccessfully to set up meetings. When she fails, she is dumped by the gang and it is a young, dark-skinned Arab girl, not particularly pretty but quite sexy, who shows up at a mobile phone shop on the Boulevard Voltaire in the 11th *arrondissement*. She's wearing a sweater over a denim shirt, tight white trousers and black boots. She asks for information, takes notes, chats to a twenty-three-year-old salesman named Ilan Halimi. The following day, 21 January 2006, they arrange to meet and Ilan goes to

Bagneux. The couple goes for a walk (and I can easily imagine Ilan trying to hit on her) when the gang jumps out of the bushes. The young man tries to run, but they are already on top of him, they gag him and drag him off.

He was held and tortured for three weeks in a studio flat the gang had access to, having bribed the building concierge. Ilan's face was completely bound with packing tape so he wouldn't recognise his captors. He was fed soup through a straw. During this time the gang demanded a ransom of 450,000 from his parents or failing that "from members of the Jewish community". This is what the kidnappers constantly repeated in their many phone calls and emails sent from various internet cafés. The Brigade Criminelle and the Brigades de Recherche et d'Intervention were alerted and tried without success to identify where the messages were coming from. On one occasion they managed to get an image of the gang leader from CCTV footage, but because the man was wearing a hoodie and a scarf, they did not realise this until later. On another occasion, reacting quickly to a message, they rushed to the internet café and saw a man running out but did not manage to apprehend him. A police officer would later say that he had never encountered such a mixture of sadism, inventiveness and technological sophistication.

Tired of getting no ransom and not knowing what to do with their victim, the kidnappers decided to release him at dawn on Monday 13 February. They later claimed that when the tape was removed, Ilan saw two of his captors and that this was why they killed him, near the station at Sante-Geneviève-des-Bois in Essonne. But, as each of them added, "It wasn't me."

Of course. In fact it wasn't anyone's fault. The young

woman used as bait didn't feel responsible because she didn't know what would happen to the young man. The concierge felt no responsibility because all he had done was rent out a studio, he hadn't known anything else. And the gang found it difficult to feel really responsible because the whole thing had been set up, according to them, by the gang leader. And as for him, he wasn't guilty because he hadn't killed Ilan Halimi. The others had...

Five days after the body was discovered, the gang was broken up. The police had changed tactics, given that they had nothing left to lose. An identikit portrait of the young blonde woman who had been used at bait in two previous attempts was circulated to the press. The girl recognised the picture and turned herself in. On Thursday night, 200 police officers went into the Pierre-Plate estate. They arrested thirteen gang members, broke down the door of the gang leader's apartment where they found neo-Nazi pamphlets but not him. Some days later, he was arrested in Côte d'Ivoire. It wasn't him, he claimed, he hadn't done it. A neighbour from his building testified that he was "an ordinary young man in jeans and trainers" while one of the gang members stated: "I didn't think what we were doing was really serious."

3

It never occurred to me to connect Ilan Halimi and my grandfather, but I knew that my morbid interest in the case clearly had its origins in my family history. The tectonic plates of violence. The thrill attached to the violence of domination. The dream of saving Richard, of saving Ilan Halimi. The ridiculous dream of justice. Whereas deep down, I was not able to save anyone.

I realised that the subject was taking up my whole life. It had been a long time now since my trip to Weimar but I still could not shake it off as though the grim gate had slammed shut on my obsessions. And yet I had no reason for lingering on these memories: my time in the sink estates of Paris was in the past, I had found my solution to the person in the photograph. With my pupils, we were even coming to the end of the topic for the term, "humanist commitment". Yet History continued to offer itself up to me from the point of view of Nazism. I was so steeped in it, it was smothering me. I had spent so long wading through this blood, with the story of my grandfather and also in various books and witness accounts that when studying Ronsard, Agrippa d'Aubigné or Montaigne, it seemed to me I was covering the same ground. I was preparing my classes and found myself writing these lines from Ronsard's *Hydra Defeated*: "You must kill the body of your adversary, / you must, my Lord, hang the remains / bloody and bleeding above the gate", in which the sensitive Ronsard of *See, Mignonne, hath not the Rose* calls for the massacre of Protestants. I looked for texts from Montaigne's *Essays* to study and stumbled on the terrifying story of the soldier held prisoner watching from his cell the "work" of the carpenters and, thinking he would be tortured, used a rusty cart-nail he found lying around to pierce his throat. He was found dying and "they hastened to pronounce sentence on him, hearing he was to be beheaded he seemed to take heart and accepted the wine he had earlier refused and thank his judges for the unhoped-for clemency of his sentence, saying that the decision to kill himself had come to him out of fear of some more cruel torture..." I opened my pupils' textbook and discovered that d'Aubigné, with his habitual prophetic flourish, had penned a horrifying picture of France torn apart by the wars of religion, with starving men feeding on grass and carrion desperate to escape "furious demons, sepulchres of their life" who hunted and slaughtered them, hung their children in cottages while they tortured the parents, "lashing their naked bodies with burning fat". Underneath the poem, the textbook reproduced a painting by the school of Antoine Caron which seemed to me to encompass every period, whether the civil wars of the Renaissance, Nazism or the war in Yugoslavia, all these conflicts born of ideologies that have seen this continent erupt with violence. The painting is called *The Triumph of Death*. Even the title reminded me of the strange love the Nazis bore death, as though taking it as a god they had worshipped. The painting is an allegory of death, a skeletal creature wielding a scythe, his gaunt, emaciated head is smiling, riding a chariot whose wheels are carved with skulls (I immediately thought of the SS Totenkopf). A pair of oxen drag the cart which rolls over bodies, crushing the men who have fallen, civilians, soldiers, priests, while, in the distance, as though come straight from hell, the head of a monstrous beast, mouth open to reveal huge teeth appearing amid coils of smoke. In this one painting, I was reminded of all the phantasmagoria of horrors I had uncovered in Nazism: hell, the beast, the worship of death, destruction. Once again I felt that Nazism was not an isolated incident, but the culmination of an Evil that had been writhing in the heart of man from the first, evident in both historical ravages and in artistic representations.

And yet, though I could not shake off Nazism, I should say that the year I had spent rooted in the past, wrapped up in my search for the identity of a vanished face, was slowly coming to an end. I had solved the riddle, the school year was nearly done. At the lycée there was talk of the trip to Berlin. It was something of an institution. Every year in the last week of June, all the final-year classes, French and German together, took a flight to Berlin where they spent a week which, by reputation, was pretty lively, not just trips to museums, but visits to bars and clubs. The teachers turned a blind eye or even went with them. Throughout the year, the pupils had been earning money to pay for the trip: selling cakes during break (they would turn up in the staff room with a plate of ruinously expensive cakes, but all in a good cause), organising a Christmas market and discos. Anything they could think of. They made enough money so that every night of the trip was a display of alcohol-fuelled fireworks in their adolescent brains.

It was now the end of May, the *conseils de classe* were being organised, we were struggling to get all our work in for the *concours d'entrée*, the obstacle that had to be passed before reaching the holy of holies, the *baccalauréat franco-allemand*.

I find the month of May particularly difficult. When I was working in the national system (as we call the French system, since being an international lycée we have a different system) it was a very pleasant month, the weather was fine, there was not much to do, I had fond memories of that. Now, it was an avalanche of homework to be corrected, tens of thousands of hurried scrawls, each proclaiming: "I'm good, I'm good, pick me, give me a good grade". It goes without saying that I wouldn't have given up my position here for any other lycée, but this yearly spring ritual where I was transformed into a homework-correcting machine was tiresome.

But this particular year, the unchanging ritual left me bewildered. As usual, I corrected homework ("Pick out three qualifying adjectives from the following sentence", or "Give your opinion of Sartre's remark 'What is the literature of an epoch but the epoch appropriated by its literature?'") when in fact my usual habits should have been shattered. I was tormented by a question: why did David Wagner's death change nothing about my life? I had been haunted by his fate for months, obsessed with the ill-fated photograph and now that I had retraced the life of my grandfather (a word I still have trouble writing) and come to the end of my interviews, it was as though he had never existed. It may sound absurd, but I felt as though something should have changed. Yet my name was still Fabre, I was still correcting homework, still teaching at the Franco-German lycée and no one had come to tap me on the shoulder and say: "You are a Wagner, come with me to Romania, your homeland. You have work to do there."

Even the first – the fundamental – shift had not taken place: I had not spoken to my father. My inability to overcome the unsaid has always depressed me. I could swallow silences like a boa constrictor, I ingested them and there they expanded, travelled their sinuous paths without ever re-emerging. So with venomous patience a situation could be slowly poisoned. My father, happy to have got off so lightly, did not raise the subject again: we talked passionately about books that had just been published, about the quality of the calf's liver, about the impact of global warming. I knew he was a bastard, I probably knew more about his father than he did which might have interested him, he knew I had been researching the subject and was probably aware of the extent of my investigation, but all we ever talked about was the calf's liver. Which was excellent. One of the great strengths of the traditional bourgeoisie is its silence. Appearances must in all cases be kept up and one should deal with adversity by hard work, hoarding and putting on a united front. It is a social class remarkable for its stubbornness, its sense of tradition and of culture: it reminds me of a large, powerful animal. A bull, perhaps, since the bull ruminates but never speaks. I was a mix of bull and greyhound, something that conjures a rather bizarre physique: since I ruminated without having the stocky resistance of my peers, my huge belly squashed in by my skinny sprinter's body.

So May passed correcting pile after pile of homework, interrupted by bouts of television, for though I was too guilty to go out, I still needed to take a break. I watched badly dubbed American made-for-TV films, programmes about health, parliamentary sessions, depressed by the mountain of little blue marks on my desk. June, warmer and feeling more like summer, flashed past and I handed in my work pile by pile, completed my weeks of correcting. Then one fine day I got up at 5 a.m. and headed for the airport to catch the plane before falling asleep, dazed, in a departure lounge full of excited pupils.

The school year was over, Berlin was about to begin.

I have been fascinated by all the capitals of Europe, they are the stony faces of History. London, Prague, Paris, Rome, Athens, Bucharest, Sofia, Madrid... Every one of them without exception. To wander through literature is to wander through capitals and great cities: the Paris of Balzac, of Hugo, of Baudelaire, the London of Dickens, the Dublin of Joyce, the Rome of du Bellay, the Florence of Dante, the Venice of Thomas Mann, the Berlin of Döblin... But the quintessence of us Europeans' relationship with our cities I witnessed in Fellini's film *Roma*, in which labourers digging a tunnel in the metro suddenly stumble on a wall of ancient frescoes. As they stare in astonishment at the mute forms, the frozen gestures hallowed by insubstantial time, the oxygen pouring into the cavity slowly obliterates the paintings which disappear into the all-consuming abyss of History. This scene has haunted me forever, not only for its tragic decay but because it depicted the layers of time of our cities, the accretion of layers of history just as the city of Troy has seven levels of ruins. Prague by night, with its brightly lit baroque streets, is a theatre of the seventeenth century expectantly waiting for a line of carriages headed for a masked ball. In Italy, most cities curl up in their history: Venice is a palace appearing from the waters through which parade unicorns, masks and the slow genuflexions of carnival, as though time itself were dissolving in a dream. To visit Rome is to visit a hotchpotch of periods, the kaleidoscopic chaos of the richest city there has ever been can turn its back on the great deserted palaces, the ruined monuments, the history on display on every street corner from the first century to the Renaissance to the baroque, skipping forward to the nineteenth and twentieth centuries, for Rome is the sum total of time. I have spent whole days roaming the streets of Paris, feeling the weight of the past in the geometric perfection our country is so fond of. Not the Roman chaos of centuries but the clean aesthetic lines of our classicism broken by arrows pointed at the heavens like dark fantasies of the Middle Ages or mysterious gallows. I have dreamed about the gargoyles of Notre-Dame, I have passed, sombre and silent, beneath the tour Saint-Jacques. I have been dazzled by the fabulous names on the walls of buildings where once they lived: Rousseau, Diderot, Hugo, Balzac, Verlaine, Baudelaire or Rimbaud... Each of these cities shows the power of History over our continent – the common work of the European people, a barbarous people refined over centuries, constantly ravaged by wars and invasions and constantly reborn: at once Dante's inferno and his paradise.

Berlin, a city destroyed in 1945, is not adorned by such immemorial monuments. It is new. But its newness reflects on History. This is why Berlin is a concept. While other cities are History, Berlin, which has no History now, reflects on it, displays it, reveals it. But this History is not that of Antiquity or the Middle Ages, it is that of the second half of the twentieth century. Berlin reflects on the fall of the continent of Europe. Berlin is our scar exposed to the world.

I have encountered History only once and it was in Berlin. I was a schoolboy in Paris eagerly listening to the evening news, following the demonstrations in Germany which had been growing to become a crashing wave, when the Wall came down in that magical fleeting moment when our continent regained its unity after forty years of division. It was 9 November 1989. I think it was a Thursday night because the following day I was on a plane to Berlin and I'm almost sure I skipped school.

It was not that I had a finely honed sense of politics but the event was such that any schoolboy you stopped in the street realised how important it was. As soon as I arrived in the city, I made my way to the Wall which Berliners were destroying with sledgehammers in an atmosphere of joyful frenzy. There was no hatred, no bitterness, and gravity could be seen only on a few elderly faces. It was a collective holiday, like the harvest of a vanished communism. Huge sections of wall were falling to the battering rams which destroyed the graffiti and everyone took a stone, a little piece of history. I think I still have mine but I've moved house at least a dozen times since then so I'm not sure.

I had been back to Berlin several times since then, but this was the first time I would be spending a whole week. We took over a youth hostel in the centre of the city: the pupils in rooms for six and the teachers each had their own small room with a shower. Breakfast and dinner were served in a canteen. For lunch, we all took a baguette stuffed with cheese and salami. The fact that I was simply an accompanying adult meant I did not have to worry about organising things, so I just wandered around chatting with my friend Robert, a Natural Sciences teacher who, like many teachers at the lycée, had spent time in various countries, notably fifteen years in Colombia where he had worked first as a vet, then as a farmer. As for the students, I was happy as long as the group seemed reasonably cohesive and I chatted with them from time to time: it has to be said, you could not hope to find a nicer bunch of teenagers. They were curious, engaged and up for anything.

Berlin had changed a lot since my last visit, its constant metamorphosis performed under conditions of open-heart surgery, with shrill building sites, scaffolding, cranes, jackhammers everywhere. The city has constantly reinvented itself, experimented with futuristic architecture, a city of glass and steel firmly dragged back into the 1970s by the globe atop the television tower on the Alexanderplatz. We walked a lot, took the U-Bahn too, I tried to pay attention but Robert was talking to me about the animals and the forests of South America, which made for a curious combination, and every now and then a student would come up to tell me they were going to get a hot-dog or a T-shirt and would be right back... I loved the relaxed, diverse atmosphere: there is nothing in the world like the ordered chaos we call the LFA (Lycée Franco-Allemand) spirit. In my year of teaching in the *banlieues* of Paris I had been struck by the constant need to enforce a rigid discipline in order to contain the suppressed violence. In the LFA, on the other hand, the school corridors were constantly teeming with kids and young adults playing cards, revising without there being any need for supervision since they never stepped out of line. I remember when I first arrived, my final-year class had sat a huge stuffed lion at least five feet tall in the front row, warning him to pay attention during French class. A little taken aback – I had just come from a school where such behaviour would have been intended to provoke and would have to be severely reprimanded – I did nothing and as I got used to the school I was grateful that I had not reacted. To have come down hard on them would have made me look ridiculous. The fun-loving LFA spirit was obvious that first day at lunch when groups split up to go and eat. A number of teachers would eat together and had arranged to meet up on a little hill. Since I was late, as always, a large group had already assembled. I thought I sensed a number of colleagues giving me strange looks as I arrived. A pupil asked if he could try on my sunglasses. I didn't think anything of it, and handed them to him. At that moment, I was charged by a dozen pupils who piled on top of me so I was a rugby ball at the bottom of the scrum.

"Welcome to the club!" my colleagues congratulated me smiling when I finally managed to extricate myself from the ruck.

Some days earlier, these same pupils had been working excitedly on a lesson so difficult I wouldn't have dared attempt it in my first year in university. This is the LFA spirit, it means nothing to anyone except the thousands who have attended the lycée who are familiar with that incredible mixture of work and play, of utter calm and a frenzied passion for study. If this spirit were spread to schools across the country, the crisis in education would be solved within three months with a broad smile and a hundred days of relentless work.

On our first night we ended up in a rather dreary nightclub – strange in a city famous for its clubs – because we picked a club where minors were admitted, always a bad idea. While the pupils danced a little and carefully hatched plans, I flirted half-heartedly with a girl of about twenty who was there with her parents. It was only because I had nothing better to do. But I was happy to practise one of my favourite sports in German. The girl lived near a lake. That's the only detail I remember about her.

I had been haunted by a curious mixture of the trivial and the tragic since the beginning of this story, since the wayward lock of hair on my visit to Buchenwald – a combination that, truth be told, governs all our lives – but History reasserted itself the following day as, joking about our night at the club, we visited the Reichstag where I was forcibly reminded of the burning of the building in 1933 and the oppression that had followed. It is enough for the present to fade for me to be suddenly plunged back into my grandfather's past. Suddenly, everything disappeared – our night at the club, the pupils – and there was nothing but overlapping black and white images, archives, photographs. I had not simply come to Berlin to look after the pupils. The Wagner shadow had come with me.

True, I had found an explanation for the original photograph but there were still gaps that I needed to fill in, areas of my grandfather's life that were incomplete. Most importantly, I had not come up with an answer for the question that constantly nagged at me: why?

Why had my grandfather died? Why had Sommer tortured and murdered those prisoners? All these "whys" were probably naive, like the insistent questions five-year-olds ask when they first begin to question the world. Though I was not stupid enough to think there was an answer to the question, I was stupid enough to think the question was not so naive. Or that at least it was worth thinking about an answer, even if one never expected to find one, that I had a sort of moral duty, as in a Greek tragedy where the dead must be buried. I paid my respects, I buried the man and I asked my questions. My question. David Wagner had never had a grave and I knew now that I would be the one to write his tomb, his epitaph, something which my father, I thought, had never done, and which had walled him up in his perpetual walks, his silences, his denial.

My tomb needed Berlin. I could feel it as I walked through the Reichstag, even with the holiday atmosphere; I needed Germany if I was to complete my project. I had returned to the source of Evil, if I can say such a thing about a country I love and which, through its memory, its furious madness, is still expiating its sins. But I know that I could never have loved it were it not, even now, a suffering country. An economically powerful, bourgeois country proud of its place as the world's leading exporter, and a country sickened by its memory, constantly revisiting its crimes, in a way both stubborn and stifling. I wandered through the Reichstag and the guide talked about the fire while we all stared, as though spellbound, at the colossal two-headed eagle looming over the parliamentary chamber that felt slightly disturbing. We left the Reichstag and passed beneath the Brandenburg Gate, a vestige of the past in an area of the city that had been completely rebuilt, and we found ourselves in a field of black concrete stelae which I had never seen before and which might have represented coffins, a maze or a prison. Though the kids dashed about as though in a maze in *Harry Potter*, these stones were a reminder of darker deeds than those of the boy wizard because, taking the stairs down beneath the ground, you come upon the long corridors of an Information Centre which testifies to the extermination policy of the Nazis. In one room were fifteen eye-witness accounts, some written just before their deaths, terrible words scrawled on yellowing paper: "They want to rid us even of our names", "Even if I survive, what will be left of life?", "What does it mean to be a man, after this?", "They are putting women into ovens". The texts are carved into the ground, we looked down at our feet to read them, as though reading the inscriptions on coffins, while on the walls were maps of Europe with figures for each country of the number of Jews murdered. I don't remember all the figures, but I can still see the figure for my own country: France, 75,000. And two other figures: Poland, 2,500,000; Denmark... 146. Then the Room of Names lists all the names of those who died, their dates of birth and death, like the Buchenwald *Book of the Dead* for a whole continent, for the entirety of European Jewry. A little pamphlet explains that in order to read all the names in this way would take six years, seven months and twenty-seven days. The Room of Places marks out 200 places where Jews were persecuted and murdered. Lastly, a computer makes it possible to look through the archives of Yad Vashem which contains the names of three million Jews. I typed in "Wagner, France". I did not find my grandfather's name. As ever, he had disappeared. But I knew that this would be the last time. From now on, those who type in Wagner will read: "David Wagner, born Paris 4 August 1915, deported to Buchenwald, died 21 March 1942."

This I know; this is why I am writing.

4

For several days we wandered through the gaping memory of Germany, a little stunned by the immense work of remembering and mourning. It seemed impossible to escape this omnipresent guilt, this brooding over the twin wounds of Nazism and communism. The scar was everywhere – the Wall, the Shoah, Nazism. In the Jüdisches Museum, the bare, sombre hall that runs through the building, sixty-six feet high, tapering as it rises towards an inaccessible slit of light, is so disturbing that the silence was like that of the concentration camps.

Everywhere we went, we stumbled upon History, repeated, displayed, a thin sliver of time from 1939 to 1989; almost infinitesimal in terms of European History yet crossed and recrossed. While other capitals casually flaunt their History, Berlin consciously, solemnly reveals hers while the city manages to maintain an energy that prevents it being crushed beneath the weight of memory. Yet it was a curious feeling, a hundred chattering Franco-Germans on a spree wandering through the city, through the maze of guilt.

I had not come to Germany empty-handed. In France, I had done some quick research on Saack and Lachmann who had accompanied Himmler on his visit to Buchenwald. These two men, or so it seemed, had no bearing on the life of David Wagner but I felt my questions could only be answered if I followed every path, even the most secret. In my adolescence, I had been fascinated by the work of the director Stanley Kubrick who took his obsession with the visual to the point of madness, who, when filming *Barry Lyndon*, attempted to ensure every detail was faithful to the period, filling the set with antique furniture that, even if not filmed, would be seen by and inspire the actors. And it is true that you can only bring a subject to life if you exhaust every possible lead, all the details that seem only tangentially related. Saack and Lachmann's paths had crossed that of David Wagner. Like an actor in *Barry Lyndon*, I would play my role as ferryman better if they were on the set. My researches on Saack were quickly concluded since he died in 1944 on the Eastern Front, sent there as the result of a perilous promotion. His descendants had also disappeared, since his only son had also been killed in France during the counter-offensive in the Ardennes which followed the liberation. As for Lachmann, who had made only a fleeting appearance in this story since, as I've mentioned, he left the dinner at the Kochs' villa early, he too had been killed on the Eastern Front a few months after his visit to Buchenwald, leaving a wife and three young children. I had phoned his wife to whom I had laboriously explained, since her hearing was very poor, that I was a French researcher studying high-ranking German civil servants during World War II. Frau Lachmann seemed fascinated by the project, something which surprised me, until I realised that, to her, nothing was more important in her life than the memory of her husband. Since we were trying to arrange to meet, not an easy task since she lived in Göttingen, a town in the centre of Germany, and I had mentioned I would shortly be visiting Berlin, she gave me the address of her granddaughter to whom, she told me, she would give photocopies of documents about her husband. A little embarrassed by this generosity, since my Kubrick-like quest had not gone so far, I thanked her awkwardly and warmly.

By the time I flew to Berlin, I had already made contact with a soft-voiced girl (a librarian's voice, I thought, one of those tranquil people who came to my rescue in anonymous libraries) who had suggested meeting me in a café. The photocopies, she told me, were ready. She hoped to be able to help me with my thesis (something I had not mentioned but I assumed Frau Lachmann did not know much about university standards).

At 9 p.m. on the day in question, the third day of my visit to Berlin, I entered a café on the Kurfürstendamm which looked less like what we call a café in France than like a living room in an apartment. The deep, quiet room was furnished with faded sofas and low tables. Ambient music swathed the place in a warm glow. I looked around for my librarian but could see no women sitting on their own so I took an armchair that faced the door. Ten minutes later a young woman rushed into the café. It wasn't my librarian: she was wearing jeans, black boots and a jacket and she was what might be called a stunner. I was looking her up and down when she turned to me and smiled. She walked over: "*Herr Fabre?*"

It was my librarian. She apologised and explained that, despite her best efforts, she was always late for everything, but that this time she had a good excuse: the chain had come off her bicycle. Then, laughing, she held out her hands in a child-like gesture – they were covered in black grease – then headed off to the bathroom. This was Sophie Lachmann and from experience I can say that she was always like this.

When she came back, I was preparing my best lines and trying to work out how the soft voice had turned out to be this rock chick who had turned the head of every man in the bar. After ordering a coffee, Sophie started talking very fast, laughing, telling stories. I didn't understand much of what she was saying, but I smiled a lot. Suddenly, she frowned.

"*Sie verstehen nichts?*"

"*Nein.*"

"*Sind sie nicht Lehrer in einem deutsch-französischen Gymnasium?*"

I told her I didn't understand. She looked surprised and said: "Let's talk in French." And she immediately carried on at the same speed but now in French.

"I teach German and French," my rock-chick librarian explained.

In a vague attempt to excuse my imperfect German, I told her that my first foreign language was English, laboriously learned over years at school and on visits to England, to suburban houses where I was put up by families who were only in it for the money and who would send me out in the morning to visit some working-class district with a soggy lettuce and tomato sandwich which I threw into the first bin I found. All this, before travelling to the United States, to Colorado. So German was only my second language, learned by listening to repeated words I didn't understand on clapped-out tape recorders operated by teachers bored out of their skulls. The worst thing about the language was that luck wasn't on your side. In English or Italian or Spanish, you could always try mangling a French word and it might make sense. Not in German where a word was either right or it wasn't. Being unable to string two sentences together after five years studying, I was forced to face the fact that I was hopeless. I did eventually pass German, having discovered to my horror that I was required to pass in a second foreign language. I swallowed dictionaries and learnt literary texts by heart (especially Zweig, whose marvellously simple vocabulary compensated for my incompetence), but without a solid foundation so that my German became a jumble of every-day words and obscure formulations. All in all, it was hopeless.

"And it hasn't improved during your time at the Franco-German lycée?"

"Oh it has... it used to be much worse."

Sophie laughed again. All this was getting us off the topic of Lachmann but I avoided the subject like the plague. Nazism is not conducive to seduction. The last time I had slept with a German girl, she had sulked for two days because I'd called her my Führerin as she was determined on leading me around Paris her way. The time before that, a girl particularly well endowed by nature in one anatomical area, I had adopted rather a risky seduction strategy by outlining my theory, pure provocation, that Germany was schizophrenic. The girl, whose name I've forgotten, was trying to convince me that the difference between our coun-tries was that Germans were frank and straightforward while the French were obsessed with appearances. Somewhat irritated, I shot back that I had discovered the secret of the Germans: for fifty years they had been pretending to be nice, boring, middle-class people with Mercedes and washing machines whereas in fact they were insane. Retarded. *Verrückt*. How did I know this? Through literature. All you had to do was compare romanticism in Germany and France. French romanticism is the literature of unease, of pent-up energy, repressed passions as in the nov-els of Chateaubriand, but an energy that asked only to spread out across the world, something which Chateaubriand, soldier, explorer, minister of foreign affairs had done with incomparable success. German romanticism, on the other hand, is bizarre, with a negative and disturbing energy, as in Goethe's *The Sorrows of Young Werther*, shot through with a death wish. In fact, there was a rash of copycat suicides after the publication of *Young Werther* and even I had sensed, beneath the soothing romantic surface, a profound madness. And if Goethe, for whom I had only a quali- fied admiration (if you're setting out to provoke, what better than to take a sledgehammer to sacred cows), was considered to be a great German writer it was because he embodied Germany's fundamental schizophrenia, the good bourgeois advisor to the prince in his beautiful house in Weimar, a rich, famous, estab- lished writer secretly troubled by strange passions.

Two hours later, after a long defence of the innocence and simplicity of the German people, which I greeted with the wry smile of one not so easily fooled, I was in her bed.

But this seemed to me to be a dangerous tactic to adopt with young Sophie. Provocation is only really possible, in my opin- ion, with girls one is half-interested in; otherwise the risk is too great. And let's be clear: I had fallen hard and fast for the beau- tiful Sophie. With her rock-chick looks and her black hands, she had just made me an ardent fan of the German nation. Any country that could produce girls like this had to be a great coun- try. I was about to deploy my most sophisticated chat-up lines when Sophie suddenly said: "Oh, I brought the documents."

Aargh. All was lost.

And she added: "They'll tell you everything about the hero of the family."

I was stunned by this remark. All clearly was lost. How could Sophie say such a thing about a high-ranking Nazi official? My confusion must have been apparent because the young woman stared at me with her piercing blue eyes and I could not help but think that she conformed completely to the Nazi idea of femininity: blonde, blue-eyed, tall and well-built, her beauty was not of a refined kind, but healthy and vivid, giving out a rare strength. This disturbed me even more. She must have read my thoughts because she quickly added: "You don't know his story, so don't rush to prejudge. And, anyway, German families need a hero, they have enough shame as it is."

"So your grandfather was a hero?"

"No, it's probably too strong a word. But he was an… interesting man. And my grandmother made him something of a myth. She never knew any other man, never wanted to remarry, though she had enough offers."

"I'm not surprised, if she was half as pretty as her granddaughter."

Sophie said nothing for a moment. Then, finding my attempt at a compliment ridiculous, she burst out laughing, making me laugh too. It really was pathetic… so clumsy it was touching.

She ordered another coffee which she sipped like some rare beverage. The pleasure she showed in sipping the liquid, her eyes half-closed, was arousing. Out of politeness, I pretended to leaf through the documents, most of which were citations and letters.

"They're letters of recommendation," Sophie said suddenly.

"Why?"

"After the death of my grandfather, my grandmother was alone and my grandfather's friends used to write to her. Von Stauffenberg was very supportive."

"The guy who led the failed July plot to assassinate Hitler? He was a friend of your grandfather?"

"Yes. They were both high-ranking civil servants and they were increasingly doubtful about the future of the Reich, as many people were. That's how the talk of the coup started."

I was surprised by what she was saying. I could understand that German families needed to dress up the truth, which seemed to be what she was doing, but I could also see that Lachmann was not a nobody and that this sexy young teacher was about to give me an object lesson in history: Von Stauffenberg was the most famous of Hitler's adversaries. And I felt intimidated to be learning about this marginal but nonetheless well-known part of German history, not through books but through the pretty girl sitting opposite who seemed miles apart from Nazism.

But, I set aside the documents. Everything in its own time. And now was not the moment for historical research. The present took the form of a beautiful young woman, which was both more attractive and more charming than a trip into the past. I was clearly not doing very well, because Sophie kept changing the subject, making it impossible for me to employ any clever linguistic manoeuvres. She would not let herself be led where I wanted to take her. Casanova was reduced to plugging the dykes, making it up as he went along. All in all, though, things went well. We were having a pleasant evening, otherwise Sophie would have left hours ago, given that it was now II p.m. Instead, she suggested we go for a walk. Night was on my side…

The Kurfürstendamm was bathed in light. The avenue looked like a yellow river lit up with flashes of red. In the distance glimmered the broken church, supported by the glass and steel belfry with its shimmering blue stained glass. From the summit arose an absurd metallic veil like the gesture of a surfer on the roof of the world. In spite of the lights, the night had lost none of its power to melt the will. Bodies are more open in the night, spirits more passionate, more tempted by impulse. It is the moment of violence and love.

I don't quite know how, but Sophie left her bicycle at the café and I walked her home. She didn't make me wait until the second date, didn't say she wasn't ready, didn't even offer me a last drink. She simply offered herself with an innocence and a directness. Casanova was petrified as he slipped into her bed. And his performance was terrible. Let's say that, for better or worse, a seasoned innocence encountered innocence of another kind. And when these innocences woke the next morning and had breakfast before leaving, they were in love, something which is the worst possible cliché in fiction but extraordinarily wonderful in real life. And I can be forgiven for only recounting what actually happened, changing only those things insisted on by punctilious heirs and legal intransigence.

We had only four days before I was due to leave. We made the most of it. And so a tall blonde woman was frequently to be seen with the Franco-German group, prompting suspicious and slightly jealous looks from some of the girls who considered me their personal (fantastical) property. The streets were sweeter with her. Our future was uncertain, which meant that we floated in an unstable bubble of pure pleasure. We never spoke of the future, only about the present and, occasionally, about a distant, obvious, past.

We swam in the lake to the west of the city. The water was cold. Sohpie undressed while I stared at her unashamedly, thinking I could sell her figure to L'Oreal for their new campaign. I stared and stared and stared. Luckily the cold water calmed me. Sophie swam breaststroke, I played the man alternating every possible swimming style. Laughing at my display of machismo, she kissed me, a long wet kiss which made us capsize in the sunshine. The earth moved a little.

With the kids, we rented bicycles and took a long ride through the city. With my heavy, solid mountain-bike, I could amuse myself on the cross streets while the group rode around the Spree and the canals, following the remains of the Wall, cutting through the woods to stop at a man-made beach where we had a drink next to some waste ground overlooking a reservoir where nobody swam. I let my feet sink into the sand. It was hot. Sweat beaded on Sophie's lip. Her sunglasses hid her eyes. I loved that, and kissed her.

As I left Berlin that radiant Sunday as the sun was setting over the Reichstag, I decided to come back. I didn't quite know how, but I was attracted to the shape of this city, the shape of this body. And since I had often thought I should change my profession – though this was the only job I had ever loved – perhaps now was the time to do so. The easiest thing, of course, would have been to decide to devote myself entirely to my book, something I could just as easily do in an igloo at the North Pole. The more realistic option was to find a job and spend my evenings writing.

The months that followed were taken up by a variety of administrative tasks. I tried to get a job at the French Embassy in Germany, which proved difficult. So I put on my best suit and went on a tour of government departments armed with a CV and a devastating smile, just as I used to when, like Pinocchio, I roamed the *banlieues* where I used to teach. The officials glanced at my achievements, mostly with sublime indifference, occasionally with a flicker of interest.

"Why don't you go and teach in Germany?"

"Why not? I'll give it some thought."

And I would leave. Finally, after a dozen such meetings, a high-ranking civil servant in the department of foreign affairs shook my hand and said: "If you're not up to the job, you'll be out within two weeks."

Having seen many movies, I replied: "I'm up to the job."

I had a ticket to Berlin in my hand. I had crossed to the other side of History. True, I was staying in the old Europe, the continent still going round in circles since the double cataclysms of 1914 and 1940, missing every train of political and economic history ever since, but from the point of view of memory, I was going to the far side of the world, towards those who lost in 1945. This is not to suggest that twenty-first-century Germans are different from the French – quite the reverse, they are very similar – but for the piece about David Wagner I was writing, it changed everything. I was stepping into the turbulent fury of the Third Reich. Obviously, I was moving to Germany for more pleasant reasons, for a smile more welcoming than a Nazi salute. But I intended, in going back to the source of Evil, to carry on with my research, to penetrate the mysteries of the Nazi regime thanks to Lachmann and his tortuous career.

Perhaps it might come as a surprise to learn how I spent my free time during those holidays – given that, while I was loitering around the corridors of the French bureaucracy, it was high summer, the two glorious months of school holidays which are viewed with animosity by those in every other profession (in fact I sometimes wondered why I was leaving a first-class, wonderful institution, with the state of education the way it was, for a job with no security). When I was not in Germany with Sophie, I was watching documentaries about the Nazis lent to me by my best friend at the lycée, a history teacher, the bouncy happy Ruellorn, as the students called him. His area of expertise was World War II. Books, as you will have realised, are my life. But there are pictures which contain secrets no book could ever reveal because they capture the moment itself. The images of the period I gorged on that summer, black and white recordings I watched lying on my bed, shutters half-closed in an apartment I was about to sell, gradually gave up their secrets. I really was going through the looking glass of history. Brooding over these fascinating, repellent images, like the character in *A Clockwork Orange*, eyes clamped open with a steel contraption, forced to watch images of violence until they produced nausea and vomiting, I endured the passage of Evil, crawling from the pit of hell that were the concentration camps to penetrate the blindness of the Third Reich. I shifted to the side of the executioners, the Kochs, the Sommers, but also to the side of the fascinated, the blind, that all-too-ordinary mass who trusted Hitler absolutely and completely.

The images revealed that I had been wrong about Hitler. And if I focus on him, it is because the Third Reich could not have existed without him. Many of the great events in history have no need of individuals: it seems self-evident that the French Revolution would have happened without Danton or Robespierre. But I am convinced that the Third Reich depends on Hitler. Even if some form of dictatorship would probably have emerged, given the economic and ideological circumstances of Germany between the wars, the bloody, savage madness of the Third Reich is the result of one individual's staggering, explosive relationship to his time. In the past, I had written that what struck me about Hitler was his coarseness, his utter ordinariness. Far from being a genius of Evil, as is often said, he was the epitome of a mediocre man who enthralled people precisely because of his mediocrity, his vulgarity. Needless to say, the piece received a barrage of criticism, but nothing that persuaded me to change my mind. I was only partly wrong: eyewitnesses at the time, the greatest historians constantly return to what they call "the Hitler mystery", by which they mean how such a lowly man could have come to power and played such an important historic role, given that from childhood he seemed destined for a life of obscurity; for thirty years he was invisible, a failed artist, an idler, sponging off his family before slipping into bankruptcy in 1909 and living in homeless shelters and on the street. And yet this man whom they refer to as "socially inept", this "non-person" – an aspect that, even in the last days in the Bunker, was still a part of this man with no private life, who, after the death of his mother, lavished his affection on his dogs – was to hold such extraordinary power that it would require the conjoined forces of every major power of the age to stop him.

But the fact is that my analysis was incomplete. A single image convinced me of this. A single, incredible vision of the Chancellor in mid-speech which is pregnant with meaning. He is in the midst of one of his grotesque gestures, shouting, spitting, his jaw unhinged from the force of his expression, jerking like a puppet. I watched him calmly, in my room decades after the event. But in the moment, the camera captures the face of a man in civilian clothes, held spellbound by this speech, his eyes rolled back like a zombie, captivated, enthralled by this rant. This man no longer had a conscience, a judgement, an identity. The image revealed its secret, the secret that the intellectual lying on his bed could not understand. Hitler had captured this man's soul. This is the only expression that seems apt. There is something in that image that is beyond understanding. It is like a voodoo ritual or a sacred rite. I don't believe in devil worship and such things, but I have seen men in a trance, in Africa, and this man presented the same symptoms. During these highly orchestrated ceremonies, a combination of sounds and colours carefully mixed by the Nazi propaganda machine, Hitler found a way, by the power of his words, to strip people of their reason. The more I think about history, the more I am aware of the irrational, of the tribal, savage forms of our societies, as though dark, secret urges are constantly waiting for some tear in the social fabric to explode. Hitler, no doubt unconsciously, discovered that tear. He came to a people with no points of reference, crushed under the weight of economic collapse, maddened by defeat, and when his voice, supported by the brutality of the SA, emerged in this chaos, everything exploded.

In these images, I saw men hypnotised, women in tears even as others were attracted to the Chancellor – a man who had always been terrified of women. Great legions were organised in perfect, serried, terrifying ranks based on the words of this man so average he had left no impression on his teachers and classmates. One day, after the Great War, Hitler spoke at a meeting of the disillusioned, the demobbed soldiers, those ignored by society, and all eyes turned to him, everyone fell silent and listened and he knew his destiny.

By early September, when I took up my post at the French Embassy in Berlin (it sounded good), I had devoured documentaries, biographies, testimonies about the Third Reich. Whether this was a professional mistake, I don't know, but I arrived through the Brandenburg Gate, which is just next to the embassy, along the avenues of the past and I am not sure this was the best way to come. But a writer is a divided creature: when you think he is focused on doing something, he is living another life, solitary, withdrawn, pensive and this shadow which follows him is just as important as the real world. As I casually strode through the metal detectors at the embassy, I was constantly, ceaselessly working on my book, this time from the German side. I was looking for explanations, I was going back to the origin of whys the way children and madmen search for the crock of gold at the end of the rainbow.

5

Sophie and I rented a large apartment in Berlin. For years I had been unhappy with the places where I'd lived which, though pleasant enough, always seemed too small, too nondescript. In Berlin, I let myself go and chose a *bourgeois* building, a *bourgeois* apartment, a *bourgeois* ostentation. Compared to Paris and certainly to London, rents were not expensive, I was earning a good living, as was Sophie, since German teachers, given the hours they work, are much better paid than teachers in France. Our apartment was everything I could wish for, a vast, unadorned, luminous space with huge windows and parquet floors.

Life with Sophie was going well. Let's say that in my somewhat tumultuous years, my departure for Berlin seemed at first like a new beginning. Sophie was still reeling from my decision: she had been charmed by my suddenly leaving my country, my profession. It was still working in my favour. Until now, aside from a couple of dubious obsessions regarding food and tidiness, I thought Sophie was the most wonderful woman in the world. I was in the radiant heart of love, contemplating our relationship with just a tinge of worry, remembering the often sudden reversals of passion. But it should be said that I would have given my soul for Sophie's smile; with her slender frame and her long blonde hair, there seemed something elfin about her.

Sophie did, however, have some trouble coping with every woman's rival – the incorporeal mistress that is literature. I told her I was working on a biography of my grandfather who had died in a concentration camp. From the first, and with a vehemence that surprised me, she was against the project. Books about the concentration camps were of no interest, everyone was bored with them, they concerned a past about which we already knew all there was to know; besides, people shouldn't make literature out of other people's sufferings. Why did I want to write something so depressing, something no one would want to read? Didn't people write books in order to be read? What literature needed were more comic novels, she declared, and no one in Europe, except maybe a couple of English writers could write good comic novels.

I told her that some day I would write a comic novel but that for the moment, I had a family debt to settle. She shrugged her shoulders.

It should be said that Sophie wasn't entirely wrong. I had embarked on a difficult project. But what choice did I have? Besides, even thinking about the idea rationally, my research was so far advanced that it would have been stupid to stop now.

"Why do you want to write about something so sick?" she went on. "It's not normal. You're the one who's sick."

I slumped into an armchair. Calmly, I explained to her that I was doing it because of my grandfather and because the period of the Nazis was a crucial period in history. A brief but terrifying period that opened up a Pandora's Box (violence, evil, destruction…), which hastened the collapse of our civilisation, sidelining us from history for decades, perhaps for ever. The fact is that, in the early twenty-first century, Europe was still on the margins of history, on the sidelines of world events, something that had not occurred since ancient Greece. These explanations should have satisfied Sophie, but she stared at me sceptically.

"*Ist es vorbei?*" "Is it over?" she would ask me in German whenever she was in a bad mood. I have to admit that even to my ears my words had sounded vapid and verbose. Clearly, I wasn't lying, but equally clearly there was something else at stake in what I was doing. Why had I been fascinated with the Nazis since I was a teenager? Why did I feel that a crucial event, not simply for humanity but for me, the teenage Fabre, had taken place that I desperately needed to understand, as though there were nothing more important in the world for me or for anyone else? I probably sensed by the animal antennae of the subconscious that some part of my history was buried there, but there was something else, something I still could not put my finger on, something that Sophie's question picked up on. I felt that, with a sixth sense I was beginning to recognise, she had touched on something important.

"*Ja, es ist vorbei,*" I said.

There was another reason for Sophie's mood. She didn't like the idea of my writing about her grandfather. Though she was happy for me to use historical documents in the context of university research, she hated the idea of them being used in a novel. She felt that she was no longer in control and that besides, to lump together Sommer, Koch, Erich Wagner and Friedrich Lachmann could only harm her family. On this point she was wrong because, in spite of my distrust of family hagiographies, it was becoming increasingly clear to me that her grandfather was utterly unlike the other Nazis. That he was a Nazi, Sophie will have to forgive me, I had to write. He had been a member of the NSDAP since 1932, so before Hitler came to power, and he had immediately been given a position of responsibility. But Lachmann was an example of what everyone in Germany knew, and what other countries, mired in clichés about the Nazis, did not know since the accounts of the Nazi they were familiar with invariably portrayed the brutal SS, Jewish victims and a passive, complicit populace. As always, and without wishing to portray Hitler as the jailer of a hostile people, which for the most part the Germans were not, the situation was more complex. Friedrich Lachmann was proof of this. His rank was the administrative equivalent of my grandfather Fabre: he was a cog of limited importance but with considerable power compared to the man in the street.

It goes without saying that, but for the unity of action, I could have devoted yet another book to Friedrich Lachmann's story. The man was certainly interesting enough. But he is just one of the people in the photograph, one character in the panorama, one of the faces of my research. He is Sophie's David Wagner, the absent figure whose death, whose sacrifice stripped all meaning from the lives of his descendants – and when I went to the vast family home in Göttingen, I truly felt that this father whose three children had barely known him (a uniform glimpsed from time to time, some affectionate gestures, a few games) had weighed upon his family, guided their lives (a life made spectral and slow by the constant weight of this absence) more completely than if he had been alive. But he is not my David Wagner, he is not my investigation – just one of the many who are part of the question and provides one part of the answer, who puts some flesh on the enigma that is Nazism because anything that goes beyond the hackneyed is a response.

It was for some family gathering that I visited the town of Göttingen – one of those pleasant but unremarkable towns that exist all over modern Germany which were destroyed during the war and replaced by those interchangeable cities that seem to have been placed on the landscape by some giant architect. The whole Lachmann family had gathered in the large three-storey villa – the father lived on the top floor, the grandmother in the middle, the largest part, and the grandson in a basement which had been renovated and was lit by high windows – all of them curious to size up the new Parisian recruit. I was warmly welcomed. A family lunch, a walk in the gardens, a tour of the villa with Sophie. Frau Lachmann was an elderly woman with a shock of white hair and permanently bloodshot eyes. She offered me her past and her library, gave me the original copy of *Defying Hitler* by Sebastian Haffner which I had just read in French and immediately realised was a work of major importance. It is celebrated in Germany but little known elsewhere. The book is a memoir of the period from 1914 to 1933 when Hitler came to power. Haffner left Germany for England in 1938, and it was there that he wrote it at the request of an editor. The war broke out and the book was never published. Such accounts always teeter on the brink of non-existence: this account narrowly missed never being published, Primo Levi's was refused by a host of major publishers, as indeed was that of Elie Wiesel, which finally appeared only after a chance meeting with François Mauriac who used his influence to get it distributed. In 1954 Sebastian Haffner moved back to Germany where he became a respected writer and journalist, every German schoolchild having read *The Meaning of Hitler* in history class, but *Defying Hitler* was not published until after his death. The perspicacity of his observations were such – he predicts the war, the defeat and the rebuilding of Germany – that a number of historians doubt the work's authenticity, which was later proved.

If I mention this author, it is not only to engrave this name among the others in my memory and my esteem, but also because it turns out that Friedrich Lachmann's career stirred certain echoes as I read the book. There were a number of paths: commitment to Nazism, resistance, exile, indifference, disaffection... Friedrich Lachmann and Sebastian Haffner chose two of these paths.

It all began with a choice. At the outset, however, the circumstances of both Haffner and Lachmann were the same: the Germany of the 1920s and 1930s. Both were born in 1907, both had a Protestant education, though Lachmann's was more devout given that his father was a pastor. He was raised in the strict observance of the law, in the harshness of Northern Westphalia, surrounded by pale, cold, austere men dressed in black. They both grew up to the sound of the drums of war, following the progress of the German armies on maps at school, knowing by heart the names of the generals, eagerly learning the outcomes of the battles as though they were football scores, the goals marked by a division being wiped out or a ship being sunk. The comparison with football is not mine but Haffner's: the pompous idiot who has buried himself in the past would have been incapable of imagining that French and German children could have thought of war as a game, a tournament with teams waging war (France, Germany, England, Russia, Austria) like a European Championship: "The truly Nazi generation was formed by those born in the decade from 1900 and 1910 who experienced war as a great game and were untouched by its realities." And this is undoubtedly one of the things that explains the Germans' extraordinary habituation to violence between the wars: that long childlike denial of conflict which translated into sudden daily beatings of random boys in the street.

I cannot penetrate the souls of these two men. But it seems clear that before making conflicting choices, their lives played out in similar fashion for many years. There is no evidence, with either Lachmann or Haffner, of any support for the Weimar republic or the democratic parties. Both men studied law; they seemed destined for glittering futures (they had forceful personalities, a developed consciousness and inner life, quick minds and were hard workers). There is one exception: Walther Rathenau, the minister for foreign affairs. But both boys were still at school when he was assassinated in 1922. Of Lachmann, I know only that he had an intellectual admiration for the man. As for Haffner, he wrote a sheaf of enthusiastic pages about Rathenau, emblematic of the Jewish intellectual bourgeoisie which had produced other great men, like Léon Blum in France who my family were so envious of because he embodied everything that they, being too uncouth, too pedestrian, could never achieve: supreme elegance and supreme sophistication. We, who had so often provided servants to the Republic, would have preferred to have been, like the young Léon Blum, a government commissioner in the Council of State, writing reports and judgements in a supple yet rigorous style rather than using the leaden bureaucratic prose of the Third Republic. We did not want to be the noble servants of the Republic – provincial officials, *préfets, sous-préfets* – but people with real power: ministers, council presidents. But it was never to be: we were one level below the supreme elegance of power.

In these spirited pages, Haffner gives a comparison between Hitler and Rathenau which I cannot resist transcribing, in the hope that his book will become as famous in France as those of Levi or Semprun: "Rathenau and Hitler are the two men who excited the imagination of the German masses to the utmost; the one by his ineffable culture, the other by his ineffable vileness. Both, and this is decisive, came from inaccessible regions, from some sort of 'beyond'. The one from a sphere of sublime spirituality where the cultures of three millennia and two continents hold a symposium, the other from a jungle far below the depths plumbed by the base penny dreadfuls, from an underworld where demons rise from a brewed-up stench of petty-bourgeois backrooms, doss-houses, barrack latrines, and the hangman's yard. From their different 'beyonds' they both drew a spellbinding power, quite irrespective of their politics." The minister, walking to the office as he did every day, was assassinated by three young men passing in a car. They belonged to the Nazi generation: one of them was a schoolboy.

But Rathenau is the only man to avoid Haffner's disdain. In these pages, written in 1938, we can sense the contempt and the disgust of Germans for all the political parties so one can easily understand the reasons why a "spellbinding" man should come to power, short-circuiting the parties by the cult of leadership. His account of the year 1923, in the mixture of story and analysis which is the book's great strength, described in tragi-comic fashion the extraordinary ups and downs of the currency which on one day had an exchange rate of 100,000 marks to the dollar and a week later 1,000,000 marks to the dollar, until finally marks were counted in billions and the daily paper cost five billion marks, in an incredible whirl in which both prices and currency were collapsing, a cynical waltz in which twenty-year-old speculators led extravagant lives of endless parties, nightclubs and sumptuous dinners while prudent family men looked on as the savings of a lifetime disappeared. In fact, rich and poor made no sense, in a single day everything could be wiped out on a risky speculation, one of life's hiccups. This was a superior brand of cynicism in which nothing meant anything, where life was a moment to be seized, a jaded, comic farce in which young girls offered themselves, and rich, disillusioned young men wandered aimlessly with lifeless eyes and hollow laughs, all this punctuated by the speeches of doomsayers haranguing people on Berlin street corners, urging them to save the world through religion, through the massacre of the Jews, through nationalism or through song and dance. In Munich, one such firebrand was called Hitler, but he was only one of the many self-appointed redeemers. "In that year," Haffner writes, "an entire generation of Germans had a spiritual organ removed: the organ that gives men steadfastness and balance, but also a certain inertia and solidity. It may variously appear as conscience, reason, experience, respect for the law, morality, fear of God. [...] The year 1923 prepared Germany, not specifically for Nazism, but for any fantastic adventure."

Here I have to part company with Haffner and his account of the resistible rise of Arturo Ui to supreme executive power of the State by a combination of threats and intimidations targeting cowardly, frightened political leaders, communists ("sheep in wolves' clothing"), while social democrats and the Catholic middle ground rallied themselves whilst the noble, heroic, nationalist right chanted "*Heil Hitler!*" as their own partisans were murdered. I will go back to Friedrich Lachmann who, far from falling in love with a young Jewish girl, as Haffner did, recognising that Hitler would bring disaster and going into exile, fell in love with an archetypal German girl,

very blonde, very traditional and a member of the NSDAP.
The other choice.

They met in 1930 at a ball in a house in the heart of the forest in Göttingen where Lachmann was studying. He had left
Westphalia to attend this prestigious university, but on that
Saturday he had abandoned his studies to go to a ball attended
by many young ladies. He met Anna, a schoolgirl of sixteen,
and I don't know whether for him it was love at first sight, but
in Frau Lachmann's account it is the most important date in
the world (which explains Sophie's obsession with the nightclub in the middle of the forest she constantly talked about):
they danced together all night. Friedrich was a fine dancer –
truth be told, in Anna's account, he was the best at everything,
and it was often difficult to separate reality from adulation.
In the family album, Anna never looks at the camera lens.
Most often, she is gazing at her husband; in one particular
photo, the love in her eyes has something of the fervour of
adoration. Anna was a rather striking woman (though not in
Sophie's league), blonde, with a slightly pronounced chin, and
in the photos she is quickly accompanied by one, then two,
and finally three small children. As for Friedrich, he is older
and although still a young man, clearly an adult: perceptive,
mature, as though from the first he has been a father, a responsible man. He has a slightly deceptive air of strength, probably due to being slightly overweight and already balding. In
most of the photos, he wears his uniform. A swastika glitters
on the lapel. And although I have seen swastikas a thousand
times, seeing it on the lapel of the grandfather of a woman
you're in love with, in a family who have nothing but love and
respect for this man, is no easy thing, especially when your
own grandfather, a Jew, died in a concentration camp.

In the four years that Anna made him wait before allowing him a first kiss (a remarkable feat of patience even for the
period), the young Friedrich did not content himself with this
platonic love. Disgusted by the situation in Germany, this son
of an upstanding, fiercely upright pastor joined the NSDAP,
as did many professors and fellow students in Göttingen, a
reactionary university quickly corrupted by the Nazis (and the
position of university professors during this period cannot be
over-stated, the most important of which, Heidegger rallying
to the cause, remains a symbol). Lachmann was hoping for
change, a change which Adolf Hitler embodied. He did not
join the party out of ambition (like those law students who
presented themselves for their exams wearing the swastika,
putting forward one absurdity after another to the despair of
the wise, elderly judges who, in spite of their misgivings, were
forced to accept them). It was too early to predict that Hitler
would come to power, but Lachmann certainly supported the
cause of the national revolution. This meant that one of the
most brilliant students at Göttingen, on the brink of passing the exams that led to the upper echelons of German legal
and governmental professions, had just joined forces with the
most brutal, the most crazed ideologue. Blinded by the period
in which he lived, Lachmann saw nothing, understood nothing. He was intelligent, cultivated, educated, honest, yet he
saw nothing.

Becoming a Nazi did not make Lachmann stupid. Let's say
that his intelligence was both blind and effective. He passed
his law exams and, as Hitler was becoming Chancellor, left
to do his training in Prussia as a trainee Landrat or district
administrator. It was at this point that things began to go
wrong and his career becomes interesting. More and more,

though unaware of it, he was fighting the battle that Haffner describes at the beginning of his book and which all upright Germans had to fight: an unequal struggle between the cruel, ruthless, all-powerful State and the weak, fragile individual. It was a battle with only one possible outcome, but one which everyone, out of conscience, had to wage nonetheless. I cannot give all the stages of the metamorphosis for the simple reason that most of the documents have since disappeared, not for glorious, epic reasons (the SS determinedly destroying the records of even a rebel Landrat…) but simply because Anna Lachmann lost all the letters in which her husband talked about the doubts and qualms of his tortuous road to independence. What remains would certainly have made many historians happy, but what they fashion is a hollow statue: not a single line by Friedrich Lachmann survives. There is much about him, but what did he think, feel, experience? I don't know. All I have are speculations, the unreliable stories of a wife who worships his memory. But I have an account of his actions, both from the letters of his friends, most of which date from the war, and witness statements from 1946 during the denazification when, in order to receive a pension to feed her children, Frau Lachmann had to prove that, though her husband was a member of the party, he did not support its aims. A subtle distinction which only witness statements could prove. I will quote only a few letters.

Firstly, the most important letter and the one that was probably decisive in getting the pension, given the identity of its author. It is written by Karen Machwitz, the widow of one of the leaders of the 20 July plot in 1944, an assassination attempt with colossal ramifications which failed, as did every attempt against Hitler, who had the luck of the devil (the house was blown up, a number of collaborators were killed, others lost limbs when the bomb in von Stauffenberg's briefcase exploded, but Hitler did not get a scratch), and which was followed by a murderous crackdown.

Karen Machwitz wrote:

The friendship between Landrat Lachmann and my husband dates from 1936, when Friedrich Lachmann was his trainee in Fischhausen in Prussia. I remember that even then, Erwin Machwitz was impressed by his intelligence, his ability to understand cases. They quickly became more than work colleagues. Their vision of the regime was the same and though the Landrat was a cadre in the party, his remarks, even at the time, were far removed from the official party line. In his clashes with the party, my husband found in Lachmann his greatest support, married to a peerless legal mind. For years, right up until the Landrat died, they continued to be firm friends and on several occasions the count informed me that, in a post-Hitler Germany, Friedrich Lachmann would hold an important post. In fact, he participated in the early discussions with von Stauffenberg which would lead to the plot of 20 July 1944. The death of the Landrat came as a terrible shock to my husband. He himself was to suffer the same fate some months later, when he was hanged for his part in the plot.

I hereby attest that Landrat Lachmann never belonged to the core of the party and that there is therefore every reason to grant the request of his wife Frau Lachmann.

I remain at your disposal should you require any further information.

The situation was obviously more complex than this well-meaning outline suggests and it is clear that Lachmann struggled with the change long after this initial turmoil. But the very fact that he had been close to Machwitz was proof enough for the Denazification Committee of the sincerity of Anna Lachmann's request. It is true that the metamorphosis must have begun in 1936–7 since, as Anna Lachmann points out in her long letter of defence, by the end of his period as a trainee, when every door was open to him, Lachmann deliberately made two mistakes which were to cost him his career and salvage his conscience: in disagreement with Himmler, he refused all offers from the SS, despite the promise of a high-ranking position; he also rejected the Gauleitung (the Reich was divided into districts administered by party delegates known as Gauleiter) who wanted to name him administrative director of Westphalia, which was the best possible position he could have hoped for at the end of his traineeship. But such a level of responsibility would have entailed working hand in hand with the party. So he declined both offers.

It was the end of his career. In retaliation, he was posted to Czechoslovakia in 1938, to Freudenthal in the Sudetenland as a humble Landrat which, at his age, was not so bad but could hardly be compared to the rank of governor or SS general which would surely have been his had he been patient for a year or two.

In the Sudetenland, he continued his inner struggle as best he could, which meant no open resistance, without any clear concept of his role, torn between the national revolution he had so hoped for and the dictates of his conscience. But he was a man of duty. It defined him. He was rigid, austere. The strict morality he had learned from his father dictated his every action. To the end, though his will was sapped and he was increasingly disillusioned, he clung to the shreds of that morality until he exploded.

His role in the Sudetenland can be summed up by the long letter written by a pastor in 1946, to my mind the most persuasive of all the letters sent to the commission. It began with these words:

> *I would first like to say that I have never been a member of the NSDAP and have never been involved in politics. I was never a friend of Landrat Lachmann.*
>
> After which the pastor writes: *"Ich bin offen und erlich, wenn ich sage, dass ich diesen Mann verehrt habe." – I am being open and honest when I say that I revered this man.*
>
> There are other possible translations of the verb "verehren", but it is a word generally reserved for kings.
>
> *In the years that he spent with us, we all admired his determination and his decency. He always supported the population of Freudenthal in their conflicts with the party and a number of Jewish families were grateful for his presence.*

The pastor goes on to cite several examples. The Landrat refused to allow the party to confiscate the property of Jews, supplied them with passports and allowed families to leave the country. This was before the Final Solution. In an astonishing passage, which seems to imply that as late as 1940 even high-ranking members of the regime knew little of the work of the SS and the concentration camps, the pastor recounts that one of Lachmann's constituents, a handicapped man, disappeared from the hospital where he was being treated.

sion of his contradictions, becoming a fighter who did not fight. This man whose political convictions had been decimated, who had seen his hoped-for revolution crumble, who had been carried along by the crimes committed around him and who, unlike many of those around him, had only his conscience left, armed himself with the most austere moral code and was the only soldier with no weapons. This means – and I am more or less certain of what I am suggesting – that he committed suicide. Like many desperate SS officers who had seen their ideals crumble in the bloody mud of the massacres, he advanced towards the enemy lines one day in November 1943 and did not even draw his pistol when he was fired on.

"He did not want to shoot a single human being," the unit commander explained in a long and moving letter to Frau Lachmann informing her of his death.

He had volunteered to enlist, but even in our first conversation when he arrived in the camp, he told me he refused to kill. He was there to defend his country, to take his place among those fighting. However, though his skills as an organizer were at the disposal of Germany, he refused to use a gun. I tried in vain to explain the problem with this position, but he would not be moved. He would not fire a gun. He was unshakeable in his resolve.

Your husband fell during difficult fighting to the north of Kiev, near Rowy. It was a foggy day. I can assure you that he did not suffer, that his death was quick and painless. Unfortunately, the fighting was so fierce that it was impossible for us to bury him. It is possible during a counter-attack we may regain this ground and give him a proper burial.

Captain Lachmann was very happy, two days before this

tragic event, to receive your letter announcing the birth of his
baby. He was thrilled at the thought of seeing you when he
was next on leave. Sadly, this is a joy he would never know.
    I hope that the knowledge that your husband gave his life
for the greater good of the people, the Führer and the Reich
will be of some comfort to you at this sad time.
    Commandant Latz

Then there were letters, lots of letters, mostly from von
Stauffenberg and from Machwitz, like a Greek chorus,
almost all of which began with the disbelieving cry: "*Landrat*
Lachmann ist gefallen! Landrat Lachmann ist gefallen!"
"Landrat Lachmann has fallen!" Yes, Lachmann was dead,
as they were all to die, whether on the Eastern Front or on 10
August 1944, when the conspirators were executed.

Es war ein nebeliger Tag. It was a foggy day, the comman-
dant wrote. *Nacht und Nebel*, this was the name given to the
forced disappearance of political activists and resistants. It was
not a gun that killed the Landrat, but all this confusion, the
fog of conscience which seems most evocative at this moment,
near Lake Constance where I have come to write my book,
where the winter fog rises in long sheets of mist all the way
to the house. This lake I love to gaze out at, when it gleams
like burnished copper in sunlight hard as metal, is grey now
and swallowed by the mist which cloaks the landscape in a
damp, sombre, blinding shroud. It looks like a mysterious
wing, frayed and ragged, then suddenly denser, floating over
the water before slithering like an animal onto the shore.

And as my thoughts suddenly scatter and drift out towards
the snowy flakes, an old memory of a Latin translation comes
back to me, awkward and mangled as all of my Latin transla-

tions were. A Roman general, whose troops are surrounded in the forests of Germania, had a hideous dream of an army emerging from the swamp as the fog recedes, their bodies broken, amputated. What the waning fog slowly reveals is the legion of Varus, wiped out by the Teutons, described in pages which show the dread terror of barbarians in the savage lands where the Romans no longer dared to venture.

This mythological fog is here before me. I think I can hear music. It is probably coming from the apartment next door. I listen. I don't know much about classical music. Mahler? Beethoven? Bloody tone deafness. After all, we are in the homeland of music and philosophy. Limpid notes, not really uplifting and yet light and shining in the greyness of my thoughts and the fog. It was not easy to write about this man. The notes glide, eddy, whirl.

6

In every school staffroom, teachers discuss their timetables compared to those in the "private sector", a generic term for the distant, phantasmagorical world paved with gold and diamonds. Those who have worked in the private sector proudly flaunt the fact: "given that I've worked in business…" like a glorious war memory. The principal argument among teachers is that an hour of class cannot be compared to an hour spent in an office where, in their imaginations, people doze over a pile of old files. And there was a time when I completely agreed with this point of view.

The problem is that, even if this were true – and I did not find my hours working at the embassy as arduous as an hour of lessons, especially when I was working in the sink estates where you are exhausted in two hours – there were, however, many hours in the day. And sadly, you didn't get to doze. I had a certain number of files I had to deal with and I could no longer simply count on my presence of mind because the intelligence required was of a more practical nature than I was used to. We were not expected to explain abstruse theories, defend ingenious theses, explore the ramifications of a text, but to manage a project from beginning to end, from the first phone call to the opening of the exhibition, for example. Oh yes, this was the job I had secured: cultural attaché. And it was anything but a rose garden because if there is one thing I have not been blessed with it is organisational skills. Unfortunately, this was precisely what was now required of me. Consequently, I sweated blood at work, got home late, which Sophie did not appreciate, even though she would sometimes sit up until midnight correcting homework.

In short, I had not resolved much about the Nazis, but I had discovered the solution to the teaching/business question. There was another metaphysical question nagging me at the time. Ever since I had met Sophie and been working on my grandfather's biography, I often thought about *Sophie's Choice,* the great novel by William Styron who had without hesitation built a pure fiction on Evil and the camps. And I wondered, crucially, whether Stingo, Styron's narrator and alter ego, would not have preferred to sleep with Sophie (despite a memorable blow-job scene) rather than write his book. In other words, what would he have said had he been given the following dilemma: "You can stay with Sophie or you can write a great novel, but the choices are irreconcilable. Which do you choose?" What response would he have made? Given the consolations afforded by literature, the question might be asked of many writers. Goethe, for example: "Would you rather have written *Werther* or slept with Charlotte?" Dante, in particular, who in my opinion wrote the *Vita Nova* simply in order to evoke his fugitive moments (a meeting in the street, a fleeting conversation with a girl who will always reject him) with Beatrice Portinari. And was *The Divine Comedy* not partly written so he could describe the face of Beatrice haloed in light? If we were to ask the Florentine the question, I am reasonably sure that humanity would have to forego one of its most celebrated literary works.

Let's reverse the position, I thought as I walked home from the embassy, a time I found particularly auspicious to mulling over ridiculous ideas: "I didn't write *Sophie's Choice*, or even the book that Stingo is supposed to be writing (*Lie Down in Darkness* I think), but at least I get to sleep with Sophie every night and that, my friend, is not something you can boast of." As you can see, I had a fascinating inner life.

Yet the fact is that my Sophie was worth the effort. Living with her was not always easy, and I sometimes wondered where she had got her teacher's diploma: she used to tell her pupils that if they had a problem, they should gently massage their earlobes (acupuncture points, she said) and she had some terrifying opinions on the subject of mobile phones and microwaves. She wore me out with her obsession with the environment which meant we had dozens of different bins and deciding which one something went in was like solving a Rubik's cube. She wanted to dance in the forest late into the night and she would say to me in her nasal accent: "Dahling, you are such a baastard!"

She would burst out laughing in the middle of something, she was unpredictable, quick-tempered, stunningly beautiful and, if the same genie had forced me to choose between my book and my love for her, I would have been in a difficult situation.

One day she swanned into the living room, her hair plastered with a concoction of oil, yoghurt and honey which she swore by and handed me the phone. It was my father.

"You're grandfather's in hospital," he said, his voice grave.

"My grandfather?" I hesitated.

"Yes, Marcel. He's in hospital, he's got cancer."

"Cancer?"

"Prostate cancer."

"Is it serious?"

"Of course it's serious," my father sounded irritated. "Cancer is always serious. What's worse, it's very advanced."

"Is he going to be all right?" I said, my heart hammering.

"Difficult to say," my father said coldly. "It would be best if you came to see him."

And he hung up. Sophie looked at me.

"Are you going to go?"

"I'll book a flight for next Saturday."

"We were supposed to be going to a concert," she said.

I shrugged. Two days later, I was on a flight to Paris. I stayed with my father for the weekend. It felt bizarre, all these years later to be coming back to the little apartment he had moved to after his divorce and where I used to come for weekends, having spent the week with my mother and her new husband (I know, I didn't mention it, the psychologists will have to work on it and I'll have to write another book). The apartment hadn't changed, it was simply greyer, more dilapidated, but still remarkably tidy. My father always did the housework himself. He had money, he could have paid someone to come in, he could have afforded to buy a new apartment. But, it's too late for him to change…

"You can have your old room," my father said, going into the room he now used as a study, though it had not changed except for the fact that the sofa had been replaced by a bed.

The furnishings were austere: sofa, desk, bookshelves. I didn't like it, because I didn't like going back to a place I had explored every square inch of as a child and later as a teenager. But in itself, it was a pleasant enough room. There was all you needed to work in peace.

That afternoon, I went to the hospital in Levallois. It was a large, inoffensive cube painted in garish colours. I'd seen worse. The smells of sickness, of bodies in agony were not too pervasive. As I came into the room, my grandfather was in bed. I had hoped he would be sitting up, calmly reading, his big glasses perched on his nose, even wearing a suit. This was how I had seen him my whole life, impeccably well dressed – tiny, badly proportioned, but impeccably dressed, as though about to go to the office.

But he was in bed and not well dressed – he was wearing pyjamas. However, he was not asleep. When I came in, he weakly rolled over onto his side, grabbed his glasses and slipped them on. As I stood in front of him, he smiled.

"Ah! my grandson! Thank you for coming from Germany."

I kissed him. The brush of his lips was imperceptible.

He asked me more questions than I asked him. It was as though I was the one who was ill. He asked me whether I had a photo of Sophie. I opened my wallet. He nodded.

"Excellent. I'm very happy," he said. "If you're happy, I'm happy."

Illness made him more accessible, warmer. Weaker, obviously, but more intimate. It almost seemed as though here in France he sometimes thought about me, something that would never have occurred to me before. We spent a pleasant time together, something we had rarely done in our lives as grandfather and grandson. I stayed for an hour until an aunt that I only ever saw at family reunions came to relieve me. My fears that she would tire him out were lifted when I saw her take out a book, sit next to my grandfather like an old hand and begin to read, while he took off his glasses and lay back with a satisfied smile.

"I'll come back tomorrow," I said as I left.

That evening, my father and I talked about Marcel. I said

that I thought he was in quite good form and that he would probably come through this. My father did not comment. But he told me what they talked about, he visited the old man three times a week.

"Three times a week? Before you hardly saw him three times a year!"

"Maybe. And maybe I regret that. In spite of everything, he is my father," he said, looking at me.

"Yes, he is," I said, "*in spite of everything*. He brought you up, took care of you."

"That's what fatherhood means."

I could tell he was not going to mention David Wagner. It was his right. Besides, I needed to grow up too, accept people's limitations, stop focusing on what was good or bad. But even as I was thinking these sensible thoughts, I felt furious. I desperately wanted to tell him what I knew, all the things he didn't know about his real father. This did not change the fact that Marcel had been his father, he was a different father, that was all. He had two fathers, a biological father and the father who had raised him. And maybe he would want to know what had happened to his father.

I went to bed a little annoyed. I still couldn't bring myself to talk because I had never spoken as a child, I clung to my secrets. Even now, as an adult, I didn't find it easy: faced with my father all the mental blocks I had had as a child closed in on me like steel doors. I wanted to talk but I couldn't, because I sensed my father did not want me to. He had shut away the past.

And I think that these words, the following day, were addressed to him: "Do you know David Wagner?"

I probably should not have asked the question because I

don't think that all truths should be spoken. Moreover, there is a time for everything and this, clearly, was not that time. But there had never been a right time, so let's just say it wasn't the right person.

"What is this, the day of judgement?" my grandfather answered in a cold ironic tone.

In a way, I was grateful for his tone. He was just as I'd always known him: ready for battle. A true Fabre.

"Not at all," I said smiling, "this is not a judgement at all. I just heard him mentioned and wanted to know more about him. And if what I've learnt is true, it might even have been good to know it sooner."

"Why?"

I was taken aback.

"Because it's important."

"So what? What's important is hearing what is good, not hearing what will weaken you. The story of David Wagner weakens us."

"Who, us?"

"Everyone. You, me, your father, the family. The story of David Wagner is a stain on our history, on our unity as a family. Not that I have anything against him, of course," said my grandfather, "but he's not one of us. He's a Wagner, not a Fabre."

These words sounded familiar. They were my own, and those of Charles. In the end, surely my grandfather was right?

"Was it your father who mentioned him?" my grandfather asked mildly.

"No. I found out about him by accident. During a visit to Buchenwald with my students I stumbled on the photograph of a man who looked exactly like my father. I did some research.

I discovered the story of David Wagner. And," I added, hesitating, "I discovered that he was a part of our history."

"School trips should be banned," Marcel muttered, turning his head away as though to go back to sleep.

There was a silence. My grandfather had closed his eyes.

"All families have their secrets," he said at length, his eyes still closed. "Mauriac and Freud built their careers on that fact. It doesn't change the fact that life goes on."

"Goes on for who?"

"David is the dark side of our history. It's a pity, what happened to him… Sad."

His words did not convince me.

"Maybe it could have been avoided," I said.

"How, exactly?" my grandfather shot back. "We were at war. Seventy-five thousand Jews from France died in the camp just like him."

"I don't know. But our family is strong, powerful. It could have intervened."

"The family?"

"Yes, the Fabres. We're a powerful family, in Normandy, in Paris we have influence. We can get things done."

"It's a myth," my grandfather shrugged. "Of course, we've got money, special contacts, influence. But that's not always enough, especially in wartime. And besides, we're not exactly united. A few family reunions don't make a clan. I had power long ago, I used it to help some people. They'd come to me at night, explain their situation. I was surprised at how many there were: brothers, nephews, nieces, friends… I offered advice, I knew people, sometimes I intervened on their behalf. But I don't believe in the power of the Fabre family. My own power, yes," my grandfather cackled, "but only for a few years, and that was long after the war. The rest is just a myth for fools and country cousins."

I hung my head.

"All the same, I'm sorry…"

"No weakness, boy," my grandfather said. "I won't have you talking like that. It doesn't mean anything. What have you got to be sorry for? You don't understand the situation, you weren't there. Do you really think you can understand something that happened half a century ago?"

"No!" I said. "These things didn't happen fifty or sixty years ago. They're happening now. They'll always be happening."

"Maybe," my grandfather nodded, he seemed to understand what I had said (though it hadn't been entirely clear to me). "But there were particular historical circumstances. Besides, we need to forget. The people in that story are dead: David, Virginie, Clémentine. I'm nearly dead myself. I'll only last a few weeks now, and I'm not feeling sorry for myself. So it's best to forget all that… Forgetting is the best thing ever discovered for secrets. It's not cowardice, it's just the voice of life. Listen to me now, because I'm going to tell you a real secret: memory is for the dead and the dying, forgetting is for the living. It's as valid for nations as it is for individuals."

"A few weeks…"

"Let's not talk about that. You can talk to the doctors about it. It's not important. I've had a full life, full of joys and sorrows. I don't want any more. But what I said to you about forgetting, that is important. You're the heir now."

"The heir? To what?"

"The Fabre heir."

"I thought you said the family didn't exist."

"It exists. It exists precisely because it isn't mythic, it isn't all-powerful. It needs an heir. Your father could not be…"

"Because he's a Wagner?" I interrupted him.

"He's a Fabre," my grandfather snapped angrily, "he's my son. But he couldn't be the heir because he is too odd, too much of a misfit. He can't bring people together."

"What about my uncles… They're normal. Captains of industry, they have money, families…"

"As you said, they're normal."

"And what about the younger generation… My cousins?"

"You know perfectly well. They're too young, and they'll always be too young. They have no soul. They'll make money, but that's all they'll make. They'll enjoy showing off. I'm fond of them, they're like young dogs, but how can you entrust a family to people who have never read Flaubert?" my grand-father smiled.

"That's the way the world turns nowadays. Soon no CEO will have read Flaubert."

"That's precisely why the world is going to hell. And I'm only half-joking."

"Honestly, Grandfather, though I feel honoured, I don't think I'm best placed to personify the family. I live abroad…"

"From now on, some part of the family will always be living abroad. There are no powerful families these days that don't have international divisions."

"But I'm no organiser, I've got no practical skills, I'm not a manager. The family needs men like you, Grandfather. All I know how to do is read and write."

"That's not true. You've never understood your greatest quality."

"What's that?"

"People love you. They follow you. So you will be the heir.

And take my word for it," my grandfather joked, "you have every reason to feel honoured. Even if the president suddenly appointed you ambassador to Berlin, you couldn't be more honoured."

On the flight back, I thought a lot about this conversation. My grandfather's weakness had unexpectedly made it possible for us to be truly close. And I won't disguise the fact that this inheritance, if only moral, made me happy. I had always thought my grandfather barely knew my name, but he had been watching me, weighing me up, and he thought me the best of us: he was entrusting the family to me – even though in practice I didn't see what that might mean. The heir... It was vague, since it had nothing to do with material things. At the same time, great families, through some intangible means, always recognise the heir.

But in spite of the sympathy I felt, I was beginning to have doubts. I also felt that my grandfather was making me his heir in order to keep me quiet. In exchange for forgetting. Grandfather's sudden warmth, he who had never been demonstrative, his pathetic mention of the few weeks he had to live, his flattery about my popularity, his insistence on forgetting, it was all slightly over the top. I'm not saying my explanation was right, but whatever the case the doubts persisted. An heir would never tear a family apart since his role was to protect it, to bind it together.

What did I have to keep quiet about? The explanation was simple and I had known it from the moment I learned the exact date David Wagner had been sent to Buchenwald. August 1941. It was very early. Before the *Nacht und Nebel* directive against the enemies of Germany. Before the massive deportations of French Jews since the first major raids

(*Opération Vent printanier* on 16–17 July 1942) took place a year later. This meant that David being sent to Buchenwald had been the work of an individual. Someone had probably turned him in. From there to inferring that my grandfather had got rid of a rival and an embarrassing future brother-in-law was a small step and one that I took without a second thought.

Some years earlier, during the Papon trial, Marcel had become incensed at a family reunion. It was the sort of subject we usually avoided because of my father's position in the Vichy administration, but on that particular day, the conversation had shifted onto dangerous ground, no one knew how, perhaps it was the doing of grandfather himself. Marcel claimed, with a sincerity that was not feigned, and which I felt had nothing to do with his own actions (Papon had been *préfet* when he had been *sous-préfet*), that it was impossible to judge history after fifty years, that even the most well-intentioned judges were incapable of untangling the precise roles of the protagonists at a time when "attitudes were not the same". I remember that phrase: "attitudes were not the same", which had seemed shaky, awkward. He went on to say that it was all very "complicated" and not something a thirty-year-old shyster was likely to understand (he was lashing out at Arno Klarsfeld, though he had only a minor role in the proceedings). "In any case," he repeated, "I'm unassailable." Could he still say such a thing? Maybe he hadn't had Jews deported during the war, but he had certainly sent one man to his death simply because of romantic rivalry. Or at least I feared he had. And even if Marcel had served up the same arguments about forgetting, about the impossibility of understanding, I was in a position to judge. Hadn't he answered my initial question with a question of his own: "What is this, judgement day?"

When I went back to Berlin, a found a poster on the ground floor of our building which read in large handwritten letters: "*ZU VERKAUFEN. Nehmen Sie was sie wollen und geben Sie soviel Geld wie sie wollen*". Small pieces of furniture, knick-knacks and dog-eared books were lying on the pavement. I had no trouble recognising the handwriting. Sophie had found something to keep her busy while I was away, gathering up all these things for sale and leaving this message: "Take whatever you want and leave whatever money you like." A suspicious Parisian, I shook my head and stared at the sign but when I opened the letterbox, coins rolled out over the floor. I went upstairs, Sophie heard me and rushed to meet me.

The following week, I didn't have time to fly back to Paris although I had resolved to go every weekend. Just because people are guilty doesn't mean we don't love them. And my grandfather was not *necessarily* guilty. The blame lay squarely with a writer I had invited to come to Berlin as part of my work at the embassy. He wasn't particularly good or particularly famous – in fact he owed his qualified success to sound marketing sense, churning out formulaic books with formulaic titles, and a talent for PR – but I had to take what I could get: not all writers were prepared to come to Berlin, especially at that time of year, just for a few days to promote a book. My writer, on the other hand, had the advantage of being available, speaking German and being quite young and entertaining, which is always useful when presenting an author. I couldn't see myself dragging some morose, unfriendly writer to a round of receptions. Besides, the ambassador loved to chat – so he needed chatty writers.

Unfortunately, though my writer was chatty, he was also unbearable. Pretentious, bitchy, he constantly looked as though he was slightly bored. I wanted to say to him what Sophie had said: "*Dahling*, you are such a *bastard!*"

But I did my job, organised his weekend which meant both promoting and entertaining him on a very tight budget. The idiot was constantly demanding I find him women: "Come on, there must be something fun to do here. Why don't you introduce me to some hot Grätchens?"

Since he annoyed me, I phoned a friend of Sophie who was very pretty and very cold. The guy spent all night trying to impress her, spoke his best German, played the smooth talker. He walked her home and she closed the door on him, telling him in perfect French, as she laughingly told us the following day: "Sorry, you're too ugly. And I thought French writers were more interesting!"

So it was not until the following week that I went back to Paris.

"I am unassailable."

7

"You don't really know, you don't really understand and as I said to you two weeks ago, you have to forget, so that's why I'm going to tell you what happened. This is not a confession, and it's not the deathbed ramblings of an old man atoning for his sins, because I have not been a believer for years now and because I've always hated clichés. It's just that you're young, you believe in black and white, you've seen too many movies. When I'm done, you have to leave without asking questions because I've had all this prepared in my head for the last two weeks, since our conversation when I realised you weren't convinced, that you needed something else, that you weren't prepared to forget. But I'm not asking you to not know, I am asking you to know but to set that knowledge aside, which isn't the same thing. It's important to know, I agree with you about that, truth is essential, but it must be forgotten, that is something else I know, something I am convinced of. So, listen to what I've got to say and go. I'm not saying you shouldn't come back, that's the last thing I want, all the more so since you are the heir, I want you to go and think and then decide to forget. I suppose all this has taken you aback a bit, you've just flown in from Berlin, your father told me you wanted to come last week but you had to hang around and look after some idiot; don't worry, I understand, I've dealt with my share in my career. As for the rest, don't visit every week, it's too far to come; what's important for me is forgetting, it is the right place for the past, somewhere between the conscious and the unconscious. Anyway, all this to say that I'm going to tell you what happened during that period, I'm not going to hide anything. I'll try to put the events in order – it's not as though any of it will really come as a surprise. But when you're ill, everything is more complicated, bringing facts together turns out to be more difficult than you thought, that's why it's taken me so long to remember this story. I had to get things clear in my head, organise things chronologically, things that for me were scattered images of Virginie, snapshots of memory. These were things I never wanted to forget, I never wanted to forget these frozen moments of my wife. I've thought of them a lot over the years, because it wasn't the way you think, beauty and the beast, and certainly not beauty, the beast and Wagner the Prince Charming. Not at all. As always, it's more complicated, it's a whole, you have to understand, so listen and try to understand.

"Taking things chronologically, I suppose I should start with David Wagner, since I knew him long before I knew Virginie. The problem is that, though I've thought long and hard about it, tried to remember, I can't remember how we met. I think he came to our house for a fitting with my mother, she was a customer at his shop. But even that seems a bit strange since he was too young to own a shop, it must have belonged to his mother, yes, I think that's right, David's mother, a tall woman, I have a vague memory of her, she was quite impressive, vague but impressive. You have to understand, we were never formally introduced to the Wagner parents – was there a father? I don't seem to remember hearing of one – because my own father couldn't abide them. He refused to have anything to do with them and was the main obstacle to David and Clémentine getting married. I'm getting ahead of myself. All this to say that I don't remember the day when David Wagner first came to our house. I'm sure my sister Clémentine remembered since from one day to the next she fell head over heels in love with him, but me... Whatever the case, David Wagner insinuated himself into our lives. At first I didn't really notice, then suddenly he was *Maman*'s boy, the messenger. He used to give her advice too, because he had taste. I remember that, he would feel a fabric like a woman, I thought there was something feminine about him and I wonder whether ladies' men – and as you can understand I was never one of those men, women have not found me attractive – aren't all slightly feminine to be able to understand women so well. Anyway, it doesn't go beyond that; that's all I remember about him until Clémentine told us that she was in love with him, was planning to marry him, which was perfectly possible, I didn't give a damn, she could easily have made a much better match but if she really did love him, well, too bad for her – don't take this the wrong way, but it wasn't a good marriage; Wagner was just a shop boy and we were the Fabres, without fighting the class war all over again, it was far from ideal. Well, anyway, Clémentine was never very pretty and she didn't have much charm, it was good to have someone who took an interest in her. But from there to marrying... But, as I said, it was her business. I didn't care. My father, on the other hand, didn't take things quite so calmly, he would fly into a rage whenever she mentioned the wedding and I wonder how it was that David Wagner ended up coming to dinner at our house so often. I suspect Clémentine must have been blackmailing our parents in some way, I have to confess I've forgotten, it's all so long ago.

"One way or another, I didn't see much of him. I'd just been appointed to the *préfecture* in Rouen, I was doing my time if you like, I was secretary general at the *préfecture*, I had a position, my parents were proud of me. There was no shortage of work but I found it interesting, I had responsibility and besides, back then a *préfecture* was a different thing, we really were the all-powerful representatives of the State. Completely different to the way things are nowadays. I met Virginie during a case of compulsory purchase. She was the daughter of a major farmer in the area who owned a large stretch of land through which we were planning to build a road. We were in negotiations with him and he invited us to lunch, two attachés and me. There were five of us at lunch, including his wife, mixing business with pleasure. The guy, père Romand, people called him, was a real *loustic*, yes, a *loustic*, a fat jolly chap, big red cheeks, very crafty like a lot of farmers in Normandy, it's not just a stereotype, believe me, he knew how to negotiate. His wife didn't say much, she was clearly under his thumb. She was an unprepossessing woman. I never really understood how she could have produced Virginie. The girl was much too pretty to be their daughter, she was in a different class… I mean, the Romands weren't stupid, they were cunning… whereas Virginie… When she came into the room, not for anything in particular, just to say hello, out of curiosity maybe because she always loved meeting people, she was like you, she liked people, well at first at least, things were different later… But when she walked into that room, I swear, I knew straight away. That it was her, I mean. It was love at first sight, just like in books and in films and in life. She was the love of my life. She was dressed casually and wore no make-up, you have to understand she was just a girl, and I wasn't much older than she was but I thought she was the most beautiful thing I'd ever seen – I don't know how to explain, I just knew that *this was it*, this was everything I wanted in life. She probably looked at me as if I was an undertaker, sitting there in a black suit and a white shirt – there wasn't much choice back then – she held out her hand and said formally "*Bonjour, monsieur*" and I did what every star-struck lover does, I held her hand a little too long. By the time we left, I knew I wanted to marry this woman. So I came back a number of times on a number of pretexts. I talked to Virginie, she was shy, always greeted me with that "*Bonjour, monsieur*" and she spoke warily as though she were talking to a teacher. Père Romand watched me ironically, he knew perfectly well why I kept coming round but it suited him because I had a great future ahead of me and besides, he liked me well enough, as he told me later he knew a fox when he saw one; he knew I was cunning just like him. More than that, I was a Fabre, our family was from Normandy, our name meant something there, it's not like it is now; back then people knew their member of parliament and a *préfet* was really someone. They were different times, things weren't all bad.

"One morning I went in and Virginie was pouring milk into a huge copper cauldron. It was white, thick, foamy... She was in short sleeves, she was flushed from the heat of the kitchen and the effort, sweat was beading on her lip. I sat down, stunned, and I just stared at her. She looked at me and a solid impenetrable silence descended. A tension. I got to my feet, went over to her, I felt her relax, let herself go, surrender. I kissed her. I'm telling you this and it probably sounds naive, but it was the best day of my life because I'd waited so long, so intensely and then everything between us resolved itself in a moment of passion, there in the heat of the kitchen. After that, the rest was a formality. I did things in the traditional way, the way people did back then, I asked Virginie's father for her hand and obviously he didn't refuse me. In July, in the midst of the summer heat and the summer balls, we had a grand wedding. *The* grand wedding. Three hundred guests at the reception at Romand's place with farmers in their Sunday best and Parisians who were slightly snooty but slightly envious too because the Romands' place was really something, a magnificent old building; it's still there in fact though it was sold on, I myself visited the place a couple of years ago, I didn't give my name, just went to look at it from a distance, choked up with memories.

"And then there was David. I knew at once. As I've said, I hadn't really paid much attention to him before. Oh, I knew he was Clémentine's fiancé, I knew he was ambitious, but those were just fleeting impressions, deep down I didn't feel it had anything to do with me. If I can't remember the first time I met him, I'll never forget the first time Virginie met him. I saw him through her eyes at that dinner my parents invited him to in Paris – Clémentine had insisted, she had been badly put out that he hadn't been invited to our wedding. Given that we had invited everyone else, she was the only one without an escort. And she would have been so happy, so proud to share that moment with him, that whisper of nostalgia and anticipation that hovers over all weddings. He arrived late, I don't know why, actually he was always late, he couldn't help it. We were all waiting, we were hungry, I remember all this as clearly as I remember my wedding, I've probably thought about it just as often since you might say this was the end of my marriage or, to be more accurate, the beginning of another union, different from what I had hoped for, though make no mistake, it was not the end of our love for each other. But it has to be said, David walked into that dinner, into my life. Virginie had asked Clémentine: 'What's he like, this David of yours?'

"My sister's answer was nonsense, she said she'd recognise him the moment she saw him, that he was the handsomest man in the world, that he was like a movie star. And Virginie laughed and walked over to the window and said she'd keep a lookout for him and it was at that moment that David came into the apartment. I knew immediately that something was wrong, that there was something wrong about the way he looked at her and worse, in the way she looked at him. He stood there stock still, Virginie could barely move either and I sat there watching; I think Clémentine was watching too. For a moment everything was frozen. Then Virginie looked away and everything began to move again. And I saw David through Virginie's eyes, through the eyes of a woman. He was a handsome man, he exuded a sort of brooding masculinity a little like your father's but without that inner absence your father has – something he didn't always have – in fact, I found it difficult to deal with your father when he was young, he reminded me so much of David. It didn't stop me loving him, though, maybe quite the opposite, but it was heartrending sometimes to look at him. David, on the other hand, had presence, he was *there* if you see what I mean. He wasn't distracted, wasn't a dreamer, he lived in the moment, revelled in the moment. He was a sensualist, to tell the truth, a man who loved pleasure: women, food, luxury. Especially women. Unfortunately for me, that was his gift.

"That dinner! Oh God, I was pitiful. I'd seen him, you understand, I knew how a woman could fall for him, especially a young woman like mine who was married to a dwarf. I'm not about to put myself down, especially having said so much about David, but I wasn't handsome, I wasn't as ugly as I am now that I'm bald and wrinkled – though even then my hair was receding – and I was short, with no grace, no good looks, I was wearing thick glasses and my dark tax inspector's suit. That's how I was, there was nothing I could do about it and it didn't bother me really, I had other qualities, after all, I was intelligent, pugnacious, determined and my looks hadn't stopped me marrying the love of my life. But compared to David… Let's just say, I didn't compare favourably. And he was a smooth talker, he joked and told stories and I couldn't keep up, I was pathetic, it wasn't my field of expertise… I was serious, a little boring probably, I was a *préfet*. He was a master of his craft, it was easy to see why women would fall for him… He showed up, he was handsome, told a few jokes and that was enough. It was so easy for him it was painful. If you'd asked me to discuss politics, economics, even literature, then maybe things would have been different… But his stories about dancers and his ability to make anything sound funny, his allusions, his irony… No, I couldn't keep up. So I clung to Virginie, I held her hand, squeezed her arm, it was pitiful, I know it was pitiful. And she laughed, he could really make her laugh… I could see a twinkle in her eye. It was a nightmare, it felt as though I was sitting an exam which was going wrong.

"And yet, nothing had happened. I'd had a bad impression, but that's all it was, an impression… Life doesn't change because of an impression. The dinner finally came to an end, David left, we'd probably never see him again, after all, my parents did not invite him often and by now I was on my father's side, we didn't want anything to do with the Jew –

I must have thought those words, though I also found anti-Semitism ridiculous, a bit like a pagan notion, a superstition, but people can be hateful when they're jealous. My father really was anti-Semitic. That's obviously not the only reason he didn't want David in the family, but it wasn't a trivial point; to overcome that flaw, he would have had to be perfect in every other respect. And no one thought he was perfect – certainly not me, by this stage. No, David Wagner was to be avoided, rebuffed, driven away, him and his dark hair and his wiry body and his jokes.

"Unfortunately, Virginie didn't see things that way. Avoided, rebuffed, driven away? No. Touched, circled, seduced. I urged her to come back to Rouen with me but she laughed and said she wanted to stay in Paris, surely I didn't want her to be an ignorant hick all her life, besides I had a lot of work and she would only be bored... Just a couple of weeks, then she'd join me in Rouen... A chance to see the sights of Paris, like a tourist. The weather was so beautiful... What could I say? After all, Paris is a big city and there had been no mention of David. And besides, Clémentine was there. I thought I'd sensed her anxiety over dinner, she wouldn't want David and Virginie meeting again.

"At the time, I didn't know it was going on. Oh, like any jealous man I spied, I watched, I tried to decode every sign. They met a couple of times, the fine weather was against me, the sun was my enemy. They went boating in the Bois de Boulogne, a boating trip I didn't go on but which, sixty years later, still haunts me like a terrible nightmare. I heard about it, about David's rowing, and I could picture him, his bare muscular arms, whereas if I'd tried to row with my thin spindly arms... I've never rowed, never took a boat with Virginie after that because I could not bear the idea of her remembering that day. I know she would have thought about it, not to compare us, but simply because those hours would have remained in her memory.

"Yes, at the time, I really didn't know anything. In spite of my jealousy. I hated the sunshine, the summer, all those things that favoured pleasure but at the same time I felt reassured because it wasn't as though they consorted much with each other – consorted, now there's an old word, one we used to use as teenagers in the last century, it's a ridiculous expression, but it's not important, though I know that you care about words; but the main thing for me was that Clémentine was there to watch over them and I came back to Paris as often as I could to prevent anything happening. Prevention rather than cure. And my fears seemed to me to be ridiculous. Virginie never so much as mentioned David, never suggested we have dinner with him. She was the same as she'd always been. The truth was, she was playing her cards close to her chest, women have a talent for such things, it's a common misogynistic cliché. Eventually, they slept together, it was inevitable, even I have to admit they were made for each other, they were so beautiful. Since then, I've grown accustomed to the idea. That they were beautiful. Beautiful people often go together, they match. Beautiful people are a race apart, they're always on the outside. They don't really like to mingle.

"When did I find out? When did I know for certain that they were *together*, that he was taking my wife from me, that he was taking her, she on top of him, he on top of her in that embrace I could not bring myself to imagine, it was so painful? When did I know for sure? Not while David was alive – you see, I'm so used to him, like an old enemy become a friend by dint of the passing years I call him David. I suspected, that terrible suspicion that heightens everything, makes everything more intense, distorts every detail so it becomes significant. I spent months, my heart breaking in a treacherous web of jealousy I hope you never know – I'm sorry, I'm being stupid, of course you know what it's like, every man goes through it at some point and you've always been a ladies' man, something that goes hand in hand with jealousy and rivalry, you can't win them all... In that, Grandson, you're like David Wagner, you love to be loved, don't deny it, I can see you shaking your head. And yet, during all this time, I loved Virginie all the more. I know, it's pathetic, it's sordidly human, jealousy binds us... Why did she want to go to Paris that weekend, why was she wearing that yellow dress? Suspicions founded and unfounded, everything took on a significance, everything was poisoned by jealousy. And then one morning in Paris, I had a suspicion that was more lucid than the others: Virginie still half-naked putting her make-up on in front of the mirror with unusual care, putting on lipstick and rouge when she was supposed to be having lunch with a girl friend. Do women really dress up to have lunch with a friend? Do they really feel the need to be beautiful standing barefoot in front of a mirror at 9 a.m.? Do they make themselves beautiful for a friend?

"Virginie never made herself beautiful for me. Never. I'm not saying she didn't love me, I don't think that at all, I'm simply saying that she never tried to make herself beautiful for me. That's all. Maybe because I wasn't handsome, maybe because she knew that I was already hers for ever, maybe because our relationship wasn't physical. She loved for other reasons – security, trust, many important things. I'm Charles Bovary, not the handsome callow Rodolphe – I don't know, perhaps literary comparisons are really helpful, I mean I was a *préfet*, nothing like Charles Bovary, an unsuccessful doctor in some godforsaken village, I don't even know why I mentioned it. It's strange, someone like me comparing myself to a pathetic character like that. Anyway, it doesn't alleviate the shock I felt that morning seeing her make herself beautiful, but it's true I didn't know for sure while David was alive. Fortunately for my soul, for my damnation as the priest used to say when I was a boy, because otherwise I would have been sorely tempted. Very sorely. One little Jew less. I don't know if I would have done it, but I would have been tempted... of course I would, a man I hated, a rival. But maybe not, because I wonder if I could really have hated him that much, because I never really hated him. I didn't like him, he hurt me, I was jealous of him, but I never hated him. Maybe because he died, maybe because like all rivals we share a certain complicity, even in hatred, the complicity of love for the same woman. You can hate the man, but she chose him too. And not by accident, not because he happened to be passing. But because he was your opposite or your younger brother or the image of you or a dream of... I suppose David was my opposite: the risk, the fusion of bodies, the brutal desire... I'll put it as simply as I can. Desire... It's true, he was handsome, he wasn't like me, pasty and... I'm sorry, I'm repeating myself, it's tough not to be handsome when your rival is. But I only had suspicions, agonising suspicions sometimes, but I never knew for certain. And in any case, he left, after war was declared, he enlisted and left for the Ardennes. There was nothing to do there, his mother was well connected, she knew people, he might even have been a second lieutenant, something like that, in a barracks in the Ardennes – you look surprised, of course he went to fight –

well, I don't know about fighting, he'd never fired a gun in his life. He was the right age and he was strong. It builds you up, constantly chasing women. A few days after war was declared… I was alone when it was declared, I was in Rouen, all the bells started ringing, but even beforehand I knew it was only a matter of hours, I wasn't surprised, I'd wanted to warn Virginie but she was in Paris and I couldn't reach her, maybe she was with *him*. Why were we never together when momentous events were taking place? War is being declared, my wife isn't there and History is about to crush us, take my word for it, History has the power, it's a pitiless millstone, I know what I'm talking about, I've lived through two world wars, the wars of decolonisation, I'm a man prone to panic and madness and I needed my wife because she was my life, my smile. I know those words probably sound ridiculous, I can't help having loved her, or loving her still years later in this hospital room where I'm going to end my days, with no regrets – well, with a thousand regrets, but not of dying, I've had my time.

"When did I know? When did the image of David fill every absence, every week in Paris, every weekend leave, my wife's every smile, every mood? When did I finally make sense of things? Of the separations, the train journeys? When did my mind picture – as every cuckold's does – the rumpled sheets, the bodies entwined?

"Do you believe we can commune with the spirits? No, of course not, neither do I. No one believes it, especially not a *préfet*. And yet when I came home on 21 March 1942, Virginie came to me in tears, utterly devastated. There in the hall, she knelt in front of me, clinging to my knees and she begged me: 'Help him!'

"And I immediately knew it was about David Wagner.

Obviously, I knew he was in the camp, Clémentine had been crying for six months, she'd asked me to do something, but what could I do? What power did I have over the Germans? I might have had some slight, superficial power in France, but in Germany... and in a concentration camp at that, in that acme of evil and Nazism that was a concentration camp... it was impossible, it was madness even to think about it, but my sister was angry with me, she blamed me. But what could I do? Nothing. Absolutely nothing. Power, let me tell you about power; we'd all like just a little more power, we'd like to have absolute power, when you're a man like me, not so that we could abuse it but to be recognised once and for all as having been divinely chosen. To act according to our desires, including our desire to save people. Had it been in my power, I think I would have done it. I was jealous, I didn't like him, maybe I was secretly happy.

"Yes, I have to admit I was secretly happy to be rid of him, but when I saw my sister weep and beg me, I would have done it. I am not a bad man, no matter what you think – and I don't really know what you think of me. I would have done it.

"When Virginie broke down in front of me, when I realised, realised everything seeing her kneeling, distraught, when all my suspicions were confirmed, I acted. I swear this, Grandson, I acted. I knew it would do no good but if only to prove my magnanimity, to prove to my wife that I was capable of saving her lover, I pulled every string I could, I went all the way up to the head of state where I was told there was nothing to be done. That's how I found out he was dead. He had died on the first day of spring. The day Virginie broke down and came to me. Communication with the spirits? Strange. She grovelled before me that day, she may even have done so at the very moment David died. I was told he'd been ill, that he'd been sent to the infirmary and never came out. Conditions there were terrible, everyone knows that now, though at the time it wasn't clear. I was told he had died in spite of the efforts of doctors and nurses. Ridiculous. A blatant lie. People were dying like flies. You know what happened, don't you? You don't look surprised.

"Anyway, whatever had happened, it was over now, he was dead. Gone. Deceased. All those polite euphemisms when in fact the truth must have been grim and sordid. And that's when I found out everything, every little detail. I wanted to know. Virginie cried herself out. I had never seen anyone so distraught. She loved him, you know, it was as simple as that. Her face was distorted from crying, her body shrivelled, broken like a broken spring under the rumpled bedsheets. And there was nothing I could do to console her, oh yes, I tried to console her, I tried to find the words to tell her her lover was dead. As if I had the words... a victory cry, maybe... No, that's not true, the truth is that, in spite of the fact that my world was falling apart, even I felt sorry for David. He was almost an abstraction. Alive, I had been haunted by him, dead, I pitied him... That squalid death, probably after months of suffering, okay, we didn't really know what went on in places like that, but we knew it was no picnic even if the truth is unimaginable, only a lunatic could imagine the reality of a camp. So I said to the crumpled woman in my arms: 'Tell me...'

"That's when I found out. Everything. When and how. She told me everything, simply, like a child telling the truth after a lie that has gone on too long, relieved to be able to confess. She wasn't crying any more, she was in her nightdress, her body had thickened, her face red and lined and still damp from the tears which she brushed away with the back of her hand, desperate not to interrupt her story. Their meeting at the dinner when everything had begun the moment that David had stepped into the apartment. That unconscious yet inexorable feeling that the die was cast. The vacillations. And then the moment when the decision was made, when everything became real, which came quite quickly, after only a few meetings even if they took place over several months, but I suppose that's what passion is. When she went to his mother's shop and they went upstairs. Untangling the skein of lies, working out the chronology as my wife, like a ghost, her eyes vacant, her tone expressionless, told me what had happened. She had to relive everything, it was all inside her and yet there were encounters that slipped out of her, the words like pearls, agonising for me, remembered pleasure for her not perhaps for the last time, but it was best to know everything both to satisfy my curiosity – even those who have been cheated on need to know the truth – and to wipe the slate clean. Once and for all. Say everything and then never talk about it again. So I could be free of my doubts and my suspicions. So that it would no longer come between us. I don't mean David, he would always be between us, but the doubts, the suspicions. Otherwise it was bound to come back to haunt us. She told me everything while I sat there trembling like a leaf... And she told me about the baby, too. I forgot to mention that... Strange that I didn't mention it earlier... Virginie was pregnant. I know, a detail... Let the shrinks make what they like of it. We had wanted a child for a long time, I was overjoyed when she told me. Overjoyed. I'd been afraid it would never happen, I thought maybe it was me, that I wasn't able – it brought to the surface all my awkwardness about my body, all my insecurities about being short, being skinny – a scrawny runt who couldn't produce a child. All that had suddenly vanished, our love had produced a child. Virginie's body had been transformed, she was bloated, she no longer went to Paris, she stayed in Rouen with me. And with good reason. Because there was no more Paris now , there was no more David, there were no encounters – he was in Buchenwald.

"'I don't know.' That's exactly what she said. That she didn't know. Because she had been sleeping with both of us. I asked her whether she had a gut feeling, it was ridiculous, like talking about a jury having a gut feeling, but that's what I asked her. She didn't. David was gone, it was over and I could hardly feel sorry about it. Can you understand that? I didn't feel sorry about it, I could feel sorry for David but without him around, everything was simpler. There was nothing to be done now – in reality, there was never anything to be done, fate rolled the dice, History is like fate – I can see you shaking your head, but you're young, you'll see, there comes a moment when the knot has to be untied one way or another, just like in a tragedy, the exposition, the knot, the resolution, and still the inexorable, the inevitable continues to loom until the final death. But with this baby, even David gone, he was still there. There was a baby whose father was uncertain, who might be my son or daughter – we didn't know – or someone else's son or daughter. His son or daughter.

"But I would have welcomed that baby with open arms. You need to understand that, I am not a bad man, there may have been times in my life when I was harsh because sometimes you have to be, I'm no choirboy, but I'm not a bad man. I was prepared to welcome that baby with open arms even if it was David's. I would have been devastated but happy. I would

flu – we all thought it was strange, sad, of course, but strange too. Dying of flu is so banal. After the years of people dying in the war, on the front, in the camps… he died of flu, looking like a dried-up prune. Was this really how a doctor, the head doctor at Pitié-Salpêtrière should die? Of flu. Strange how some deaths can be so banal. I'm dying of cancer, that's slightly more dignified. Actually, I'm dying of old age, I've had my time, that's all there is to it. But at least it's not flu. I mean why not a cold? One sneeze and I drop down dead. I suppose you'll say I had become the heir – in practice I already was. Don't laugh, it's important, being the heir, it's the highest responsibility… We are a family, there has to be a man to hold families together, otherwise they fall apart, everyone goes their own way.

"Why did they all still love him? Virginie, Clémentine. Why did they go on loving him? Clémentine grew old alone, she never wanted to marry after that. It's true men weren't exactly queuing up, but all the same, if she'd wanted to marry… She was intelligent and she was rich… We weren't poor, especially back then! Things were going well. Things have gone a bit sour since then, you'll have to do something about that, the family's too traditional – investing in land and property – you need to shake things up. Back then, things were different. Clémentine was a good catch but no one wanted her. She still worshipped the man who had been sent to the camps. Why are some men so loved? I swear to you, there was nothing extraordinary about him, not physically or intellectually. As I said, he was good looking, he wasn't stupid, but he was nothing exceptional. He was not handsome the way Virginie was beautiful. He was quick-witted, but not deep, not original – it was all jokes and innuendo. And yet he could have any woman he wanted. He would see them and carry them off. Like an ogre from some legend. You'll have to explain it to me. What do men like him have that other men don't? I was respected, maybe even admired sometimes, my efficiency was noted – but loved? No, I wasn't loved. Oh, I'm not going to play the ugly duckling… well, maybe a little, because there's one point I want to clear up, because to me it's the most important point. The issue, the only issue that matters was whether Virginie loved me. That she had loved David went without saying. But me? The duckling, the *préfet*, did she love me? And I can tell you now that she did love me. Not like she loved David, not that union of bodies, that passion. She loved me the way one loves a husband, more soberly, more patiently. Or maybe the way one loves a father or an older brother. Obviously that doesn't sound as good, I know that. But is it really nothing to have someone you can count on, a man who is always there, watching over you? Is it nothing to live with the same man for years, sharing his joys and his pains. Because that's how it was, we shared things, we didn't cut ourselves off, it wasn't that, the old fogey and the young captive. She wasn't even that much younger than I was, though I'm sure people thought she was… But it was the suit, the job, it aged me. I can assure you, she wouldn't have been able to live without me. David had been her passion, her soul, that most secret part of a human being. He was her secret. I'm not sure that her secret wouldn't have melted if exposed to the sunlight. Could she have lived with David? I'm not sure. Could they have stayed together all that time, for all time? I was time, I was what was *real*, he was an illusion. You have to understand. It wasn't David and Virginie the way you might say Romeo and Juliet, Tristan and Isolde, all those love stories. Instead it was the more humdrum couple Marcel and Virginie who muddled along. No passion but they had position, togetherness, love. When I say they had no passion, I did feel a vast undying passion for her, I was constantly pulling my beloved back from the brink, constantly looking after the *département* I was running, and later the region, all the while cultivating my own passion, my wife, her beautiful face ravaged with frailty, her insomnia and her dreams. My wife, Virginie Fabre.

"That's what you need to know, you can't give in to images, to self-delusion. I'm not dismissing David out of hand. He was there, he mattered, they had a child together. Whether that was a good thing or a bad thing doesn't matter. David Wagner existed. But all through those years, the long struggle that is life, in this case Virginie's life, I was there, me, Marcel Fabre, her husband, no more unworthy than the next man, even if I was an ugly duckling. It was hard, because she got sick, but I was there. Would David have stayed with her? A lover isn't cut out for sickness, for soiled sheets and fevers. A husband is. Or at least I was.

"It is strange, all this, when you think about it… He's dead, she's dead… They were the picture of health, they were strong and beautiful. He waited in the Ardennes; the German tanks crashed through the mountains, but then nothing, his unit retreated. He said himself that he never felt a moment of fear, it all happened so quickly… the defeat happened so quickly, it was as though someone had waved a magic wand… a magic that cost hundreds of lives, hundreds of tanks, but he came through it without a scratch, came back to Paris, came back to Virginie, the strong and the beautiful, but me, the ugly duckling, short, fat, with thick glasses, I survived; even now I survive because I'm more than a match for life. Life has never touched me. I moved through it like a tank, crashing through the Ardennes of life. I wasn't handsome, I wasn't strong, but I took everything it dished out and I survived. Life pounded me but I got up again – I say I got up again, but I was never really down, I may have stumbled, I may have reeled but I never went down; even now, I'm dying on my feet, take my word for it, I have no fear, no fear and no regrets… But were they strong enough to face up to life? Was David a match for life in the camp? Is such a thing even possible in a concentration camp? And Virginie, didn't she crumble? Wasn't that what her illness was, the chaos of her life. Are not the beautiful and the strong weak in the face of life? She stumbled, she staggered, she fell and she never got up again. She wasn't that strong. She fell.

"There you go, now you know everything, well, not everything, that would be impossible, you weren't there, and even when you are those things are never straightforward. But at least you know the essential, you have the missing piece, the only one that I can give you, the others can't tell you anything any more. It's been good, talking to you like this, all these things have been going round and round in my head for the past two weeks. I can tell you that this speech was more important to me than when I spoke to the president. Not particularly well structured, I admit, but you'll have to make allowances, weakness, illness and lucidity don't make an ideal partnership; the most important thing is to forget, to know everything so you can forget because life is in forgetting, life is forgetting things, not brooding over them. David, Virginie, they're like that, they're the past, we're not to blame, it's fate.

"I'd like you to go now because I'm very tired, but it's been a pleasure, honestly, it's truly been a pleasure to talk to my grandson. You needed to know these things. Obviously, you've heard other rumours, but who is there who can talk to you? Who can really tell you anything? To be able to say something, you have to have lived it. I lived it, I'm the only one who sees Virginie's smile in my dreams, in my memories as she comes towards me, then moves away, counting every step. Give me a kiss, take care of yourself and give the beautiful Sophie a kiss. It's a pretty name, that. A name for every nation. In the end, women are all that is best in the world. Its greatest pleasure and its greatest sorrow. Give your father my love. He's my son."

8

At twenty, Antonin Artaud had the face of a ragged angel, mellowed by the soft grain of the photographs of the period until his face exploded, his teeth all lost, a face caved and cracked beneath the shock of tattered hair.

It was this dual image I thought about as I left the hospital, stumbling, reeling slightly, but not falling.

Sometimes I wonder whether my literary references aren't simply a mask for my emotions, channelling, focusing, diverting my gaze towards the paper beings that are writers and their characters.

Who was the face of Artaud? David as he lay down in the infirmary to wait for death? Absolutely not. He was still a handsome man. Not as handsome as he had been, probably thinner, more emaciated, but in the photograph his face is still handsome. Marcel as he lay down in the hospital to wait for death? Absolutely not. He's still an ugly man. Illness has barely changed him because short ugly men don't change much. My grandfather had always been ugly, in his youth as in old age. Me? Absolutely not. I haven't yet got to the point of imagining my own ruin and I certainly hope to avoid the terrifying fate of Artaud. Even if perhaps I am projecting slightly in my fear when faced with the image of Artaud ruined and mad.

Virginie, then? Because I knew what her illness was. What my grandfather refused to name and what was simply her madness. I had had to dig. I am not here simply to dig a bland grave for David Wagner. When Charles, my great-uncle Wagner, his hands trembling, had talked about Virginie, whom he met at the end of the war and who had summoned him every year – to talk about David, obviously, but also to see a brother in his brother's face, before she disappeared and died, I wanted to know what had happened. And Charles was a doctor. He told me.

"She was schizophrenic – in the clinical sense of the term, which is meaningless really because most specialists in the disease reject this catch-all term since there are a thousand different degrees of schizophrenia, from someone barely affected who might be slightly eccentric but go through life without ever being diagnosed to the psychotic interned in an asylum in a straitjacket."

He talked to me about the illness for a long time in that neutral, medical tone doctors use.

"Schizophrenia depends on both genetic and environmental factors. Constant stress and the use of certain substances, cannabis in particular, can trigger the psychotic crisis that indicates the illness, though it has been there all the time. In general, the crisis occurs between the ages of fifteen and thirty-five. It's easy to imagine that David's death triggered the crisis in Virginie; once the illness was established, it never left her, though there were probably healthy phases until towards the end of her life, when she had to be institutionalised. Personally I haven't come across it often, and even then usually in patients in remission, so I couldn't diagnose it but I did notice that she sometimes had problems ordering her thoughts, which is one of the symptoms of schizophrenia and can lead to cognitive problems. She was a beautiful woman, witty, elegant. She lost that wittiness. Schizophrenics live in an opaque, threatening world, a world that imprisons and tyrannises them. The outside world, other people, cause them to suffer. Psychologically, it's a very painful illness. So they cut themselves off, which is what Virginie did, she cut herself off from the world, withdrew into herself and, from what I know, her husband protected her and looked after her until she reached what's called the cataleptic stage of the illness, a complete absence of reactions, of movement. Virginie became a statue. She wasn't dangerous to those around her, but she was a danger to herself. It must have been harrowing, watching her slowly disappear."

I had asked Charles lots of questions. I was captivated by this image of Virginie, frozen, withdrawn, her eyes dead. This image that, for all I knew, had never existed. But I could see her, from her first appearance walking quickly towards the window when David came into the apartment, a blur of movement, and, then, later, prostrate. The strong and the beautiful. The weak and the vanquished. Just as the photograph of David Wagner had brought together several destinies, I would have liked a last snapshot that brought David and Virginie together in death. If the writer could be a magician which, in essence, he is, I would bring to life three images: the dinner, the boating trip in the Bois de Boulogne, and a parting glance which never took place, between the prisoner in the concentration camp and the prisoner in the asylum, a last glance that fascinates and repels me, and, more than anything, terrifies me.

"There was no treatment?"

"No. In Virginie's day, the treatments were horrifying – electroshock, which could sometimes bring about a certain improvement but, more often than not, caused even more damage."

"You think she really was given shocks?"

"Probably. That was the treatment at the time. These days, there's no cure but certain forms of it can be managed. The illness is still there, but its effects moderated. People can live an almost normal life. But back then for the sufferer and their family, it was terrible. When I met your father…"

"You know my father?"

"Of course. All the Wagners know him."

"You mean he met the rest of the family?"

"Of course, at a big dinner. It was normal. He might have been a Fabre but he was a Wagner too, at least partly. And besides, he looked so much like my brother… It was astonishing. We were all struck by it. He probably didn't realise."

"I don't quite understand… how did he get in touch with you?"

"It was easy… I knew him already. He was very young when I met him the first time. He must have been about eighteen. The phone rang in my surgery. My secretary answered it, he said he wanted to speak to me and she told him I was with a patient but said she would take his name. At that point there was a silence. Then he said he would call back. About an hour later I was on the phone to him. What he was saying didn't make much sense, he seemed lost, he said that he wanted to meet me. I asked him if he was ill, he told me he wasn't. Told me it was something more serious. I laughed. I asked him what could be more serious than illness. There was a pause. Then he told me he was David Wagner's son. And at that point I was the one who was speechless. I suggested he come to the surgery. He told me he was just across the street, that he would come up. He came up."

"How had he found out who his father was?"

"I don't know. He never told me. Which is strange because he talked to me for hours, said that he had always suspected something because he didn't resemble anyone in the family, because his brothers were so different, because his father was short and bald. He told me that he felt on the margins, that he had never really felt as if he was part of the family, that he had sensed there was some secret. Adolescents are very drawn to secrets. They are always the bastard child of some deposed king. Well, in this case, the king in question was Wagner the Jew who had died in a concentration camp. Actually I think he had had an argument with his father or his stepfather, I'm not sure what to call him. He'd run away. He stayed at my place for a few days. I put him up. He was troubled, confused. He had obviously just found out the truth. I advised him to send a message home so that his *family* wouldn't be worried. The word made him shudder, but he did it anyway. After three days, I thought it was time for him to leave. I was touched by his situation, and we'd never had children of our own so having a nephew suddenly appear out of nowhere, well, it stirred things up, we could very easily have taken him in. But I thought it was for the best. He had to go home or to find his own place. I think he was hurt by that. I asked him to keep in touch and, a few months later, he wrote to thank us. It was a kind letter. A few months after that, he phoned. I told him I'd talked about him to the rest of the family and that they were all eager to meet him. They were overjoyed at the idea. He hesitated, he said: 'Maybe, yes, I think it's a good idea, but not right now.' And then one day, some months later still, Adrien said: 'About dinner, I'd love to come.' We held it at my house. Obviously, there too many people were missing – my father, my mother Natacha, Adrien's grandparents and, of course, my brother David. They were like empty chairs, I felt their absence. But everyone else was there, my sister Sophie and her husband, their four children, yes four of them, my nieces and nephews of various ages and sizes who delighted us with their joy and their mayhem. Four adults, four children. The Wagner family, you might say, though of course my sister and her family were called Stern, and since we had no children the Wagner name was destined to die out. There was no Wagner heir. But as far as Adrien, the ninth guest, was concerned, he was meeting the Wagner family."

"And was he really happy to be meeting everyone? I mean, I know my father, he dreads family reunions…"

"That dread may have been the result of that dinner," Charles said smiling. "It would be difficult to imagine a worse dinner. Not that my wife, who was a very good cook, didn't prepare a lovely meal – the food was delicious – but the family reunion was a fiasco. It was strange because we were so happy to meet him, my sister talked about it every day… It's true that when he arrived, he looked so much like David that it took her breath away. God knows, my brother and sister never really got on for a whole host of reasons, all of which came down to the fact that they were opposites like fire and water. And yet, the moment she saw Adrien, her eyes filled with tears. He didn't notice, but I knew my sister, I was stunned. Later she told me she thought she was looking at David: 'He's the spitting image of him, it's almost unbelievable.' Unfortunately, after that everything was a disaster, more than that it was ridiculous: Adrien and my sister had an argument."

"They argued? About what?"

"I can't rightly say… A conversation about politics that turned ugly."

"They were talking about politics? An aunt who'd just met her disappeared brother's son for the first time?"

"I know, it's incredible. But that's what happened. Actually, we didn't talk about David, about the family, about your childhood. I think everyone felt awkward, uneasy. From the start, the conversation was banal, run of the mill. It quickly became obvious that Adrien was left wing, my sister was right wing and it all came out of that. Tensions were running high, they talked about the government, I think, and about communism, and when they got on to the subject of Algeria, Adrien got up and left."

"And he never came back?"

"Never. I never saw him again. We wrote once in a while, but that was all."

"I can't believe it."

"It does seem unbelievable when you look at what happened, but I think that the truth was Adrien didn't really want to meet up. Or at least not all of us together at a formal family meal. He had enough to deal with in his own family. He wasn't a Fabre any more, he wasn't really a Wagner, his mother had died insane, all of this was too much for a teenage boy. In a sense, the argument suited him and later, when I thought about that meal, I remember that he was the one who had steered the conversation, the one who raised his voice, adopted extreme positions. Of course, they were difficult times, people were polarised, but it was him too, caught up in his problems and his questions. He was young and very alone. With no sense of belonging. Certainly not to a new family. So he left."

Deep down, my father hadn't changed. By starting an argument with his aunt, he had rejected memory and explanation, just as he refused to explain anything to me although I'd given him a perfect opportunity to do so. By chance, I found myself at the heart of his story but again he got up and left the table. And I didn't know if one day he would stay and talk.

9

My father was not the only one to turn his back on memory. Sophie – not the right-wing aunt, but my Sophie, who I was certain my father, with his eye for a beautiful woman, would not have dismissed so quickly, in a piece of political sleight of hand, was becoming more and more hostile to my book. Aside from the inevitable antipathy between the life of a writer, hunched over his computer, and life in a couple, she was deeply opposed to the subject of my work.

"It's not normal, writing about the Nazis," she said over and over.

"I'm not writing about the Nazis, I'm writing about my family."

"Then why do you mention my grandfather?"

"Because he is a part of my family now," I said, half-lying.

"So your family includes the whole world?"

And other fascinating conversations like this.

"The real reason is you," Sophie said one day.

"What do you mean?"

"You're the one who's the Nazi."

I was dumbfounded by this staggering statement.

"It's true," she went on. "You don't start delving into documents and archives unless you've got some personal reason."

"In that case, I could just as easily say 'I am that Jew'. That would make more sense, after all David Wagner is my grandfather. Not everyone is lucky enough to have a Nazi grandfather."

She blushed.

"You know perfectly well he wasn't a Nazi."

"That's right, he was only a National Socialist."

The conversation was turning ugly.

"What I meant," said Sophie, "and I'm not saying this to hurt you, is that the reason you're writing about your grandfather is not necessarily the reason you think."

"That's ridiculous."

"No, it's not ridiculous. What is it about this story that fascinates you? Is it David Wagner or the Nazi regime?"

I didn't answer. I could understand that Sophie was uncomfortable with the subject. It was the most terrible period of her country's history, it was her grandfather and it was a murky story which clashed with the bright, smiling love story she had planned for us. But I was convinced that I was not fascinated by Nazism itself, though there was something mythic in the forces that had clashed in that war, as though primeval monsters buried in the depths of humanity had woken.

Yet I could not simply dismiss out of hand the opinions of a woman who was sharing my life, a woman whose keen intuition I had noted more than once. It is all very well talking about other people, about David Wagner, about Adrien Fabre-Wagner, Marcel Fabre, Clémentine Fabre; there comes a moment when you have to question yourself. And that is what I did. I can see myself, as night creeps into the living room, feet propped up on the coffee table, thinking. I was playing the game. The truth game. And of course there was another truth, one deeper and more personal than my search for my grandfather and I didn't need to think about it to know that this deeper, more personal reason concerned my father; it was obvious. And yet, even that meant nothing.

Was there something else? Something in my original research, something which coalesced in a photo in which a father mirrored his son who mirrored his son. Some obscure reason that would make sense of Sophie's suspicions. The one troubling aspect of my investigation, it seemed to me, the one point that wavered like visions in a heat haze, was Martin Sommer. Obviously I use this name as emblematic of a more all-encompassing violence. If I truly tried to probe myself to search for hidden reasons that would support Sophie's suspicions, if I played devil's advocate, became my own worst enemy, the one murky point was Martin Sommer. I could clearly remember how I had tried to depict this man as emblematic of Nazism whereas everyone claims that Nazism is precisely not that brutal violence which is characteristic of every war; that there have always been, will always be, men like Martin Sommer in the world. What marks out the Nazis, people say, is the bureaucratic violence, not the wild fury of one individual but a sweeping, mechanised violence, devoid of hatred, of rage. And yet the fact remains that I took a character who played a negligible role in my grandfather's life and made him a key part of my representation of Nazism. Even if the chronology forced me not to overly exaggerate his role, to me Martin Sommer was a central element, the emotional key to the writing of a book. The narrow prison trench that was his bestial domain, his savage sadistic violence, provided a ferment for thoughts and images more crucial than analyses of the banality of evil and the workings of the complicated Nazi machinery of destruction.

There, walking through that dark prison sixty years later, with the impenetrable, meaningless reverence one accords to bare walls, is perhaps what Sophie sensed in me.

It is there, perhaps, that my relationship with violence, with fear, becomes clear. I will never say that writing this book was prompted by the dark room of Martin Sommer. The cause, the true cause, was the discovery of a photograph and all the revelations that ensued. But at the same time, I know that that dark room is buried within me, in the depths of my being and that there is a child shut up in there. I know, if I am prepared to face them, dark images of violence and suffocation are buried deep within me where a Martin Sommer is constantly threatening to kill me. And if he does not kill me, he terrifies me, his huge hands have clutched at me since childhood.

Once these hands close round you, they never release their grip. The fear never leaves you, and nor does the violence. You for ever remain a terrified child – and consequently a wounded adult, aggressive, violent. You can try to bury the fear, encase it in a block of steel and marble, it will never leave you. There is no cure for evil.

Whatever conclusions I had drawn from my soul-searching were not easy to reveal to Sophie. Fear and violence are not exactly popular subjects when you're in a relationship. So I decided to respond to her suspicions with a three-day holiday which, though hardly heroic, would at least be enjoyable. I bought two plane tickets to Munich where I planned to visit the magnificent galleries, Bavaria also being a splendid place for walks, and on Thursday we left for a long weekend.

Once we arrived in Munich, I realised the extent of the problems my subject had stirred up. It had not been a particularly clever choice of destination. A weekend in Venice would have been more romantic, a night of masks and bergamasques, rather than a weekend in the capital of the Third Reich. But I had previously been to Munich, "one of the most interesting cities in Germany" as my guidebook prudently put it, without thinking about the Nazis and all the issues I wanted to leave behind. This time I was like a rat in a maze of references. In the Alte Pinakothek, a Rubens painting depicting hell with its legions of devils and its tortures in a confusion of flesh and teeth and pain, all perspective suspended, up and down abolished, made me think of Buchenwald. If I had wanted to depict a concentration camp it would have to be like this: mysterious, manifold, teeming. An idea that would obviously never lead to anything but one I spent an hour thinking about, imagining how I would go about it.

That wasn't all. That would have been nothing. That night, I gave in to Sophie who wanted us to use Servas, a pacifist association founded just after the war that she was a member of, which claimed to foster peace between peoples by encouraging person-to-person contacts. Such encounters, the founders piously believed, would reduce the risk of conflict. Hence the birth of Servas, a worldwide association in which members opened their homes to other members. All she needed to do was phone to ask if local members were happy to have us stay. In return, obviously everyone had to agree to accept foreign visitors. So, after a couple of phone calls, we stayed in a pleasant suburb of Munich. But I realised it would be impossible to avoid my subject as we chatted to our hosts, whose story was fascinating in itself, but it brought me back to the war, something I was trying to avoid. Years earlier, this couple who were in their fifties and had two charming daughters (one of whom was supposedly learning French, though she could only utter a few sentences), had received a curious delegation of four Americans aged from seventy-five to eighty-six, who were on a tour of Europe. In a beat-up, second-hand Citroën which was constantly about to give up the ghost, they drove from country to country, staying with members of Servas, wearing their garish clothes, hauling camping gear which they set up in every apartment, laying down groundsheets and sleeping bags. As the Americans and the Germans were chatting over the traditional evening meal, the symbolic breaking of bread intended to bring them together, the four old men explained that, now they were coming to the end of their lives, they had decided to visit a continent they hadn't seen since World War II. As very young men they had enlisted in the American army to fight in Europe. One of them said simply that he had been a bomber pilot and for years and years afterwards he had thought about the bombs that had destroyed whole districts, each time killing hundreds of people. Their hostess said that her mother had been killed during a bombing raid in Stuttgart. The man asked when her mother had died, she told him and the man responded that he had been on a bombing raid over the city at the time. They both thought that he had probably killed the woman though they did not say as much because it was obvious and because, as our hostess explained, she didn't feel any anger towards this man, she felt it had brought them closer together as though they had come through a common tragedy.

When we went to bed, I said to Sophie: "You see? It's not my fault. We can't get away from the subject."

"Not at all," she said. "I thought it was a beautiful story. I thought the four old men were touching. It's a story that reminds us to make peace with the past, not drag it up again."

My arguments with Sophie about my work were the tip of an iceberg of other unspoken disagreements which might simply have been teething troubles in settling into the relationship after our initial burst of passion, but they worried me nonetheless. There was a constant tension, sudden flashes of rage on both sides, which did not bode well. I had left France for Sophie, we had moved in together expecting a future of happy days, gurgling babies and other joyful future events but the reality was more complicated. If the love between us was clear, our day-to-day life was less so. Some of our hopes were deferred, as though wavering in the face of the tension between us, and it was with a certain disenchantment that we now considered our dazzling love which seemed less brilliant, less radiant than we first thought. In short, love at first sight had come face to face with reality, and we were no longer sure of ourselves.

As we walked through the yellowing autumn forests of Bavaria, the branches bending above us evoked the gilded arches of a wedding, but also the melancholy of decay. The sudden showers thundered like drums on the leaves of the trees which were thankfully so dense that they protected us from the rain. In the past, I had often had to face relationships that suddenly crumbled, I knew the signs, and I could see them now in ours. But the difference here, and it was huge, was the love we felt and which we believed would help us to overcome these problems. I would have liked everything to melt in the immense harmony of the ripening sun, a sun with no past and no future, yielding simply to languid pleasure. I would have liked my life to be that summer sun, that sun at dusk, sinking, radiant, which I loved more than anything and which made me hug Sophie to me, filled with love, with tenderness. And she hugged me too and we waited for our next argument.

Life went on with that necessary unpredictability I had

always found exasperating, the endless coincidences that still seem somehow to be written into our personalities as though everything were inevitable, as though the detours of our lives led back only to the same sinuous disposition of being. I was who I was, just as I am now, with my wanderings, my fleeting affairs, my bursts of anger. And I had to follow the path that had been set out.

The following weekend, my father and I went to see my grandfather Fabre, who was now in a nursing home. I was thrilled by this news. I had always expected my grandfather to survive: what was cancer compared to this man?

The nursing home was not far from Chateaubriand's house in the Vallée-aux-Loups. This seemed to me a good sign. Chateaubriand, who had survived everything, who had drawn unquenchable strength from his childhood dreams, the terrible desire that destroyed him in the loneliness of his domain in Brittany, an insatiable energy that encompassed history, women, and literature, was my grandfather's sort of man, a man of the old world emerging from the old culture which he studied passionately at his lycée in Normandy. The nursing home, a large stone building set in a vast domain surrounded by walls, was itself encircled by nature. There was no noise; a river ran through the grounds flanked by linden trees. It was idyllic. As we entered the grounds, my father stopped and stared at the landscape, already familiar since he visited my grandfather every other day.

"I'll leave you to it," he said. "So you can have him to yourself."

"We can see him together," I said.

"No, it's better this way. Make the most of it, you don't get the chance to talk with him as often as I do."

I went into the building alone. At reception, they told me where his room was. Climbing the stairs, which seemed strangely worn to me, I wondered how I would find my grandfather. The door to his room was open. He was sitting in a chair, dressed, reading a book. I smiled. It was like finding him again. I glanced around the room, a little dilapidated, a little Spartan, which surprised me, but bathed in warm autumn sunshine. There was a washbasin and a small mirror which reflected the little figure bent over his book. And, in the same moment I saw this, my grandfather realised I was there and looked up. And I saw his smile, marked by a black hole, in a gaunt and ravaged face.

He closed his eyes happily like a cat screwing up its face. I kissed him.

"Missing a tooth," he said. "One of my crowns broke. I look terrible."

"Let's just say it's a new look, Grandfather. It makes a change."

"You're right. Let's be positive. It's new," he said. "I'm glad you're here."

"How are you? You look well."

"Very well. I'm happy, I've got my books, the nurses are pretty, what more could I ask for?"

"Pretty? I thought that was a myth?"

"It is a myth, but at my age any woman of twenty is pretty."

A nurse came in. Short, thin, dark-haired, very plain.

"How are we today, Monsieur Fabre, have you got everything you need?"

"Everything. My grandson is here, I'm happy. He's come from Germany to visit me."

The nurse smiled.

"He's the one whose book you didn't buy."

The young woman blushed and disappeared.

"I gave her money to buy your last novel," my grandfather explained, "and she came back with some rubbish. You can imagine how happy I was…"

I nodded.

"What would you like to do?"

"See you."

"In that case you can see me just as well in the garden."

"In the garden?"

"Yes. I'm back on my feet, I go for walks."

"Lead on."

Marcel struggled to his feet, walked over to the little wardrobe and took out a large coat which I helped him put on. We went down in a little lift. There was no one else about.

We walked in the garden. My father was nowhere to be seen, I wondered where he'd got to. Marcel walked with difficulty, holding on to my arm. He walked about a hundred metres, looking at the scenery, breathing deeply. He didn't say anything. He was looking.

He stopped by the river and sat on a garden chair, something that seemed to be a habit. I took a chair next to him.

"Nice place," he said. "I'll miss it."

I didn't say anything. This stretch of the stream felt damp and I was wondering if it was the right place to stop.

"Another month and I think I'll be fit to go home," he said. "It's beautiful here, but I like my own river, my own fields."

"What about looking after yourself?" I asked.

"I'll have a full-time nurse. I talked to the doctor, he doesn't think it will be a problem."

"I can see why," I said. "You really seem to be in good form."

"I am. You see, the only thing the cancer has done is make me more likely to reveal secrets. You know a lot about that now. And it's no bad thing. I haven't done enough talking in my life. What about you? Still happy with your German girl?"

I told him there was tension between us but that the relationship was settling down. And that Berlin was an exciting city. And I was enjoying my job. Meeting lots of people.

My grandfather considered me sagely. "Yes. These things are never easy," he said. "But you need to work things out. Family is important."

We talked about one thing and another. We talked about Chateaubriand. And then my grandfather shivered. I suggested we go back to his room. He walked, better now, as far as the lift.

"I'll have to have one of these fitted at home," he said staring at the steel walls. "It's very practical."

When we went into his room, my father was waiting for us. Marcel and Adrien hugged.

"It's the first time in years I've seen the two of you together," said Marcel. "It's good. You're very alike. More so than Adrien and me."

There was an awkward silence. The comment was out of place. Then my father asked him about his health. Marcel said it was tough.

"When I die, have a lovely ceremony. Not that I believed in all that religious drivel… but a nice funeral couldn't do any harm."

"You don't need to think about things like that now, Papa," said Adrien. "You've had good news."

The word "Papa" made me shudder.

"Not such good news," said Marcel. "Cancer is still cancer."

"Maybe, but prostate cancer progresses very slowly. You could live to a hundred with cancer."

"In my case, I'd be surprised."

I didn't understand what was going on. My grandfather was not the same man. We helped him onto his bed.

"I don't feel very well. I think I overestimated my strength. The joy of seeing my grandson probably..."

His voice was more feeble, he seemed weaker but most importantly the tone of his conversation had changed, it was as though he were doing his best to convince my father he was about to die whereas talking to me five minutes earlier he'd been full of good news.

"It's not good for me, taking on too much. It was cold in the garden. And it's damp down there by the river..."

The impression that Marcel Fabre was constantly playing a role came back to me. The feeling that I was being constantly manipulated, as when he offered to make me the heir the way you might ennoble a rival you're trying to get around. I had been thrilled for us to finally be grandfather and grandson, with the sudden closeness between us after his coldness throughout my childhood and adolescence, the family Christmases... "My grandson is here, I'm happy..." Was he lying? Was he playing a part?

"Did you talk to the doctor?"

"Yes," my father said. "He said you're in good shape, much better than last month. It's a good sign."

"I think it's just temporary," my grandfather closed his eyes. "It's still cancer..."

This sadistic game of cat and mouse carried on until we left. I was so surprised, I didn't say much, my grandfather went on insisting this was the end and my father kept saying the opposite. The whole thing seemed increasingly difficult for Adrien, my grandfather's insistence he was dying seemed to hurt him. But he didn't want to go, he stayed where he was, arguing, counter-attacking, trying to joke. I cut the ordeal short, pointing out that we had been there for quite a while and that Grandfather needed his rest.

On the stairs, my father turned to me, his body racked with terrible sobs. Shocked, I couldn't bring myself to do anything. My father had never cried in front of me. I made to do something, but how could I put my arms around this man who for years, for ever, had been walled up in his solitude? Frozen and reserved, my family had never taught me such gestures. Caught between this chilly formality and my father's towering silence, the silence of those who have too much to say, I now realised that I had never said anything, never made the first move. And what every woman I had ever known had first to teach me was how to take her in my arms.

So how could I hug this silence that was my father? We were separated by so many years of silence. Besides, he quickly regained his composure. He wiped his eyes – and again I was shocked at the gesture, and shocked to see his eyes were red and watery.

"Why?" I asked.

And this question which sounds so ordinary, so banal, required an enormous effort on my part. I was asking for an explanation. This was probably the first time I had ever asked my father to explain anything.

"He's dying."

"What? He seemed fine to me," I said. "He even went for a walk. He couldn't have managed that two weeks ago."

"He will be dead within two months."

"Who told you that?"

"The doctors are all agreed. It's only a brief remission, it often happens with cancer. It's over."

"I don't believe it," I said dully.

"Talk to the doctors," my father shrugged his shoulders.

"Okay, that's their diagnosis, but that doesn't mean they're right. I saw him walking, making plans. He's going home."

My father started down the stairs.

IO

My grandfather never came home. A month after my visit, he died. His condition had stabilised for three weeks, I phoned him, he told me again that he was making plans to go home. What was the point of all this pretence? I still don't know. He had played two different roles with me and with my father, changing what he said according to who he was talking to and it's probable that neither of us got the real version. He wasn't a man to spare us grief, nor was he a man to look the other way. In the end, no one would ever know what this masquerade was about, but I'm left with the painful image of a sinister game played with my father, like a Venetian masked ball, the morbid menace in all those frozen faces. But Marcel Fabre would not have been himself, and I would not have respected him as much as I did, had he not been a man of a thousand masks.

After those three weeks of fleeting remission, he quickly deteriorated. I had phoned, and someone answered then hung up. I didn't understand, I thought I'd misdialled.

He died holding a nurse's hand. Perhaps for the sake of beauty and pathos we should assume he was thinking about Virginie. But it's more likely that he held the hand of this young woman, this 'pretty' young woman as he would have said, out of love for life. What my grandfather had, the profound instinctive wisdom, over and above the sorrows and weakness of other men, was this savage, animal love. Although he had been in a kind of limbo after the death of Virginie, especially in his relationships with other women, he was still profoundly attached to life. And to forgetting.

His funeral, as he had requested, was a "beautiful ceremony"; Sophie came with me and her presence calmed me. I felt stronger when I was with her, and her coming meant that I could formally introduce her to the family. Everyone was at the service: uncles, aunts, cousins... As a mark of honour, the bishop himself offered to have the funeral in Rouen cathedral, which was filled with distinguished guests, the minister of the interior sitting in the front pew. Though the ruddy-faced, pot-bellied old men all around me looked almost like caricatures, I didn't feel like smiling. These men had not come because they were bored, they had come out of respect for my grandfather. Business colleagues, friends, VIPs united by their supposed importance, family members made up a black silent throng. The bishop paid tribute to Marcel Fabre, recalling certain details which made me understand that this Parisian bourgeois truly was a local boy. When the crowd rose to pray, I felt a surge of emotion, part religious, part humane.

At the cemetery, in the chill winter wind, I was about to fall into line when my aunt came over to me and, without a word, pushed me to the front, earning me a strange, almost menacing glare from my father. I hesitated, not knowing what to do and then, with my father and my uncles on either side, I accepted the condolences – hesitantly at first, then more confidently as though adjusting to my new status, as my fathers and uncles were.

"You're the heir now."

Mechanically, I shook the hands of people who, for the most part, I didn't know. Some clapped me on the shoulder, a sorrowful, almost sheepish hug. One woman put her arms round me. I gave each one the same mournful smile, I played my role.

And then there was no role to play, just shovelfuls of earth to stare at.

The family went back to the great house. As many as the house would hold were staying there, with distant cousins staying in a hotel in town. My grandfather's room remained empty.

"It's yours now," my father said, somewhat tongue in cheek.

I pretended I hadn't heard.

Dinner was rather a sombre affair. My aunts did their best to keep the conversation going, which made Sophie the centre of attention. As the newest recruit, she was an endless source of questions about her job, her country. She answered with a disarming ease and tenderness. In spite of everything, it was difficult to forget the coffin.

Then everyone went to their rooms. I talked to Sophie for a while, she asked me if I was sad. I told her I had been, that I'd cried when my grandfather died but that I didn't really feel sad any more because I knew that he'd felt he'd had a good innings. He had had a long, full life. His death was natural. I added that the one thing I regretted was not having known him better until those last months. In fact, until I asked him about David Wagner, he had been an august mysterious figure about whom I could bring to mind only a handful of moments of intimacy from my childhood. And once again I mentioned the long poems he used to recite to me. I tried to recite one myself, whispering it into Sophie's ear as if telling a child a bedtime story. My imagination compensated for my memory. Sophie fell asleep smiling.

I couldn't get to sleep. I went downstairs to the living room. There was a figure still there, reading. My father.

"I couldn't sleep," I said.

He nodded.

"I don't sleep much myself."

He had stoked the fire and a log was blazing.

"Pleasant, the fire."

"Yes."

A beat.

"That'll be your role now," my father added. "You're the heir, it's your job to tend the fire."

Clearly he wasn't going to give up on this.

"I can see the title bothers you. Don't worry, I don't intend to lay claim to it. Anyone here would make a better job of it than me.

"Marcel named you. He told me, he told my brothers. You're the heir. I have to say than we were surprised to say the least. Me less than the others, obviously, for reasons you understand, but my brothers…"

"He didn't pass you over for that reason. Other than that, I don't understand what he was thinking."

"It's unbelievable," my father said in anger. "When you consider your youth, your circumstances, the fact that you don't live here… You've never had any responsibilities, you don't even have a family of your own. Think how humiliating this was for your uncles, men who've made something of their lives, who have important jobs, wives, children."

"Maybe that was it, maybe Marcel couldn't choose between his sons?"

"That's the most logical explanation. We all thought of that… but I have to confess, we don't really believe it. You were chosen for some reason we can't fathom."

The conversation was beginning to be hurtful.

"I didn't realise everyone thought I was incompetent. Especially given that the heir is simply a figurehead. I'm not going to be running the family affairs. Everyone handles their own very well."

"You're wrong. Being the heir isn't entirely symbolic. You have to take care of the house and the lands. Who'll live here now?"

"Not me. I work in Germany, I'm not planning to move here. Besides, your issue with this whole thing isn't material, it's abstract. You all feel passed over, belittled by Grandfather's decision. You feel as if he didn't think enough of you to give you the responsibility."

"Absolutely," said my father. "Again, for me it's one thing, but for my brothers... Besides, you know your own weaknesses... The responsibility should go to the strongest in the family."

Traitor.

"What do you mean, weakness?"

My father leaned back in his chair and launched into his speech, each attack delivered in his soft, almost mellifluous voice.

"Your mother and I have always worried that you were nervous and highly strung. You know the family history, you know what happened to my own mother, all that meant we were always very careful. You were a nervous child, intelligent but frail. We thought that your sense of self never fully developed, you were constantly searching for something. You buried yourself in your books, you wrote. You set yourself apart. And that isolation... Why aren't you married? That girl you're seeing, the German girl, she's very pretty. Why don't you marry her? Women fall for you. You've had a lot of girlfriends. That's fine, that's good, in fact at first we were reassured. You'd engaged with life. Women. But why do you never stay with one of them? Why do you always refuse to take on any responsibility? You can't just float through your whole life a teenager. Maybe you're worried about your fragility? It's not as though I didn't make an effort. That's why I tried to discourage you when you started researching our origins. No point making things worse. At least you were born into a solid, stable family. You weren't the son of a bastard brought up by force of circumstances in a family that wasn't his. It's not good, being a bastard, and it's not good to be a bastard's son. Rootlessness is hereditary."

Stunned, I raised my voice.

"We've finally got to the point, haven't we? Roots. That's the crux of the matter. Otherwise, it sounded to me as if you were talking about yourself: floating through life, the lack of identity, that's you all over. As for your fatherly fears, this is the first time I've heard you mention them, or my mother for that matter, you haven't talked about her in years. So I'll ignore all of that and go back to what is important, to this conversation we should have had long ago and which you've constantly avoided."

"I haven't avoided it. I've deliberately tried to spare you. But when I knew you'd been to Buchenwald, well, it was down to fate: either you'd see the photograph or you wouldn't."

I fell silent, suddenly completely calm.

"You knew about the photograph?"

"Of course. I've known about it for years."

"But you seemed so surprised when I showed it to you."

"Well, I wasn't."

"You'd already done your research?"

"Of course."

"You know all about David Wagner?"

"I've known for a long time. Before you were even born."

"I suppose you were the person who phoned Vincent Mallet?"

"Vincent Mallet? Yes, I think I remember him. An idiot. He wasn't much use either."

"If you know Vincent Mallet, you must know Serge Kolb, but he never mentioned you."

"Hardly surprising, since I don't know him."

"In that case, how did you find out the whole story?"

"My father told me everything the day I turned eighteen."

"That explains why you ran away."

Adrien tensed.

"Ran away?"

"Charles Wagner told me that you called him one night at his surgery and you went and stayed with him."

"I don't know anything about that. On my birthday, Marcel called me into his study and he explained everything. Most of it I already suspected for various reasons. Who David Wagner was, what had happened. Obviously I didn't run away, I thanked him for his generosity, for always having treated me like his own son. In fact I've always thought of him as my real father, David Wagner was only my biological father. And my whole life I've had a close relationship with Marcel."

"Sure you have, so much so you ran away to your uncle's place and never attended a single family reunion."

He gave me a long, dark look.

"I thought I told you, that story about running away was

pure invention. Marcel Fabre is my real father and I'll love him my whole life."

"Why did you run away from the family dinner at the Wagners'?"

"What are you talking about? If you're referring to that dinner with my biological family, I didn't run away from anything. I was curious to meet this family, which, though not mine, had played a role in my life. I met them, we ate together, and that was that."

"That was that? Nothing else. You meet your father's family and that's that. Case closed."

"Who do you think you are?" my father got to his feet. "What is this, a court?"

"It's not a court. I'm just trying to understand. All my life, I've been part of a tightly knit family, the Fabres, okay, my father was a bit distant, but anyway… a family. Then one day, I discover that my father is the son of a man named David Wagner, a Jew who was deported to a concentration camp. That's no crime, it's not even shocking, and I can understand how Virginie could have loved two men at the same time, but you have to admit as news goes it's not exactly trivial. It might have had a bearing on your life. And therefore on mine."

"As I told you earlier, I was trying to protect you."

"Protect me from what? From which secret? The fact that my Jewish grandfather was sent to the camps? That my grandmother was mad? Great! What was terrible was what happened to those people, not their secrets. And silence is a harder burden to bear than a secret."

"Maybe. But I still thought it was for the best not to tell you."

"And you never tried to find out anything else? I feel like I know more about your real father than you do."

Adrien smiled. "I very much doubt that."

"You have no idea," I said in a burst of stupid pride, "I've spent the past year collecting information about his life, I've met everyone, I can tell you every detail about his life, I can even tell you what happened on his last day."

"Really?" said my father mockingly. "A remarkable piece of work! I'd expect nothing less from you. I've always thought you'd make a better researcher than writer. You never did have much imagination."

I got to my feet and as I left the room, I said: "I'm going to write the whole story. It'll have taken you sixty years, but at least you'll finally know your father. Thanks to me."

"Erich Wagner, does that mean anything to you?"

I turned on my heel. "How do you know?"

"You see, that's the problem with young people," my father said derisively. "They think they're better than everyone else. You did your little investigation, you chatted to a couple of people, read a few books and you think that means you know everything about David Wagner. Me? I acted."

II

In the mutability of people and things, the shifting flux of appearances and images, of roles and lies, my father once again took his place. From the first, I had sensed that his misgivings about my research veiled secret silences. Now, suddenly, in a grotesque twist of fate, a window had been opened. A window that opened onto other windows, other illusions, an endless labyrinthine story. Every time I reached for something to hold on to, it swivelled to reveal a sinister mask that sent me off in new directions, all of which were true and yet false.

If there was a lesson to be learned from this, it was that I had to see things as though on a ghost train at a fair, spectral figures coming towards me, each suddenly revealing a different face so I could never know which face was real until finally I saw the figure of myself unmasked to reveal a new face just as alien, as grotesque as all the others. The fact that I was on a ghost train, alone amid the screeching, the gibbering faces of the puppets, lashed by these shifting images told me only that I would be the last to know and would know myself only after everyone else – or perhaps never.

Together with the automatons living in solitude and isolation for decades, my father now revealed that he had another face, one which brought me back to Weimar, a place I had managed to leave behind. It brought me back to the main gate at Buchenwald, to the infirmary, to the Parable of the Jew, to Erich Wagner. It brought me back to my trip there with the

students as we were wandering through Weimar and its sur-
roundings, taking the coach to Buchenwald and discovering
the photograph that began all this. A German colleague who
lived with her husband in a tiny house in a beautiful part of
the city had agreed to put me up. So I shared the evening *Brot*
– bread and sausages, cold meats, cheese washed down with a
small glass of beer (or for her slightly caricatural, pot-bellied,
moustachioed husband, a large bottle). The conversation
lapsed into long silences as my hosts took it for granted that I
was fascinated by local folklore and wrongly assumed I knew a
lot about football, German teams in particular. Like the idiot
in the fable, I smiled at the lengthy homilies of my host, who
would surface from his beer to give a long detailed explanation
about some local site because, being a hotel manager, it was a
point of pride for him to thoroughly inform his customers. I
was the unfortunate customer.

One evening, however, the conversation took an interesting
turn as I realised that I was in the company of former communists. Perhaps it should have been obvious, but I had not realised
the fact. Let's say, I had a vague idea: the GDR was communist,
therefore my hosts had lived under the communist regime.
Then suddenly, for no reason except perhaps that I felt the
strange relationship with history which in Weimar is like a
dense, treacherous mist seeping into me, I no longer thought
it was trivial that I was breaking bread with former communists. Particularly with a woman who, though she taught
French, also taught Russian, as attested by the number of
Russian books in their library, almost as many as there were
German and many more than there were French. Given that
I had just come back from visiting a camp that had been first
Nazi and later Soviet, it did not seem *banal* at all. Commonplace,

probably, since it had been the fate of all the peoples of Eastern Europe, but not banal. I realised that the lives these people lived, in their tiny house with its tiny garden, could not have been more ordinary, that they had clearly not been opponents of the dictatorship or apparatchiks, that they had been content to live a humdrum life in the bureaucratic tedium that was the GDR for those who walked the straight and narrow, but still it did not seem to me to be *banal* to be talking to people who had learned Russian, who could speak it as fluently as they did German, who had read Marx, Lenin and Stalin – in the way that American children read the bible – and had been bombarded for years by propaganda denouncing West Germany as a corrupt country under the tyranny of capitalism where the working classes were oppressed. No, none of these things seemed to me to be *banal*.

Why was I suddenly reminded of this? Why had my father brought me back to Weimar? Because he had been there during the communist dictatorship. In the end, I had simply followed in his footsteps, retraced his steps towards Erich Wagner. There was, however, a difference of scale: we had not been looking for the same Wagner. And we were not obsessed by the same regime. When I went looking for David Wagner, I was also looking for that first collapse of the continent (even if the First World War had already resulted in the collapse of the nation) that had been Nazism. My father's hunt had taken the place of the bleak, corrupt greyness of communism, the second collapse of the continent of Europe.

The other difference had been our ages: I am older than Adrien had been at the time, a young man barely twenty, younger than his father had been when he died. The sixty-year-old man sitting opposite me in the living room of the great house was telling me the story of a young man so different, so distant that he seemed like another person. If he was the same person to Adrien, for my part, I found it difficult to picture him. I suppose that if you superimposed a photo of David over one of me, you would get something like him.

Adrien had quickly learned the story of his father. When Marcel told him David had died in Buchenwald, it was only fifteen years since his death, so many witnesses were still alive. And everyone in the camp knew that Erich Wagner had killed David. It was at this point that my father felt the irresistible urge to find Erich Wagner and let everyone know about his Nazi past. He was very young, he had no desire to forgive and this concerned his own father (even if he insisted he was simply his biological father). I discovered he knew almost nothing about other details of David's life – he was not interested in the fact that he had worked as *Kalfaktor* for the Kochs. All he wanted was to get his hands on the murderer. I don't know where this idea came from since, from what I could tell, he had no love for his biological father, felt no filial duty to avenge him. And if someone had to be blamed for David's death, I'm not sure that Doctor Wagner was the obvious choice. David was dead from the moment he got into the wagon that took him to the camp, so I feel that the real blame falls on the man who denounced him to the French police.

Adrien did not share this opinion. For him, Erich Wagner was the guilty party. It goes without saying that he was not the calm young man who claimed he had rushed into his stepfather's arms on his eighteenth birthday. On the contrary, he was a sombre, solitary young man whose suspicions about his origins throughout his adolescence cast their shadows. He was tormented by demons – something that deep down I knew, after all he was my father and I felt the weight of this repressed violence like dark bubblings that ravaged his whole being. He had been a highly politicised law student, ready to rebel today and start the revolution tomorrow. He was friends with the man who founded the magistrates' union, later nicknamed "the Red Judge", and had he been a judge himself he would have been utterly inflexible. But my father did not become a judge; he had assumed the role of judge only in his role as a son, condemning Erich Wagner to death on circumstantial evidence alone.

For this, he would first have to find him. "I was the youngest Nazi hunter," Adrien told me one day. "Younger than Simon Wiesenthal or the Klarsfelds. But nobody has heard of me, because I only hunted one, that was enough to satisfy my rage." The word "rage" seems somehow inappropriate because my father went about it with painstaking precision. He knew that Wagner had escaped from prison in 1948, that the Allies were looking for him and consequently he had probably left West Germany. Franco's Spain would have been a possible refuge, as would Argentina, a land of exile for a whole community of Nazis who were still making pathetic salutes, plotting the return of the Führer. But before looking into these possibilities, Adrien first checked to see whether Wagner was in East Germany. Patiently he extended his network, his investigation. Bearing in mind Wagner's occupation, he searched lists of doctors: there was no reason for the Buchenwald doctor to have changed his profession. He had to make a living. True, Wagner had obtained his doctorate thanks to a thesis written for him by a camp prisoner, but his years of practice, gassing, eviscerating, experimenting, trepanning, had no doubt served him well. He would be more than capable of dealing with the coughs, the colds and the stomach aches of a small undemanding clientele. Adrien searched, examined, was kept informed about symposia and conferences through a doctor connected with the communist party he had known since high school. Not just any conferences: those on dermatology – scars, marks, tattoos. And so, one day, almost two years after beginning his research, Adrien read an article about tattoos by a certain Karl Grüber. Reading the article, which was dense, detailed and referred to an astonishing number of cases, he was immediately suspicious. And when he discovered Grüber's address, he knew there could be no doubt: the doctor lived in Weimar.

Erich Wagner had never left Weimar. Apart from his time in prison after the Nazi doctors trial (in which other doctors at Buchenwald had been sentenced to hang while he, for no known reason, had been sentenced to life imprisonment), he had stayed in the town, returning to the swamp of memory on the Ettersberg where he had killed. He had remained in the mire of guilt. Obviously, when old friends encountered the former camp doctor Erich Wagner in the street, they were not taken in by the slightly plumper figure of Doctor Grüber, but though they may have glared at him, stared a little too long, they would doff their hats and walk on. And so Karl Grüber took his daily constitutional just as Goethe had walked these streets with his small quick strides, thinking the thoughts of a writer, scientist and counsellor to the king. David Wagner's murderer, and this was what my father could not bear, walked around this small provincial town like some dignitary, this town that was so pleasant, so unassuming yet bathed in culture. He looked left, looked right, walking along slowly in his grey suit, his grey fedora, his grey overcoat. He would pick a rose and stroll beneath the tree with the unpronounceable name which every German knows since Goethe wrote a poem about it: the ginkgo biloba.

My father knew Erich Wagner's route very well because he had followed him. He had gone to Weimar and immediately found the address of the doctor's surgery and set about following him.

He had come to denounce this man. He was sweating with fear and with impatience at the thought that he would finally get justice. Crime and punishment. But more than anything, he wanted the doctor to realise he had committed a crime. He intended to turn him away from his too-peaceful walk.

He began with anonymous notes written in German: "You are a criminal." "You are a killer." "Your crimes will be avenged." Late every night, he would slip a note into the doctor's letterbox. He would have liked to work more slowly, to leave a week between each note, leave time for doubts to take root, but he could not stay in the GDR indefinitely. Grüber's demeanour changed immediately: his walks were now more troubled, he constantly glanced around him, he felt he was being followed, threatened. This was the first reason to feel satisfied. The doctor's sleep was disturbed too, the porch light of the house was left on all night and behind the curtains it was possible to make him out, peering through the window, wondering where the threat would come from.

Then Adrien began to send him letters in French by post. "Why did you kill?" "What pleasure did you feel when you murdered?" and lastly one, childlike but ominous, that read: "Who are you? Who am I?"

The following day, Adrien made an appointment with Grüber's secretary under the name David Wagner. He arrived in the doctor's waiting room in the late afternoon. It was deserted. The receptionist showed him in, then disappeared. For ten minutes there was silence. Adrien was not afraid. It's possible that avengers feel no fear, that they feel protected by their vengeance: right walks side by side with them. Hence their implacable severity, their faces like marble. Adrien was the statue of Justice.

The doctor came into the room. He was wearing a white coat.

"I'd like to have my tattoos removed," said Adrien in his crude German.

Grüber said nothing but simply stared at him.

"My name is David Wagner. I'd like to have my tattoos removed," Adrien said again. "Do you remember me?"

"A little," said Grüber. "David Wagner worked as *Kalfaktor* for the Kochs, is that who you are?"

"That's right. I'm glad you remember me."

"You can stop your games. David Wagner is dead."

Now it was Adrien's turn to say nothing and stare fixedly at the doctor. "How do you know he's dead?" he asked finally.

"He was a Jew. He's dead. All the Jews died back then."

His words were brusque, terse. "Who are you?" Grüber went on.

"I am David Wagner."

"Are you the person who's been sending messages?"

"Yes."

"Are you a relative of David Wagner?"

"I am David Wagner."

"Have it your own way. Why have you been sending me vile messages?"

"Because they're the truth. You need to hear the truth. Everyone needs to hear the truth."

"I didn't kill David Wagner."

"You killed him. The proof is that I am here."

Neither man had moved, they were frozen, the doctor standing by the door, Adrien sitting in an armchair.

"Why did you kill him?" he asked.

"I didn't kill him."

"We're all alone here. You, me and the truth. You can tell us everything."

"Truth is something invented by fools. You weren't in the camp. You don't know what happened."

"I was there. I am David Wagner. I know you murdered me."

"You're insane!"

"No. I'm telling the truth. It's as horrible as madness. But you haven't answered: why?"

"There is no why," whispered Grüber.

"What did you say?"

"There is no why," Grüber said aloud. "There is no explanation, there never will be an explanation for what happened. You could force every German to confess, the guilty and the innocent, the brave, the cowards, no one can give you the reason for what happened. There are factors, explanations, but when you get down to it there is nothing. Nothing at all. Even I don't know what I did. It was war, the worst war there has ever been. That's all anyone can say."

"I'm not asking what anyone can say," Adrien said softly, "I'm not talking about the brave and the cowards. I'm asking what you can say. You. Why did you kill David Wagner?"

"I didn't..."

"You killed David Wagner in the infirmary, you gave him an injection on a spring day in 1942. I was there. I am David

Wagner."

"Stop this farce!" Grüber roared. "All right, I killed him. But it didn't change anything, he would have died anyway. All the Jews had to die!"

"Finally. You see, you can tell the truth when you want to. So, why?"

"Because his name was Wagner, like mine," the doctor said in a monotone. "Because his name was Wagner, because he was a Jew, because he had a beautiful wife."

"A wife? He wasn't married."

"I'd seen a photograph. He'd managed to keep it with him. I don't know why they all tried to hang on to some personal memento. He kept a photograph of a woman, I assumed it was his wife, a young blonde woman smiling. I thought she was extraordinarily beautiful. I thought it was an insult that this Jew with my name should have such a beautiful wife."

"You killed him," Adrien repeated slowly, "because his name was Wagner and his wife was beautiful?"

"No," Grüber said as though suddenly exhausted. "As I said, there is no reason. You don't kill a man for something like that. It's just that in the madness of the Third Reich, when we were all caught up in the madness, I became obsessed with a Jew named Wagner and a photograph. But he would have died in any case."

"That doesn't excuse anything."

"Nothing excuses the death of a man, I suppose."

"Except revenge."

"So you're going to pull out a toy gun and shoot me?"

"That's why I came," Adrien said simply.

"Just like that? You kill me and you just leave the country… You think it's that easy."

"It was easy for you, wasn't it?"

"That was a different time. Communists like order. Disappearances. Prison. All done in triplicate for the bureaucrats. A murder outside of that strict order would perturb them."

"I didn't say I was going to kill you myself. The communists will do that for me."

Grüber stared at him, dumbfounded.

"I've already spoken to the police," Adrien explained. "They were very interested in my story. An escaped Nazi doctor using an assumed name. They're young men, like me. Twenty, twenty-five. You know how people are at that age: idealistic, maybe a little extreme. They were surprised to hear that a Buchenwald doctor was still living in Weimar. I let it slip that you were responsible for experimenting on Russians using gas. It's very unfortunate. They won't like that. Over there, I mean – in the East. My young friends in the police have probably already made a phone call. You see, in this world, all it can take is one word and everything explodes. Silence is much more restful."

Grüber was staring at him, not saying a word. His face was expressionless. No hatred, no despair. He seemed simply to be passively registering my father's words.

"Have you got a wife and children?" Adrien asked.

The question unsettled the doctor.

"Erich Wagner had. I don't have one any more. After my escape, my new identity…"

Adrien nodded.

"Are you David Wagner's son?" asked Grüber.

Adrien seemed to struggle for a moment, he opened his mouth, closed it again then said simply: "I'll leave you. You should have a little time yet."

He got up, walked past the doctor and, when he reached the door, he turned and, like a teenage boy apologising, said: "Don't hold it against me. It's justice, that's all. Justice has to be done."

The following day, Grüber was dead. He had committed suicide during the night. Two days later, my father went back to France to begin the strange, solitary existence that he would lead – aside from the bizarre interlude of being married for three years and fathering a child – for the rest of his life. Once he had made this concession to "normality", he withdrew into himself, hid away with his silences and his secrets.

12

I'd like to talk about something else.

Listen to the resonances, weave the threads of violence, at the risk of losing my way.

Reconsider the fate of Europe.

But how could I do so? How can I launch into the tangle of history when my father has just stepped out of his habitual walk through the Quartier Latin, when I have just realised that his winding route via the rue des Écoles, the Jardin des Plantes, the rue Monge, la place de la Contrescarpe, takes place in a small town in East Germany? That the man who sits alone with the radio every morning confronted his father's murderer, played out that strange scene, the final tragi-comic act?

Sometimes, I thought that this confession by my father was a joke, that he had never gone to Weimar, and it's true that I have no proof. Maybe he got carried away by his fantasies, maybe he really believed he had punished the murderer the way I believed for years that I had saved my friend Richard from his tormentors. And it's true there's something farcical about the scene, the constant refrain: "I am David Wagner". But it is also true that Doctor Wagner killed himself under the name Karl Grüber. And I don't know if one should constantly doubt the word of others.

This is why I would find it difficult to talk about other subjects. Though one last question crept into the conversation with my father. A question he answered without a moment's hesitation, like someone crossing out the past at a single stroke. And his answer revealed such a stupid mistake that it made my blood run cold. A murderous stupidity. And I wonder if it is not that answer that makes it impossible for me to write any more.

I'd asked the question half-heartedly. Firstly, because I thought that Adrien wouldn't be able to answer it. Also, because I believed that in the unlikely event that he did answer, he wouldn't say anything against Marcel who had always seemed to me the guilty party in this whole business. Always ask who profits from the crime.

To my half-hearted question, Adrien gave the only obvious answer. Obvious in its stupidity. Obvious in the weight of the times that it reveals. One which explains the collapse of the European nation. Because no country could ever recover from such an answer.

My question was: "Who denounced David?"

The answer was: "Marcel's father, because he despised this ambitious Jewish son-in-law. He wanted rid of him."

As Adrien said the words, the folly of the period was revealed to me in all its vile duplicity. A bourgeois man of the 1930s, a respected doctor, sent a man to his death out of anti-Semitism and self-interest. David Wagner had no money, he was taking the man's daughter from him though he did not love her, and he was a Jew. He had to be punished – or at least sent away for as long as possible. To give him the benefit of the doubt, he may not have known what life was really like in the concentration camps.

It was not an anonymous letter. A lot of neighbours, rivals and unpleasant sons-in-law were got rid of that way. But that was later. At least a year later. At the time, while Vichy was still dragging its heels, baulking at the idea of sending French Jews to the camps, preferring to send the foreigners, the stateless, all the refugees who had taken refuge in the land of human rights, to have a French Jew sent there, you had to try very hard. Doctor Fabre, the man with no first name, the man Adrien referred to as "Marcel's father" met a civil servant from the *préfecture de Paris* (a senior doctor at Pitié-Salpêtrière obviously ended up treating everyone at some point, which meant that everyone owed him something), one of those grey, faceless men who bring order and misery to a nation. The civil servant was happy to do the favour, but he asked for a signed letter. Bureaucracies are fond of paperwork. To his shame, the doctor signed. Years later, Marcel had no difficulty tracing it. Another grey faceless man, perhaps the same man, perhaps his son, showed him the signed letter. It is the job of bureaucracy to preserve documents.

I had said all there was to say about my twin families, about the Fabre-Wagners and the Wagner-Fabres, the men and women with and without first names, with and without histories, the good and the bad and those who were neither good nor bad, the beautiful and the ugly, the sane and the mad. They were David, Adrien, Marcel, Virginie, Charles, Clémentine, Ulrich, Natacha, Sophie. Like all of us, they are of no particular importance and yet each of them is the soul of the world, meaning that David's death is utterly without consequence while also being the greatest tragedy in history.

I was in the living room of the great house. I was in Weimar in 1962, I was in Buchenwald in 1942, I was in the dining room the day David met Virginie and I was in the nursing home of my grandfather Fabre.

I was dazed. I think I was standing facing my father but I'm not sure. I think he was saying something, but I'm not sure. I think he was talking about our family, but I'm not sure.

I should probably have put my arms around my father and hugged him. I don't know, it's all a bit complicated. Some families hug, kiss, others never hug or kiss. The Germans have a word: "*umarmen*". To enfold in your arms. We have a beautiful word too: embrace.

Rather than writing a book, maybe I should go round the cafés of Europe and tell the banal and terrifying story of a man who wanted to marry a woman for her money, loved another because he loved her and was deported to a camp by his future father-in-law.

I could leave tomorrow. Instead of going back to Germany, I could start my European tour. I'd first go to Britain, tour the misty green roads, then I would go to Austria, thereby launching my tour in countries whose language I can speak. I would ask people to help me. We have all lived through the same history, we are all the grandchildren of war and carnage, people will help. The good and the evil. The neither good nor evil. They will tell me my story in the languages I hardly speak, like Italian and Dutch; the languages I can imagine, like Spanish or Romanian, or those I can only dream in like Greek, Czech, Swedish, Danish, all the languages of the European Babel. I would go from the southern tip of Portugal to the Baltics, to the borders of Russia, deep into the empire of myth, the historic dreams of all the nations that make us up. And every night, in the inns that welcomed me, I would tell this story. People would quickly start to yawn, they'd think I was a lunatic, but soon they would carry on themselves. Over the parched hills of Greece, past the frozen, translucent lakes of Nordic countries, through vast forests, I would walk and tell my story, both without interest and fascinating. The ravings of a madman, told by an idiot?

13

I imagined them in a hotel room in Paris as the autumn sunshine flooded through the window. They were naked, pale skin pressed to olive skin. They were motionless. David's hand, fingers splayed, stroking Virginie's cheek as she closed her eyes like a contented cat. The sun traced a square of light, illuminating the woman's thighs, her belly. There was no sound, no movement. Even the hotel seemed to be dozing in the frozen, immortalised image of an instant that was fleeting and destined for death.

They were the strong and the beautiful.

But they were neither strong nor beautiful, they were lovers. Lovers basking in the pleasure of the sun and the presence of the other. At the very moment, perhaps, that a bitter anti-Semitic doctor was meeting a civil servant in Paris. Perhaps. This I could not know. But the image lingered, lingered. David's hand was immense; sunlight played on Virginie's thigh. And she always closed her eyes. David kept his eyes open, as though spellbound.

We were at the beginning of the world, before the fall.

ACKNOWLEDGEMENTS

Usually, I prefer a book to spring from nowhere, unconnected with anything or anyone which proscribes dedications or acknowledgements. But given the very particular nature of this book I feel obliged to thank a number of people:

My father, first and foremost, who was always my first reader and who today, is necessarily the last;

My family, for their presence;

Serge Ruellan for his historical editing and Caroline Géraud for her corrections to my decidedly approximate German;

Floréal Barrier, a former inmate of the camp, a member of the *Association française Buchenwald Dora et Vanina Brière*, of the *Fondation pour la mémoire de la déportation* in Caen, whose knowledge and help was invaluable;

All the team of Le Passage for their encouragement and support.

TRANSLATOR'S NOTE

I have used the following translations in the text, with thanks to the publishers:

Primo Levi, *If This is a Man*, translated by Stuart Woolf, 1958; Abacus, 1987

Sebastian Haffner *Defying Hitler*, translated by Oliver Pretzel, Weidenfeld & Nicolson, 2002